Katherine gasped as the horse began to move through the trees.

She was riding faster than she ever had before and every muscle screamed in protest. Just as she thought she'd collide with another tree, Jarin used his skilled horsemanship to avoid it.

"Move with me," Jarin yelled.

"I can't," she shouted back. "I don't know how."

Jarin yanked her back in the saddle until she was sitting flush against his thighs. She gasped at the contact, and the strange tingly feeling she kept having every time they touched started up again. This time it swept through her whole body. She tried to pull away from him; she shouldn't be feeling like this right now.

"Now isn't the time to be modest," he said into her ear, his breath whispering across her skin. He pulled her even tighter against him. "Follow my movements and we'll ride faster."

Katherine's stomach fell away as Eira leaped over a fallen log but she wasn't jolted by the action. Her whole body was now pressed against Jarin. It was much easier to ride when he took over their movement. His strong arms surrounded her, protecting her from the world around them.

Author Note

Thank you so much for choosing to read Jarin and Katherine's story in *Under the Warrior's Protection*.

I first met these characters in *The Warrior Knight and the Widow*. I loved Jarin from the first moment he smiled; Katherine made me laugh with her terrible attempts at embroidery.

Jarin is the most honorable man I have ever met. He is always striving to do the right thing even if that goes against his true heart's desire. He fiercely protects those he cares about while not expecting anyone to do the same for him.

Katherine has lived her early life in almost virtual seclusion, and she is ripe for adventure. She has been constantly let down by the very people who should have protected her, and she finds it very difficult to trust anyone. When she meets Jarin, she finds it hard to believe that such a man can be honorable, let alone that he has begun to care for her.

I hope you enjoy going on an adventure with these two as much as I have.

I love hearing from readers, so please do get in touch with me on Twitter, @ellamattauthor, or at my website, www.ellamatthews.co.uk.

ELLA MATTHEWS

Under the Warrior's Protection

ISBN-13: 978-1-335-50586-6

Under the Warrior's Protection

This edition published by arrangement with Harlequin Books S.A.

For questions and comments about the quality of this book, please contact us at CustomerService@Harlequin.com.

Harlequin Enterprises ULC
22 Adelaide St. West, 40th Floor
Toronto, Ontario M5H 4E3, Canada
www.Harlequin.com

Printed in U.S.A.

Ella Matthews lives and works in beautiful South Wales. When not thinking about handsome heroes, she can be found walking along the coast with her husband and their two children (probably still thinking about heroes, but at least pretending to be interested in everyone else).

Books by Ella Matthews

Harlequin Historical

The Warrior Knight and the Widow
Under the Warrior's Protection

Visit the Author Profile page
at Harlequin.com.

To Linda and John,
with thanks.

Chapter One

The Earl of Ogmore's fortress—1331

Their boot-clad feet whispered across the stone floor as the sisters ran, their breath coming in hurried gasps. Katherine rubbed her ribs, where a stitch dug into her side, but she didn't slow—not even when they rounded a corner and came face to face with a stern guard, his expression contorted in a scowl.

'Excuse me!' called Katherine as they hurried past.

She heard Linota's surprised giggle from behind her and reached back to grab her sister's hand.

'He didn't stop us,' gasped Linota as they rounded another corner.

'Nothing will stop me going to our brother's wedding,' wheezed Katherine, although she was going to have to cease running soon or her pounding heart would give up.

They rounded yet another corner and found the corridor deserted. Katherine slowed to a walk and then stopped altogether as Linota doubled over, trying to catch her breath.

'I can't believe we did it,' said Linota, clutching her side.

'We did.' Katherine grinned, pulling her sister into a tight hug, and the two girls laughed in delight.

For the first time in their lives they had defied their draconian mother and escaped the rooms in which the older lady normally kept them confined. Katherine couldn't quite believe they'd had the nerve, but they had and now they were on their way to their brother's wedding, no matter what the future consequences might be.

'Where do you think everyone is?' Linota asked, looking around the unusually quiet corridor.

'They're probably already waiting for the service to begin. We'd best hurry; we don't want to miss anything.'

Linota pulled a face.

'What's the matter?' asked Katherine.

'I need to use the privy.'

'Now? Can't you wait?'

'No. It's not as though I had time before. We were busy running for our lives.'

Katherine let the exaggeration slide. 'Fine, but don't be long.'

'I won't, there's one down there.' Linota indicated the way they'd just come.

'I'll wait here,' said Katherine.

Linota was already hurrying away, her golden plait bouncing against her back as she dashed back down the corridor.

Katherine smiled. It was impossible to stay irritated with Linota. Out of the three Leofric children to survive into adulthood Linota was the one blessed with both looks and charm. Katherine tilted her head to one side. Perhaps that wasn't fair. Braedan probably would have been a handsome man if his face hadn't been so badly disfigured with scars.

It was only Katherine who had been born plain. Her brown hair, neither light nor dark, never did anything to particularly enhance her rather round face. She was so small and slight, she had no chest to speak of, and could easily have passed for a boy if it weren't for her long hair. It didn't matter. At twenty-four she was too old to be considering marriage and so what she looked like was irrelevant.

What she wanted was to see Linota settled and then she would consider her own future. She imagined herself somewhere with a little space all to herself. Maybe a small dwelling she could call her own on the edge of a village near Linota's home so that she could be a doting aunt to her sister's children. She'd dreamed so often of being able to escape into the wilderness whenever she wanted. As soon as Linota found her place in the world, that was what she would do.

She scuffed her slipper against the floor—what was taking her sister such a long time?

A prickle of unease ran through her. What if their mother had found her? Katherine was used to withstanding the punishments their parent meted out, but Linota was a gentle soul. She would be destroyed if she had to withstand the full force of their mother's anger alone.

Katherine hurried back the way Linota had disappeared. She turned a corner and came to an abrupt stop as she heard her sister's name spoken in a deep masculine voice.

Her heart froze. If her sister had been compromised the first time she had been left on her own, it would all be Katherine's fault and her mother's punishment would be nothing in comparison with how much she would hate herself.

She crept forward. A deeper voice said something she couldn't quite make out. There was no sound of a struggle or any type of movement, so perhaps the men were talking *about* Linota rather than *to* her, but why?

Katherine stepped closer to the voices.

'It's not as if it would be a hardship to be married to Linota Leofric,' said one of the deep voices. 'I know the Leofric sisters don't come out of their rooms much, but have you seen her, Jarin? A man would be a fool to turn down the chance to bed a creature like that.'

Katherine clenched her fists. The desire to storm into the room and wallop the man talking so casually about bedding her sister was almost overwhelming.

'I'm not talking about a quick tumble, Erik. I'm talking about being shackled to a woman for the rest of my life. I've married once before and you know how badly that turned out.'

'Not every woman is a scheming harpy like Viola. Look, I know you thought marriage to Ogmore's daughter was the solution, but I still don't see why you're acting as if you're on the way to your execution now there's a different option. You get a beautiful wife and an alliance with Ogmore. Many men would kill to be in your position.'

'Ogmore didn't specify which sister. It could just as easily be the older one.'

'It's not as though you would *choose* the plain one, is it? I believe her name is Lady Katherine,' said the man named Erik incredulously.

Katherine had heard herself be described as plain before, but it didn't stop the heat travelling up her neck as she heard the casual dismissal.

'It's not the girls' looks that are bothering me,' growled Jarin's voice. 'I can't marry into *that* family.'

'Ogmore doesn't seem bothered by the family's lineage. His only daughter is marrying into it after all.'

'Sir Braedan Leofric is good enough for a daughter. It's not as if she will ever inherit his vast estate, he's got plenty of healthy sons to do that. It makes good strategic defence to have a man like Leofric on Ogmore's side, but the girls…'

There was a brief silence.

'The pretty one is supposed to be quite charming and docile. You will be able to mould her into the perfect wife,' said Erik.

'You don't understand, Erik. It doesn't matter how beautiful or charming either of them is, her father was still executed for treason for plotting against the King and their mother will still be insane. If my father were alive, he would have started a war with Ogmore for even suggesting such an alliance.'

'Your father's dead. What he wants is no longer an issue,' said Erik bluntly. 'I thought you needed the alliance with Ogmore.'

'I do, but not to the extent of sullying the Borwyn line with…'

Katherine gasped and the rest of the sentence was lost as blood pounded in her ears. She knew she'd recognised the name, but she hadn't connected the dots. One of the men, the one skewering her family, was Jarin Ashdown, the Earl of Borwyn, a guest at the fortress.

To think only yesterday she'd spied the man riding his horse from her chamber window and had marvelled at the way he'd held himself in the saddle. He'd effortlessly ridden around the training ground, spearing the targets from atop his horse, his muscular arms never missing a target. She was like all the other foolish girls in the castle, casting doe eyes at the man because of his high cheekbones and the way he filled out his clothes so well. From now on she would know that his beauty was only skin-deep and that underneath he was rude and obnoxious and firmly beneath her notice, despite him believing it was the other way around.

The sound of Linota's hurried footsteps reached her and she stepped forward to greet her sister.

'Come on, we must hurry,' she whispered.

'What's wrong?' said Linota quietly, a small frown creased her forehead.

'Nothing.'

'If that's true, why do you look as if you've swallowed a bee?'

Katherine would rather die than tell Linota what she had just heard. There was no point ruining the day for both of them.

'I'm worried we're going to miss the ceremony,' she said, tugging Linota along in her wake.

'I wasn't gone that long,' said Linota, tucking her arm companionably through Katherine's.

Katherine didn't respond. She was too busy seething. The words she'd heard Jarin Ashdown utter swam round and round her head, taunting her with every step. How dare he speak about her family like that! Yes, her father had been executed for treason and, yes, that horrific event had changed their mother for the worse, but there was nothing wrong with Katherine or her siblings. A man who listened to spiteful gossip wasn't worth bothering with, no matter the distracting strength of his broad shoulders.

Her fury carried her all the way to the Great Hall where people were swarming around the large entrance in a great chattering mass. Over the buzz of conversation, Katherine could just make out the strains of fiddlers entertaining the crowds. Even on tiptoes she couldn't see over the heads of the other guests. Tears pricked her eyes; even after everything that had happened this morning she still wasn't going to see her brother get married.

A young page pushed his way through the crowds and stumbled to a stop in front of them. His ruddy face flushed an unbecoming red. 'You're to come with me,' he mumbled.

Katherine's heart stumbled, 'Why?'

She wasn't going to follow the boy if he was going to lead them straight to their mother. She hadn't come so far only to return meekly to her chamber. If she refused to come, she had to hope that not even their mother would cause a scene in front of this many people.

The page flushed an even deeper red at her question. 'You...you've got s-seats at the front,' he stuttered.

Katherine couldn't have been more surprised if he'd

told her she'd been about to marry the King of England himself.

She opened her mouth to respond that he must be mistaken, but the boy didn't wait for her to question him again and began threading his way through the mass of people. Katherine hurried after him, tugging Linota in her wake, murmuring apologies as they bumped into finely dressed noblemen and elegant ladies.

She was aware of people turning to stare as they made their way to the front, but for the first time that she could remember she couldn't hear unkind whispers and sniggers following in their wake. Even so, she was grateful when they finally reached their seats.

'This is…well, this is incredible,' said Linota, sinking into her seat and looking around at the other guests.

'It is,' said Katherine, arranging her skirts. 'It's almost hard to believe.'

'Our brother is going to be Ogmore's son-in-law.' Linota glanced around the hall again. 'I suppose that has elevated our status a bit.'

Katherine snorted, quickly turning it into a cough; she didn't want to draw attention to her lack of feminine behaviour now that they were in front of everyone. 'A bit!' she said when she had got herself under control. 'We're sitting at the front, Lin. As honoured guests. I think it's safe to say our status has changed quite dramatically. What a shame our mother couldn't see past her foolish pride and refused to come.'

The raised dais, which normally hosted Ogmore and his close family, had been completely cleared of the grand chairs which normally took centre stage. The only thing that remained was Ogmore's family crest, which stood proudly at the centre of the platform. But what had Katherine gasping in surprise was the smaller crest that rested next to it.

For the first time in eight years her family's heraldic emblem was on display. The two swords and the falcon were there for everyone to see, no longer hiding in some darkened room, a symbol of their family's shame.

She raised her chin.

She hoped Jarin Ashdown got a good look at where her family was today. Yes, they'd endured years of misery, but now their fortunes were changing. The Earl of Borwyn would rue the day he dismissed the Leofric sisters as beneath him.

Chapter Two

Jarin shifted his weight on the wooden bench trying to find a position that would allow him to stretch his legs out; his body wasn't designed for such cramped conditions. He bit back a sigh when the man sitting next to him glared in annoyance. It wasn't Jarin's fault that the guests were crammed into the Great Hall shoulder to shoulder to watch the only daughter of the influential Earl of Ogmore marry a hulking, scarred knight.

Normally Jarin loved a wedding. Hosts often went to great lengths to prove their wealth and status to the benefit of their willing guests. Feasts could go on for hours and in the relaxed atmosphere that followed it was never too difficult to find a willing woman for an enjoyable, no-commitment tumble.

Today was different. He should have been the groom. The fact that he was a mere guest, and not a particularly honoured one at that, had his guts twisted into knots. Not that he was broken-hearted. He'd only met the bride a handful of times. She was intelligent, kind and pretty in a classic way, but he couldn't honestly say he was sad to have been usurped. It was the loss of the alliance with her father that was causing the tight knot of tension to form across his shoulders. He tried rolling his neck to relieve it, but the movement only caused his neighbour to frown at him again. He was damned if he didn't come up with a solution to his problems soon, but did that solution *have* to come in the shape of the disgraced Leofric sisters?

'Stop fidgeting,' said Erik, who was sitting on his other side, a slight smirk crossing his lips.

Jarin ran his fingers through his hair, 'When do you think it's all going to start? This bench wasn't designed to be sat on for very long.'

'I suspect it will start when Ogmore is good and ready. You know how he likes to make an entrance. Your grumbling isn't going to speed anything up.' Erik's grin turned wide when he saw Jarin's deeper scowl at his words.

Some people might find their relationship odd. Jarin was an earl with a large estate which went with his recently inherited title. Erik was his closest confidant, steward and all-round right-hand man of unknown parentage. According to the laws of society, Erik should have treated Jarin with deference, but he never had. Jarin wouldn't want it any other way. They'd been friends ever since their tumultuous childhoods and Erik felt more like a brother than a steward, the position Jarin had given his close friend as soon as he'd been able.

'Look,' murmured Erik, nodding towards the front of the room. 'There's Linota Leofric. You cannot deny that she is a fine-looking woman.'

Jarin looked in the direction Erik was indicating.

Linota Leofric did stand out amongst the other guests, her pale blonde hair seeming to shimmer in the dimly lit room and her beatific smile lighting up her face. Jarin waited for even a slight flicker of desire for the beautiful woman, but there was nothing, not even the slightest urge to touch her skin or hear her moan, which he supposed was a good thing. He'd allowed himself to be led by his cock once before and it had brought him no end of grief. Still, it would be good to feel some stirrings of vague attraction for the woman he must get with child.

He straightened the end of his sleeve; the strain of his position must be getting to him. He couldn't remember the last time he'd slept through a night. Every time he closed his eyes the weight of his responsibilities settled on his chest, making it difficult to breathe, and nothing he did seemed to relieve the pressure.

He hadn't had a woman for some time; he hadn't even wanted to, let alone had the opportunity. He should feel something at the sight of such radiant beauty. Perhaps his desire had died and he'd never get it back. Right now, it didn't seem important.

His gaze wandered to the tiny woman sitting next to her. Unlike Linota, this woman wasn't smiling and a deep frown marred her forehead. Although no one was speaking to her, she suddenly muttered something, shook her head and smoothed out her skirts.

'The crazy one's her sister,' said Erik quietly.

Jarin nodded thoughtfully. So this was Katherine Leofric, the other Leofric sister whom Erik had described as plain. As he watched, Katherine turned to her sister and smiled.

He inhaled sharply. Desire he'd thought long dormant swept through him, licking through his blood and making his body tighten. His fingers itched with the need to trace the pale skin of her cheeks and those wide, smiling lips.

No one could describe Katherine as beautiful. Even from this distance he could see she had no figure to speak of. Her face was too round to be fashionable and her hair did nothing to help as it was bound in elaborate braids that hung around her face like a thick curtain. Her cheekbones stood out sharply in a way that suggested a lack of food rather than a desire to be thin. But her smile promised laughter and surprise and he wanted to taste it. He could easily picture his hands undoing those unflattering braids and seeing her hair spill around her bare shoulders in thick waves, that smile directed only at him.

He shifted on his seat again and dragged his gaze away, only to find it returning to her almost immediately. She was no longer looking at her sister and though the frown was back in place, it didn't detract from her attractiveness. He wanted to rub his fingers along the crease and massage it away, all the while trying to coax that smile back to life.

He wondered what could be causing her to look cross at her brother's wedding. Surely this should be a day of immense happiness for her and her family. They were finally being accepted after being shunned for so long.

'I think marriage to a beauty like that would be worth betraying the oath you made to your father, don't you agree?' said Erik.

For a moment Jarin thought his friend was talking about Katherine and his right hand flexed with the urge to punch the man. He glanced down at it in surprise and stretched his fingers. He had never wanted to hit anyone, especially not his closest confidant. His whole reputation was built on his ability to remain calm in a crisis, a trait his father had abhorred, but of which Jarin was inordinately proud. His body had clearly run crazy with the lack of a good woman. His body turned cold as he realised what this meant. He knew extreme desire was bad for him. It made him act differently. He must not let it happen to him again. He would control his body's actions whatever it took.

When he turned he realised Erik wasn't looking at Katherine anyway; his gaze was fixed solely on Linota. He had obviously dismissed Katherine as uninteresting and seemed to think only Linota was a suitable bride. Erik didn't think much about the oath Jarin had made his father about honouring the Borwyn family's heraldic motto *Give Strength to Honour.*

In reality, Jarin didn't much care about the one he had made his father either, but he wouldn't tell his friend that, even though he'd made no secret of the fact that he hadn't liked the bastard when he was alive and his feelings hadn't improved after his father's death.

It was, instead, the soft, secret promise he'd made to the only woman he'd ever truly loved: his mother. The promise to be better than his deceased brothers, to make sure he always followed reason, the trait she'd so admired in him and the one she had nurtured even as his father had tried to beat it out of him.

His mother had wanted him to be the kind of earl who was respected because of the decisions he made and not because he had forced his subjects to act that way. He intended to live up to that ideal. He'd already had one disastrous marriage based on lust and only been released from it when Viola had died in childbirth. A second marriage like that was not something he would ever contemplate. It seemed his famous reasoning couldn't be trusted when he followed his body's desires instead of his mind.

The ceremony finally got underway and Jarin found his gaze wandering back to Katherine. She was back to muttering under her breath and shaking her head. It appeared she was having a full-blown argument with someone who wasn't there.

'What's so funny?' whispered Erik.

Jarin touched his mouth; he hadn't been aware he was grinning like an idiot.

'I'm just enjoying the wedding,' he said.

Erik raised an eyebrow.

'It's very moving.'

Jarin turned his attention to the couple binding their lives together forever and tried to adopt a pleased expression. He was glad when Erik didn't ask him what he'd found moving because he couldn't recall a single word of the ceremony.

The tables groaned under the weight of food Ogmore thought appropriate for celebrating his only daughter's wedding. As a high-ranking guest, Jarin was sitting at the top table but, unusually, the space opposite him was empty.

Conversation flowed around him, but he felt oddly separate, as if he wasn't really there; this sensation was getting far too frequent for him. He had to spend so much time pretending, lying to all those around him that he was as calm and collected as always, which meant that dread and uncertainty weren't burning away beneath his skin. Outwardly he had to portray that inheriting a vast estate hadn't changed him from the man he'd always intended to be, one who was always in control of every situation no matter his own feelings. It was as if the real him was disappearing behind the weight of the earldom and in his place was a sophisticated puppet.

To the left of him sat a beautiful widow who'd made it abundantly clear she'd be interested in spending time with him after the feast had ended. He'd hoped the raging desire he'd felt earlier for the unusual Leofric girl meant that he would once again be able to take enjoyment in women. There was no reason, after all, for one woman to appeal to him so much. It didn't seem to matter, though, how many times the widow—whose name he could not remember—brushed up against him, his body didn't tighten in anticipation. He could no more imagine bedding her than he could picture sprouting wings and flying out of here.

He glanced down the hall. Erik was laughing uproariously at something his neighbour was saying and it looked as if his friend was going to have company this evening. He turned back to the trencher in front of him, piled high with roasted goose, and tried to squash down the envy that was rising up inside him. He knew he was in a position of privilege, a position that some would kill for, but sometimes he felt he would like to swap places with Erik.

A movement to his right caught his attention.

The Leofric sisters were standing huddled together

a few steps away, having an intense conversation. Nobody else was paying their strange behaviour any attention but, once again, he couldn't take his eyes off Katherine. She was tiny. He was sure that the palm of his hand would cover her waist. He'd been wrong about her body, too. She wasn't well endowed, but he could see delicate curves through her shapeless dress and desire tugged at him once more.

She was evidently furious about something; her sister tried to placate her by putting a hand on her arm, but she shook it off.

Linota shook her head and suddenly broke away, walking towards the space opposite him. Katherine stood for a moment, frowning, then quickly followed her.

Linota slid into the space on the bench opposite him; she smiled sweetly at him and he responded in kind. Behind her, seemingly unwilling to take the last place at the table, Katherine hovered like a dark cloud. She was visibly vibrating with some kind of strong emotion. He knew he shouldn't stare at her, but he seemed to be unable to pull his eyes away. In contrast, she looked anywhere but at him. Why?

'Are you enjoying the feast, my lord?' asked Linota.

Jarin jumped. He'd forgotten Linota was there, so focused was he on her sister.

'Very much so,' lied Jarin, who'd yet to take a bite of the rich food spread out in front of him.

Katherine climbed gracelessly on to the bench next to her sister, her slender shoulders rigid beneath the fabric of her dress. He wanted to reach out and knead the tense muscles until she moaned in pleasure. Shocked at his own reaction, he took a swig from his tankard, spluttering as the drink went down the wrong way.

'Are you all right, my lord?' asked Linota.

Katherine said nothing.

'I'm fine, thank you,' he said, feeling heat rush over his skin.

He was acting like a young boy who had never spoken to a woman in his life. What was wrong with him?

'Do try some of this goose, Katherine. It looks delicious,' said Linota, handing her sister a cut of meat.

Katherine took it, but didn't raise it to her mouth. Jarin wondered if she was so tiny because she didn't like to eat. He'd heard of such a thing before, but he'd never witnessed it. She looked almost starved and her sister was not much better.

'If it's not to your liking, Mistress Leofric, perhaps you would like to try the venison.'

He pushed the trencher towards her.

She still said nothing, glaring instead at the cut of meat in her hand as if it had done her a great wrong.

Linota shifted uncomfortably in her seat, finally hissing her sister's name to get her attention. At last it worked and Katherine looked up and straight at him.

Her gaze was like a punch to the chest. He momentarily forgot how to breathe as her unusual-coloured eyes took him in. It was as if with one look she could see the real him. Not the man he portrayed to the world, but the man underneath the rich clothes. The one who was feeling his way blindly through a whole host of problems he wasn't sure he would ever be able to fix.

'No, thank you,' she said coldly and the spell was broken.

The noise of the room rushed back in and he found he was able to breathe again.

He turned away from her then, giving his attention to the widow, whose inviting eyes did nothing to disturb his equilibrium. It didn't matter that he didn't turn to Katherine again because all through the long feast he could sense her every movement.

He was in trouble.

Chapter Three

The Great Hall was packed with people. Katherine squeezed between two groups and stood on her tiptoes, trying to get a glimpse of Linota. It was no use; even with the extra height the other guests still towered over her.

'Can I help you, Mistress Leofric?' asked a deep voice from behind her.

Katherine didn't need to turn to know who spoke to her. Ever since the feast earlier she hadn't been able to shake off an awareness of the Earl of Borwyn. She only had to turn and she knew her gaze would immediately fall on him as if some invisible force was tying her to the impossible man.

She wanted to walk away, to get as far from him as possible, but her feet refused to move.

'Mistress Leofric?' he said again and she slowly turned to face him.

The press of people around them pushed them close together. Her head only came up to his chest and she watched the steady rise and fall of his breath. She knew she should look up at his face, but she didn't want to be distracted by his good looks—if she did she might forget how angry she was with him.

He cleared his throat. Slowly, she looked up until their eyes met and locked. She couldn't have torn her gaze away even if she'd wanted to. Up close his face wasn't as perfect as she'd thought. A thin scar cut across his left eyebrow and carried on across his cheekbone. It should have marred his looks, but instead it only added to his attractiveness. She curled her hand to stop her strange impulse to reach up and trace it with her fingertips.

'Well?' he asked.

'Well what?'

His lips lifted in a half-smile and her heart stuttered. 'Can I help you?'

'I'm looking for my sister, but I'm too short to see,' she blurted out and then cringed. She hadn't wanted to talk to him at all, but his intense gaze was unsettling. Now she sounded like a silly little girl in front of the very person to whom she was trying to appear clear-headed and aloof.

He stretched and looked over the crowd for her.

'She's talking to your brother's new wife,' he said.

'Oh,' she said. 'I should go to her.'

But still her feet refused to move.

He didn't move either.

She stared at him and he looked right back. The noise of the room faded away until the only sound she was aware of was the loud thumping of her heart.

A slim hand slipped around Borwyn's arm. 'Borwyn,' purred the widow from earlier, 'there you are. I've been looking all over.'

Borwyn turned to smile down at the woman and the hold he'd had over Katherine snapped. She turned and ran before he could catch her in his gaze again.

But instead of heading towards Linota, she hurried towards the entrance of the keep, desperate for the cold night air to soothe her fevered skin.

She'd obviously had too much wine with the feast; that explained the light-headed sensation she was experiencing.

She certainly hoped it was nothing to do with Borwyn and his unsettling gaze. Ogmore had told her and Linota earlier that Borwyn would be escorting them to their new home with their brother and his bride. She'd been looking forward to the journey, to seeing new parts of the world, but now she wasn't so sure. It would take at least five days; five days in which she couldn't escape from Borwyn and his disconcerting presence.

She took a deep breath as she neared the entrance. Everyone was different this evening, the normal rules seemed relaxed and people spilled out of the Great Hall in a great chattering mass. She glanced around, but no one was watching her; the plain Leofric sister was easy to ignore. It was no problem to slip outside unseen and into the shadows.

Her heart beat loudly in her chest as she crept around the edge of the keep. She'd never been so daring as to be outside without anyone knowing where she was before, but everything was changing now and she wasn't going to deny herself this liberty.

She walked, hidden in the shadows, without much

thought of where she was going. The further she got away from the keep's entrance, the quieter the night became.

Heavy footsteps from behind her had her darting into a narrow alley. She held her breath as the person passed by, but the walker didn't discover her hiding place. She poked her head out as the person carried on their way. Oddly, whoever was in front of her was also hiding in the shadows.

She looked back the way she had come, but there was no one else to be seen. Without giving herself a chance to think, she followed the stranger into the darkness.

From the person's height and build she decided she was following a man. Why she was doing so rather than returning to the safety of the castle was beyond her, but this was her first opportunity for adventure and she was taking it.

A shout of laughter had the man in front of her pressing himself into the wall ahead. She followed suit. What was he up to and why did he seem so familiar?

The man briefly stepped into the light and she gasped. She'd spent so long looking at the Earl of Borwyn from her chamber window she felt she would recognise him anywhere. This person had the same height and build as him, but…surely Borwyn was enjoying the attention of the widow and not skulking about outside?

She held her breath. Suddenly, a much smaller man appeared from a side alley, his body covered in a long, dark cloak. The two men spoke intently to one another, the man she thought might be Borwyn making short, sharp gestures with his hand. A package exchanged hands and he started nodding. Katherine waited for more, but it appeared the meeting had come to an end. The shorter man turned on his heel and headed back the way he had come.

Katherine kept her eyes on the taller man as he folded the mysterious package into his cloak, all the while keeping his head turned in the direction of the guards. Just as she thought she wouldn't see his face he stepped out of the shadows, no longer appearing to need to hide.

She inhaled sharply. It wasn't Jarin Ashdown creeping around, but his right-hand man, Erik Ward. Erik straightened his clothes and looked towards the guards once more. None of them paid him any attention. She held her breath, waiting to see what he would do next, but he only sauntered away as if he didn't have a care in the world.

Chapter Four

'This is a bad idea,' muttered Jarin, the cool morning air biting against his face. Beneath him his horse, Eira, shifted, her hooves crunching on the ice underfoot.

'You can't make a reasonable decision about marrying one of the Leofric sisters if you don't spend any time with either of them,' argued Erik reasonably. 'You'd be a fool to turn down Ogmore's offer.'

Jarin tightened his grip on his reins; Erik had a point, but he didn't want to hear it. He didn't think he could manage five long days under Katherine Leofric's unsettling scrutiny. He wasn't sure he'd be able to control his body's impulse when it came to her either. It was not a prospect he relished.

'What's taking them so long? I instructed them to be ready to leave at daybreak. We need to leave promptly if we're going to make it to Abbotston by nightfall.'

Eira whinnied restlessly underneath him, picking up on his tension. He patted her neck to soothe her.

'I'd imagine it takes more than a few hours to pack up one's entire life,' said Erik drily.

'Their belongings are already in the cart. It must be something else holding them up.'

Jarin had been shocked by the pitiful amount of luggage the sisters were taking. Just one small bag of clothes between them; hardly the amount you would expect from two ladies of their rank, even taking into consideration their family's fall from grace. Most of the cart was taken up with provisions for the trip and a few gifts for the newly married couple.

'You need to relax. You're escorting two young women to their new home, not going into battle. Neither of them knows about Ogmore's offer of a marriage settlement. At least the old goat promised to keep that to himself.'

Jarin leaned forward to smooth Eira's neck as once again Katherine's piercing gaze sprang to mind. He closed his eyes tightly. Why couldn't he stop thinking about the way she'd looked at him? He didn't want anyone to know the real him underneath his cool exterior so why, when it felt as if she had peered into his soul, did he want her to do it again?

'It's a simple solution, Jarin,' continued Erik, oblivious to his mood.

Jarin shook his head, dispelling the image of Katherine's gentle curves; he needed to approach this problem with his normal, rational decision-making. One of the sisters might make him a decent wife and, with Ogmore's dowry for them thrown in, some of his problems would be sorted.

All around him his men busied themselves getting ready for their departure. Last-minute items were being added to the cart and horses were being walked backwards and forward to keep them from getting cold while they waited for the Leofric sisters to emerge.

A flurry of activity appeared around the keep's entrance as the sisters burst out into the open. Wearing plain, dark travelling cloaks, the pair hurried towards the waiting horses. As they approached, some of Jarin's ire at their lateness dissipated. There was no sign of excitement from either woman. Instead of whispering and giggling together, they walked hurriedly with their heads bowed.

'They don't look happy, do they?' commented Erik.

'If even half of the rumours are true, living with their mother must have taken its toll on them,' said Jarin.

'Their mother isn't weeping and wailing as she watches the girls off so perhaps relations are as badly strained as rumours suggest.'

'Surely this is yet another reason to steer clear of the family,' said Jarin wryly.

He'd had enough of family tensions to last him a lifetime. His brief marriage had been a web of lies and deceit that had turned him inside out, leaving him drained and desperate not to make the same mistake. Becoming involved in someone else's family dramas was something he actively wanted to avoid.

'I'm sure they will blossom when they are out of their mother's iron grip,' said Erik optimistically.

Jarin wasn't convinced. Katherine's tight mouth and rigid shoulders certainly didn't make it look as though she was happy and excited to start her new life.

'Good morning, ladies,' he said as they were helped on to their horses.

Linota replied sunnily enough, although her smile

didn't quite reach her blue eyes. Katherine merely nodded in his direction. Her long, light brown hair was tied tightly in more unflattering braids and her plain cloak was shapeless, almost as if she were wearing a sack. He knew that underneath that unflattering outfit she had a trim figure, but there was no sign of it today. There was no earthly reason for his attraction to her, but he couldn't deny that it simmered beneath his skin, urging him to tug her hair from her braids and watch it fly into the wind as she rode her horse.

Perhaps it was her obvious indifference to him that had him intrigued. Women normally fawned over him, whether it was something he encouraged or not. It didn't seem to matter what age or social standing a lady had, he was always subject to some sort of simpering behaviour, flickering eyelashes or coy giggles. He didn't delude himself that it was always because of the way he looked. He knew he wasn't ugly. He'd had his fair share of female attention before his older brothers had died and left him the heir to the vast Borwyn estate, enough to know that he was physically appealing to women.

His title normally ensured that even those not swayed by his face still treated him well. Katherine Leofric didn't seem to fall into the category of most women. Despite the fact she was above what most people would consider a marriageable age and he was a single, eligible man, she showed no interest in him at all. Perhaps that was part of her attraction. Now that she was seated on her horse she wasn't sparing him a second glance. Her uneasy gaze flickered between the gate and the keep as if she was expecting the portcullis to be slammed shut before she could get out.

He cleared his throat and her head whipped round to face him. He'd been about to make a light-hearted quip about leaving, but his words died in his throat as her eyes locked with his again. In the weak morning sunlight they looked moss green and he couldn't have torn his gaze away even if he'd been forced at sword-point. For several heartbeats neither of them moved and then her lips twisted in disgust and she turned away again.

He frowned. What had he done to cause such a look? They'd hardly spoken so she had no reason to dislike him. Perhaps she was mad like her mother. Or worse, his desire might be written all over his face, making him look like some sort of salivating beast. The back of his neck heated and he vowed again to rein in his reaction to her.

Her obvious dislike shouldn't bother him. If he was going to marry one of the women, then the fact that Katherine couldn't stand him should make the decision easy. Unfortunately, it wasn't Linota's hair he fantasised about tugging from tight braids to watch it fall around her face. It wasn't Linota who could capture his interest in just one look. He frowned again; this was going to be a long five days.

'Erik, you ride out front and I'll take the back,' he commanded. 'I want to reach Abbotston before it gets dark.'

Gradually the group of riders started moving; the heavily laden cart creaked as the wheels finally began to turn. He sighed as they progressed slowly out of the heavily fortified gates and into the wide-open countryside. Far into the distance, hills glistened white under a layer of frost and the ground crunched underfoot as they started their journey.

Riding at the back of the group was slow progress, but it meant Jarin could keep an eye on stragglers. His men knew how much he hated dawdling and would keep up a brisk pace, especially if he was watching their movements from behind.

It soon became very apparent that Katherine was not a natural rider. Her movements were jerky and she kept pulling on the reins to slow her horse down even though the rate at which they were progressing was so laboured Jarin was sure he could walk backwards faster. Katherine slipped around in the saddle, her plaits bouncing wildly. Her technique had to be causing her discomfort and she was already falling behind the rest of the group. Her mount was a placid creature, but Jarin knew it would only be a matter of time before the animal lost patience at such mishandling.

'Try loosening your grip on the reins,' he said as he rode up beside her.

'Pardon?' She twisted on her saddle to glare at him, causing her mount to skitter sideways.

'Careful,' he said, grabbing her reins and bringing the horse back under control.

She frowned at him as she clutched the pommel in front of her. 'You spooked her. What were you thinking sneaking up on her like that?'

He snorted with laughter and passed the reins back to her. His fingers grazed the skin on the back of her hand as he did so, the brief, gentle touch causing his body to tighten. He snatched his hand away. How strange he should react like that to the briefest of contact, especially with someone so bad-tempered. It really had been too long since he'd had a woman. As soon as the opportunity presented itself he would take a woman to his bed and lose himself for a couple of hours. That would satisfy this strange, unwanted craving he was having for a woman who couldn't stand him.

'I don't think Braith is spooked easily.' He looked at the squat mount that was now plodding placidly along. 'I think it's your erratic riding that's upsetting her.'

He snapped his mouth closed in surprise. He'd never been so rude to a young lady. Katherine was making him act unlike himself. He really should offer her an apology, but his mind refused to come up with one.

'My riding?' she gasped. 'There's nothing wrong with it.'

'You're all over the place. It's upsetting Braith and it can't be comfortable for you.'

She sat up straighter in her seat. 'I am perfectly comfortable, thank you very much.'

She raised her chin and focused her gaze on a distant point in the horizon. Every line of her body was rigid. He really should fall back and allow her to ride alone. That would be the chivalrous thing to do, but for some reason he couldn't do it, she drew him in without even trying. His mind warred with his body, telling him to act sensibly and retreat; his mind lost.

'If you change your grip slightly, you'll have a lot more control over the direction in which your horse is travelling.'

The glare she sent him would have killed a lesser man.

'We are travelling in a straight line,' she ground out through clenched teeth.

'We are, but if you want to travel around an obstacle you will have greater success if you hold the reins like this.' He held up his hands to demonstrate.

She didn't respond. Her grip only tightened, causing Braith to toss her head. He didn't know Katherine, they'd never spoken before this brief altercation, but something told him she wouldn't be able to bear him having the last word. They rode in silence while he waited.

'Are you always rude?' she asked as they passed a small copse of trees.

Jarin flung back his head and laughed.

No one had ever called him rude before. Good manners had been drummed into him before he could even talk. He always acted on the rules he'd been taught during his upbringing and, even if he had inadvertently insulted someone, no one ever commented. He was the Earl of Borwyn, one of the largest landowners in the country. Everyone wanted to be on his good side. Women wanted to marry him; men wanted his favour. Or at least they did at the moment. If they ever found out the truth about his strained finances, he knew he'd fall out of favour. Her unguarded response was refreshing. At least if he married her he would know from the outset that she didn't like him. That had to be better than finding out several months after they were wed, as he'd learned from bitter experience.

'Well?' she demanded.

'Well, what?'

'You didn't answer my question.'

'Ah, you want to know if I'm always rude. No, I've never been accused of that before. I think, when you've had time to reflect, you'll find I'm not being rude right now, merely helpful.'

He really shouldn't tease her, but the deep frown across her forehead was extremely entertaining and it was going to be a long ride to Abbotston.

'Can't you go and be helpful to someone else?' she asked, still not looking at him.

He grinned. 'No one else needs my assistance with their riding.'

He nodded to the rest of their party who were moving in a solid line ahead, her own sister riding comfortably at their centre seemingly deep in conversation with Erik.

'I don't need your assistance.'

Something scurried in the undergrowth and Braith snorted in distress. Katherine squeaked and pulled on the reins, causing the horse to stagger sideways. Katherine yelped in distress as she slowly slid from her saddle.

Before she could become completely unseated he reached over and instinctively grabbed her. She gave a cry of pain as his hand encircled her upper arm. He released her quickly; he hadn't held her that hard, but her cry had been genuine. She continued to slide and so he slid his arms around her waist and held on. Underneath her bulky cloak he could feel her slim figure trembling.

'It's all right; I've got hold of you. You're not going to fall. I'm going to sit you upright.'

She nodded against his chest, the gesture oddly vulnerable. As gently as he could, given that their horses were still moving beneath them, he helped her back on to her saddle. When he was sure she was balanced, he slowly removed his arms and transferred his weight back on to his own horse.

She turned her face away from him which meant he couldn't see her expression, but her whole body curled up in misery. She reminded him of a wounded animal. Was it because he had upset her by insulting her riding or was she in tremendous pain? Was she hurt elsewhere? The thought caused his fingers to curl into fists. She was a tiny woman who wouldn't be able to defend herself, but someone had obviously hurt her badly. Anger throbbed through his veins and he had an insane urge to turn his horse around and demand answers from Ogmore, the man whose care she'd been under for many years.

He'd been a boor to tease her. She was obviously distressed for a reason that had nothing at all to do with him.

'If you have need of me, I'll be right here,' he said gravely.

A brief nod was all the indication he got that she'd heard him. He slowed and allowed her to pull ahead, noting with a slight smile that she altered the way she held the reins to the way he'd shown her. She might be stubborn, but she wasn't an idiot.

He kept his eyes on her throughout the long, dull morning of riding. Her miserable posture didn't relax at all but, although her riding technique didn't improve, she did remain in her saddle. He wanted to talk to her again, to engage her, even if it was through argument. He'd rather see her angry than such a sad, miserable figure plodding along in front of him.

All through the long day of riding his brain kept conjuring up scenarios of him rescuing her again, images that showed him holding her in his arms once more. He kept ruthlessly pushing them to one side. It was obvious she did not want to cast herself as a damsel in distress and, even if she were, for some reason he was the last person she'd want to rescue her.

Chapter Five

Jarin blew into the palms of his hands, but the gesture did little to alleviate the numbing cold slowly turning his fingers white. Each morning of the journey the temperature had dropped a little further. He pulled his cloak tighter and made his way over to his men who were busy preparing for today's departure.

As he got closer, William, one his guards, nodded over to a spot a little further on. 'Mistress Leofric,' he said gruffly.

Jarin looked in the direction William indicated. Katherine Leofric was sitting on her haunches, apparently staring into a thicket of wild brambles. Her hair shone dark gold in the early winter light—an unhelpful observation, thought Jarin as he made his way over to her.

'Is everything all right, Mistress Leofric?' he asked as he approached.

She glanced up at him fleetingly before turning back to the hedgerow. He sighed softly. She didn't seem to be warming to him after three days of travelling together.

In direct contrast, he was spending an inordinate amount of time riding behind her and watching the way she moved. She was still a terrible rider, but she never complained or asked for help. He'd have gladly given it just to see her smile at him the way she did at other people, but never at him.

'Mistress Leofric,' he said again. 'We need to be going, so if you've quite finished…um, whatever it is that you are doing, then…'

She turned back to look up at him, 'There's a little bird stuck in the brambles. I'm trying to help, but every time I go near she goes wild.'

Jarin crouched down next to her and looked in the direction she was pointing. A slight breeze picked up and he caught the smell of lavender. Katherine must use it when she washed because he caught the tantalising perfume whenever she was around. He clenched his fists as he resisted the impulse to pull her closer and press his lips to her neck so he could inhale her.

A frantic flapping thankfully brought him back to the problem.

'See,' she said.

'Ah, yes. Perhaps if I…'

He reached into the brambles and managed to pull a few apart. It only sent the bird wilder in her efforts to escape. Beside him Katherine gasped.

'It's all right. I don't think she's hurt,' he reassured her. 'Perhaps if you lift that branch there, we'll create enough space for her to get free. No, not that one, the one further back.'

Katherine stretched, revealing the pale underside of her delicate wrist. Jarin forced himself to concentrate on the brambles even as his gaze strayed to soft skin, the urge to run his fingers along it almost overwhelming.

The bird, now free from its trap, took off in a flurry of wings. Next to him Katherine laughed, the sound so joyous and unexpected that Jarin dropped the branches he was holding. They sprang quickly back into their original position. Katherine jumped and hissed in surprise as thorns grazed her arm.

'I'm so sorry,' said Jarin, cursing himself as a damned idiot. What was it about this woman that made him so clumsy? It was amazing that someone so small could have such a massive impact on his equilibrium. It was time he took charge of the situation and remembered who he was. He was the Earl of Borwyn, master of a vast estate with hundreds of men and women at his command. He was not a inexperienced page with his first crush.

'It's fine,' she said, pulling her arm towards her, but not so fast that he missed the bead of blood trickling down her arm.

'It's not fine,' he said, capturing her wrist gently in his hand and pulling her arm towards him again. 'You're hurt because of me. Please let me look.'

Without waiting for an answer, he swept the material of her cloak up and out of the way. Three angry, red lines marred the soft skin, but they weren't deep and the bleeding had already stopped.

'It's not as bad as I feared,' he said. 'We'll bandage it up to stop it getting inflamed, but you should be fine. You'll heal without a scar.'

He knew he should release her arm. He shouldn't have taken hold of it at all. But now that he was touching her, his baser instincts were taking over. Desire pounded through his body, stronger than ever now that he was close to her. The long, graceful column of her neck was so close to his lips. The wrist he held was so delicate. It would be a matter of moments to pull her into his arms. Only the thought that she wouldn't welcome his advances held him back. As it was he wanted to skim his fingers over the crease of her elbow and up past the hem of her sleeve to feel if her skin was as soft as it looked.

She tugged her hand and he let her go, heat creeping up his neck as she broke the contact. Here he was, pawing at her like a callow youth while she was in pain.

'Sorry,' he muttered again.

As Katherine moved to twitch her clothing back into place he caught a glimpse of the back of her arm. It was covered in a large green and yellow bruise from wrist to elbow.

'What happened there?' he demanded, reaching out to enclose her wrist once more.

She twisted away from him, moving her arm out of reach. 'It's nothing.'

She stood quickly and tugged her clothes back into position.

Rage bubbled up from his stomach and spread through his body, making him clench his fists and want to pound them into the person who had done such a thing to her. The pain she must be experiencing was far greater than anything he'd imagined. That bruise must be the result of a serious attack against a vulnerable young woman. It was definitely not 'nothing'.

'Mistress Leofric, I—'

'You said we needed to set off. I'm ready now,' she said, averting her eyes from his.

He wanted to argue with her, to find out who had committed such an act of violence against a small, defenceless woman so that he could return to Ogmore and mete out a suitable punishment—preferably instant death. The force of his rage shook him to the core, but he could see from the way she was half-turned away from him that he wouldn't get any answers from her and he knew he mustn't pry.

'Very well, let's return to the others, but if at any point you need to rest today you only have to say the word.'

She turned to look at him, her eyes wary. He wanted to say something charming, something that would put her at her ease with him and allow confidences between them. But words failed him once again and they returned to his men in silence.

Chapter Six

Katherine stared at the cracked ceiling above her bed. It hadn't been cleaned in a while, if ever, and cobwebs laced the gaps. Next to her Linota snored softly. Outside their room the inn slowly settled into the sounds of night-time: the occasional bursts of masculine laughter from the taproom, the creak of the wooden stairs as guests climbed up to their chambers; the rattle of a cart arriving as it pulled up outside.

How strange that, after only four nights, these sounds should be familiar to her. She hadn't travelled outside Ogmore's castle for over eight years, but with each day passing the oppressive nightmare of their cramped chamber fell away from her, leaving her feeling lighter than she had in years.

She ran her fingers over her body. The bruises from her mother's last beating were finally starting to fade and in a few days they would be gone for good. God willing, she would never see the woman again nor feel the pain of her displeasure.

Now, instead of her skin burning with the reminders

of sharp slaps, her muscles ached with a bone-weary tiredness from all the riding they were doing. That Linota felt none of the agony Katherine was experiencing led her to the unwelcome realisation that Jarin Ashdown was right to criticise her riding skills. If she could only remain upright and seated properly on Braith, then perhaps she wouldn't ache so abominably at the end of every day.

The Earl knew exactly what he was doing in the saddle. To her eternal irritation her gaze would stray to him whenever he rode in front of her. His wide shoulders never sagged. He seemed to be able to change Eira's direction with barely a twitch of his strong thighs. She rolled on to her side; she shouldn't be looking at his legs in the first place. Annoyingly, she had to keep reminding herself that it didn't matter how attractive the outside of him was, he was rude underneath.

The only problem was, that argument was starting to wear thin. He hadn't been rude to her or Linota once since the start of the journey. He had been constantly kind and solicitous to both of them and then there had been yesterday morning…

She'd known he was heading her way, not because she'd seen him coming, but because she still couldn't shake off an awareness of him. No matter where they were or what they were doing, she only had to turn slightly and know that her eyes would rest on him. It had been that way since she'd first set eyes on him.

As he'd approached, she'd expected him to scold her for keeping the party waiting. She'd expected him to ridicule her care of one tiny bird among thousands. What she hadn't anticipated was for him to crouch down beside her. He didn't even question her desire to free the animal, merely reaching forward and helping her with ease.

Her heart had clanged around in her ribs, caught off guard by his nearness and the sheer size of him. His care, when he had spotted one the bruises from her last beating, had almost been her undoing. She'd wanted to lean against his broad chest and allow him to protect her. She'd almost swayed towards him, but then she'd stopped.

She couldn't take Jarin's concern at face value. Ogmore had offered him a substantial dowry to marry one of the Leofric sisters. His concern seemed genuine, but it could easily have been pretence. Was he this man who was tender and considerate, or the one who had scathingly referred to the Leofrics as '*that family*'? Who was the real Jarin Ashdown? Better to guard against him and not risk the inevitable disappointment of being let down by yet another person.

She pushed back the covers. It was no use. She couldn't fall asleep. It had been the same for the last three nights. Whenever she closed her eyes, images from the day would surge to the forefront. Wide-open countryside, mysterious woods with gnarled tangled trees, smoke rising from the chimneys of distant dwellings—there was a whole world out there that she had never seen. There was so much for her to explore. She pulled on her woollen cloak and crept over to the doorway. She glanced back at Linota—one arm was flung over her head, her lips slightly parted as she breathed heavily. She was sleeping deeply; these days of constant fresh air and relentless riding meant she slept like the dead during the night. She wouldn't wake while Katherine was gone.

Katherine slipped from the room and stepped lightly to the bottom of the stairs, her heart pounding wildly. She'd never done anything this risky before, but no one need ever find out and she could easily pass for a boy if anyone saw her. All she wanted was to look at the stars once more and feel the fresh night air against her face.

She pulled her hood over her head and entered the taproom; smoke was thick in the air and the only light came from flickering candles and a roaring fire. In the far corner, a group of men muttered into their tankards. Her heart leapt when she unerringly picked out Jarin Ashdown again, this time staring moodily into the fire. She was sure he would be able to hear the pounding in her chest, but he didn't look up in her direction.

She wanted to stay and watch him when he didn't know she was there. Perhaps that way she could figure out who he really was. But did she actually want to know? It was better to think badly of him because it would be all too easy to fall for his good looks and easy charm. Once she had, she would not be able to protect her heart and when he too proved to be as disappointing as her father she would be devastated.

She had promised herself she would see the night sky, so before she could lose her nerve she raced to the doorway and pulled it open.

The night air hit her lungs and caused her to gasp. She'd never experienced cold like it. Her exhalation came out as a white puff of smoke. She giggled and stepped away from the tavern, watching as her breath disappeared into the air around her.

Beedon was a tiny hamlet with only a few houses dotted around. She made her way to the edge of the settlement, hoping for a good vantage point to see the night sky.

Before she had gone many paces, an arm gripped her wrist and spun her around. She didn't have a second to be afraid before a familiar voice demanded, 'What in God's name do you think you are doing?'

Jarin Ashdown stood glaring down at her, his dark eyebrows an angry slash across his forehead. She tried to pull free of his grip, but although he didn't hurt her his hand was like a circle of iron.

'I'm…' she started to say.

'This had better be good, because from where I'm standing it looks as though you have wilfully put yourself in extreme danger,' he growled.

'I don't have to answer to you,' she snapped. 'I'm a free woman and can do whatever I please.'

He laughed, the sound bitter and harsh and not at all like the charming one he deployed on a daily basis. He was always so calm; she had never seen him be anything but controlled, until now. 'You are a young woman under my protection. Do you have any idea, any idea at all, of what could have happened to you if you had been found out here by any man other than myself?'

'I…'

'Do you?' he growled again.

Heat travelled over Katherine's face and she was glad for the darkness to hide it. 'I know what happens between a man and a woman, if that's what you're asking, but it is highly unlikely to happen to me.'

He took a step backwards. 'Are you actually insane?'

Katherine tried to wrench her hand free as she cried, 'I am not crazy! Don't ever accuse me of that again.'

He nodded brusquely, keeping her arm in a vice-like grip. 'Fine. I will call you foolish instead, because that is also a very apt description. What makes you think you are any different from every other woman? Do you have some inhuman strength you are hiding from the rest of the world? It doesn't feel like it to me.' He gave her a little shake to demonstrate her physical inferiority. It only served to infuriate her further. How dare he treat her like a scrap of linen to be tossed around as if she were nothing!

'Men don't find me attractive. I never have been, nor ever will be, the object of a man's lust. So there, you see, I have nothing to worry about.'

He looked down at her for a long moment, anger burning in his eyes. 'You are even more foolish than I thought,' he said eventually. 'A man doesn't have to find a woman attractive to hurt her in the most basic way possible. To think otherwise is beyond ludicrous.'

A tiny part of her, a part she pushed down ruthlessly, was hurt that he hadn't denied her inability to be the object of a man's lust. Of course, a man as beautiful as he was wouldn't think that way about someone as plain as her.

'Come, I must return you to your room.' He began to tug her back towards the tavern.

'No,' she said, digging her heels into the dirt track. Gone were the days when people could tell her what to do. She had come out to see the night sky and that was what she was going to do.

He stopped tugging her, but didn't release his grip.

'No?' he repeated. 'Please don't think you have a choice in the matter. We are returning to your room even if I have to fling you over my shoulder and carry you there myself.'

'I am not going back in until I have done what I came out to do,' she stated.

'And what, pray tell, is that?'

She was grateful to the darkness for hiding the heat she felt spreading over her face. She tilted her chin up. 'I have come to look at the night sky.'

She heard him take a deep breath. 'You have come out here, risked your life and your…your…for that?' Incredulity laced his words.

With his freedom to come and go as he pleased he wouldn't understand her yearning for this simple pleasure, but suddenly it was important to try and make him understand.

'I have only ever seen it once before, so, yes, I have decided to see it this evening. It might seem like a small thing to you, but to me…to me it is everything,' she said simply.

His stance softened at her words and she felt his grip at her wrist relax although he didn't let her go.

'Fine,' he said eventually. 'We'll take a minute to look at the night sky on the condition that I stay with you the whole time. When I say it is time to return to the tavern you shall do so without argument.'

She bristled under his dictatorial commands, but she didn't utter any further comment. If she quibbled with him now, he could easily throw her over his shoulder as he'd threatened and there wasn't a great deal she could do about it.

His palm slid gently down her arm and his long, firm fingers curled around her hand. She found herself linking her fingers with his, the gesture coming naturally. 'Come,' he said softly, 'you'll get a better view from the ridge over there.'

They didn't speak as they made their way over to a small outcrop which looked out over the valley below. Her hand felt tiny in his and the warmth of his skin against hers slowly heated her. A strange, tingly sensation unfurled from where they connected and spread up her arm and over her body.

She glanced up at his face to see whether he was feeling the same effect, but it was impossible to make out his expression in the darkness. The new, unusual sensation was probably all one-sided. He was a deliciously handsome man used to mingling with sophisticated women while she was a spinster who'd spoken more to him than any other man, including her own brother. She had so little experience with the opposite sex it was as if they were a different species altogether. He probably barely even realised they were holding hands and merely thought of the connection as another way to keep control of her.

They reached the outcrop and he allowed her to step in front of him so she had the better view.

It was difficult to see where the stars ended and the edge of the valley began; the vast emptiness called to something in her soul. 'It's so beautiful,' she murmured.

'Did you know,' he said softly, all trace of anger gone from his voice, 'that the Romans believed their gods lived among the stars?'

'No, I didn't know that.'

'Do you see that red star, shimmering amongst the white?'

He leaned over, his face coming level with hers. A brief brush of stubble grazed her cheek and the strange, tingly feeling started up again.

'Yes,' she croaked.

'That's their god of war, Mars.'

'Really,' she breathed out. How amazing that over a thousand years ago people had looked up at the same sky and made stories about what they had seen. For this small moment in time, the sky reached across the years and connected them.

Jarin kept his hand curled around hers as they stared at the red dot which appeared to be winking straight at them. She wondered briefly if he realised he was still holding her hand. She should pull it away, but it was very pleasant to be held by someone.

Once again, he'd been remarkably kind and she was surprised to find he was more learned than she'd imagined. From the width of his shoulders she'd believed him to be interested in jousting and sword play rather than learning, but he must have studied Roman texts if he knew so much about their gods. Perhaps he wasn't an ignorant boor after all. The thought did nothing to ease her conflicting feelings about the man.

'Thank you,' she said eventually when the cold began to seep into her toes despite her practical boots.

'My pleasure. May we return to the tavern now?'

'Do I have a choice?' she asked lightly.

She felt him laugh. 'Not really.'

'Then, yes, I will allow you to escort me back.'

This time she heard him laugh.

'I think you are going to be the death of me, Mistress Leofric,' he said as they turned and began to walk back towards the inn.

'Why ever do you think that?' she asked, shocked.

'I think...' Jarin said. 'Wait, what's that noise?'

Katherine bumped into his side as he came to a complete stop.

'Some people are coming,' he said, pulling her behind the wall of the nearest dwelling.

'What does it matter if someone sees us?' she asked as he pushed her body against the building, shielding her with his own. 'With my hood up we could just be two men walking.'

'You look nothing like a man,' growled Jarin.

'That's not true. I have virtually no female shape and this cloak covers me completely.'

'I knew you were a woman as soon as you stepped into the taproom and I knew it was you before you reached the door. Your cloak is not as good a disguise as you think it is.'

'That doesn't count. You know what I look like from riding behind me for—'

His free hand came up and closed over her mouth. 'Could you stop arguing with me for one moment?' he ground out. 'You look like a woman, you move like a woman, you are a woman and a sheltered, naive one at that. It is dangerous outside in the dark, even for me. Now let's wait here, in complete silence, until whoever is out there has passed and then we can be on our way again.'

His hand remained over her mouth. Katherine's heart began to beat faster in a way that had nothing to do with the strangers approaching and everything to do with Jarin's proximity. She'd never been so close to a man. Never had one touch her face. She could feel the ridges of his palm against her lips. This close she could smell him: the rich smoky scent of the tavern's fire mixed with something spicy. She clamped her lips shut before she gave into the overwhelming urge to taste his skin. He'd likely think she really was insane if she indulged in that behaviour. Even through layers of thick clothing she could feel his hard, lean body and her stomach squirmed in a whole new way she didn't recognise or understand.

The footsteps were coming nearer and Jarin's hard body tensed against hers.

'It's a two-day ride from here,' said a deep voice she didn't recognise.

An answering grunt and a murmur she couldn't make out followed.

'Borwyn will have to stay in Swein for at least a day to rest his horses and get provisions,' continued the voice. 'I'd guess at two and then it's another three days to Borwyn's fortress from there.'

'So we've got almost a week to get it done.'

'I'd say five days to be on the safe side.'

There was a grunt of agreement and two sets of footsteps passed them, gradually fading into the distance.

When they could hear nothing more, Jarin slowly removed his hand from Katherine's face.

'What was that about?' she whispered when it became apparent he wasn't going to say anything.

He didn't answer. Instead, he set off back to the tavern, tugging her along in his wake, his fingers locked firmly but gently around her wrist again.

'That was strange,' Katherine said again. 'What do you think they were talking about?'

'It's nothing for you to worry about,' he said tersely.

'So you know about it, then?'

He stopped abruptly, his hand briefly tightening on her wrist, 'What do you mean by "it"? Do you know what they were talking about?'

'Of course I don't. How could I? Until a week ago I had barely left my room in eight years. I didn't even realise how close we are to your land until a moment ago. You said it was nothing, so *I* assumed *you* knew.'

Some of the tension left his body. Had he really believed she'd know about a plot against him? How would she have found out about anything from her chamber?

'We're on my land already. We'll pass into Swein's territory at some point tomorrow. Do you think you and Linota could be ready to leave early in the morning? I'd like to try and shave a day off the journey and arrive at Swein tomorrow.'

Katherine's heart dropped. She'd so enjoyed seeing the country and now it was coming to an end even earlier than she'd expected. Unless… 'Why don't we go straight to your fortress?'

'What?'

'Those men were clearly planning to do something in the next five days. Why not take them by surprise and arrive earlier than expected? You'll be able to catch them at whatever they're doing. I mean, it might be nothing, but it sounded odd, didn't it?'

He paused for a moment and appeared to consider

her suggestion, but then shook his head, 'I can't leave you and your sister to travel without me.'

'We'll come with you. It's only a day or two out of the way. You can write to my brother and tell him something unexpected has turned up and that we'll be delayed by a few days. I dare say he and his new bride will enjoy having more time to themselves.'

'They're hardly alone. They're in a castle full of people.'

Katherine held her breath. If that was his best argument, then it shouldn't take much to persuade him to take her and Linota with him. She'd be able to see so much more of the country—even the Borwyns' ancestral home, which was rumoured to be magnificent. Perhaps, when she'd seen all that, the strange, restless feeling that was growing inside her with every day that passed would be satisfied.

As his silence lengthened, her heart thrilled in excitement. The Borwyn fortress was rumoured to be so much more luxurious than Ogmore's. Jarin's late mother apparently had exquisite taste in decoration and his father had splashed out on every comfort. She would love the chance to see it as a guest and, if she was lucky, explore the surrounding countryside. Even with a guard that would be more freedom than she'd experienced in her whole life.

She looked up at Jarin. He was staring in the direction the men had taken, anxiety crinkling the corners of his eyes. Guilt hit her hard. While she was imagining adventures, he was worrying about his home, perhaps even his life.

'Going there first will set your mind at ease,' she

said quietly. 'Linota and I won't mind a few extra days' travelling.'

His lips curled into a small smile. 'I'm not sure Braith can take it. Your riding is putting the poor horse through its paces.' Her heart thudded at his gentle teasing.

Then he sobered. 'If you think you and Linota will be all right travelling for a little longer, then I would prefer to go to Borwyn first, thank you. I don't know what those two men are up to, but I would like to check that everything is as it should be.'

It was only later, as Katherine lay in bed, still unable to sleep, that she remembered she'd witnessed Erik Ward's strange behaviour at Ogmore. She should have told Borwyn what she'd seen, but she'd watched the two men together over the few days they'd all been travelling together. It was obvious the two of them were close and she was hard pressed to believe that Erik Ward was acting against Borwyn's best interests. Still, she would have to try and find time to speak with Jarin privately over the next day to tell him what she had seen.

The thought caused an odd fluttering sensation in her stomach. She touched the spot lightly. What did that mean? Surely it wasn't excitement about talking to Borwyn. If it was, then he was right: she was very foolish.

She rolled on to her side and stared at the wall. She definitely wasn't excited about speaking to Jarin Ashdown. The fluttery feeling was down to nerves. She didn't want to accuse his friend of something and cause a rift between the two men. She'd seen enough strife to last a lifetime. Reassured, she drifted off to sleep.

Chapter Seven

Jarin looked at the riders around him. Signs of strain were beginning to show themselves in sagging bodies and tight-lipped grimaces. Not that anyone had complained to him or shown any surprise that they were now heading, at speed, towards Borwyn instead of Swein. One of the benefits of being an earl was that his orders were always obeyed without question. He began to slow his pace; for once he was riding up front, setting the rate of travel he expected everyone to follow. His mood must have been apparent because there were no lingerers today.

He turned in his saddle; well, there was one. Riding at the back of the pack was Katherine Leofric. Even from a distance he could see that her white face was etched with pain, but she hadn't once complained or asked to slow or stop. She had more grit than her slight frame would suggest.

'We'll rest here,' he said to Erik.

Katherine needed a break. Even if her riding skills were fantastic—and they were far from that—the bruises he'd seen yesterday must be hurting her as she moved. He didn't want to stop and think how much her physical comfort meant to him. She was effectively his guest and so, of course, he had to make sure she was cared for; it had nothing to do with his rampaging desire. He was working to control that and he *would* succeed. Even if she did turn out to be the ideal wife for him, she would never know how much his body craved her. No one would ever have the kind of power his first wife had wielded over him for a short but brutal time in his past. Those days were over.

The whole party slowed and gradually came to a standstill near to a slow-moving stream. Erik set about giving orders to everyone while Jarin took Eira for a drink.

Erik was the only one who knew the reason behind the change of plan, apart from Katherine. He had tried to talk Jarin out of returning to Borwyn, saying that he could go by himself to investigate the strange plot Jarin had overheard last night. He argued that Jarin was placing himself in unnecessary danger by returning home in the middle of something. Jarin didn't see it like that. The two men had not talked about a threat to his person. Whatever they were planning specifically required him not to be at the formidable Borwyn fortress and after all the problems he'd experienced over the last year he wasn't taking any chances. If this was the plot that finally pushed him over the edge, he wanted to face it head on.

He slipped from Eira's back. Her coat was slick with sweat and he rubbed her neck. Hopefully she would forgive him this rough ride across the country. He relinquished her to his master of horses and made his way over to Katherine.

'How are you faring?' he asked as he held up a hand to help her down.

She eyed his outstretched hand. For a moment he thought she was going to refuse to take it, but then she placed her slender fingers in his and his soul roared in triumph. Last night he'd held her hand and he'd enjoyed the way it had made him feel: protective and warm. He'd wondered if she'd noticed that he hadn't wanted to let go of her. He'd felt pathetic afterwards. Had he become so starved of companionship that holding the hand of someone who couldn't stand him brought him joy? No, joy wasn't quite the right word. Their contact had made his blood sing and he'd had to fight to keep things chaste between them. She would never know how much he had wanted to place his lips against hers as she'd stared up at the night sky, her eyes alight with excitement.

He'd sworn to avoid her today. Despite all his efforts, she had a way of making him forget his vows. He was once again caught up lusting after a woman and if he wasn't careful he could find himself in another marriage straight from hell. He'd given himself a stern talking to after he'd seen Katherine to her chamber last night. *Stay away from Katherine until you can judge the situation with cold, practical reasoning.* But at the first opportunity he'd had, he was already holding hands with her again and the strange sensation was whipping through his blood once more. He was a fool.

She swung her leg over the saddle and slipped down

from Braith. He caught her around her middle and gently lowered her to the ground.

'Thank you,' she said breathlessly.

His hand rested on her waist for a fraction longer than necessary before he remembered himself and stepped away.

'I trust you are not too fatigued by today's riding,' he said.

'It's not so much that I am tired,' she said. 'I'm afraid I'm going to have to confess that you are right. I'm not very good on a horse.'

He managed to swallow his laughter, although it took some effort.

'You don't have to pretend not to laugh,' she said, picking up on his mood despite his efforts.

'I thought I was hiding it quite well.' He smiled down at her and got locked in her gaze.

In the afternoon winter sunlight her eyes seemed to burn a golden colour. He'd never known eyes to look so different depending on the surroundings. Jarin spent far too long wondering what they would look like next time he looked at her.

'You're not as good at hiding it as you think you are,' she said in a light parody of his own words to her the night before, a soft smile taking the sting out of her words.

She stepped away from him, breaking the strange hold her eyes seemed to have. He let out a long breath. It seemed she had no problem keeping away from him, a fact he would do well to remember.

'Are we nearly there?' she asked, hope filling her eyes.

'I'm afraid not.'

Her shoulders drooped.

'Would you find a slower pace easier? Perhaps we could split into two groups. Erik could ride with you and Linota along with several others who have slower mounts.'

'No, thank you, my lord,' she said quickly. 'I will do my best to keep up with everyone. But…there is something I would like to discuss with you.' She glanced around. 'It's private,' she whispered.

He looked around them. Several of his men were dotted nearby tending to their horses.

'Let's lead Braith down to the stream. I'm sure she would appreciate a drink,' he said, taking her horse's reins from her and leading them both down towards the narrow river.

They walked in silence for a few steps.

'Well?' he said when they were out of earshot.

'On the night of my brother's wedding I was outside the keep.'

Jarin groaned. 'Please tell me you had a guard with you.'

She didn't respond. He glanced down at her and saw a blush spreading across her cheeks.

'Mistress Leofric, you really ought to take better care of yourself.'

'It was the first time I'd ever done anything like that,' she muttered.

'And your last.'

He heard her hiss of annoyance.

'Do you want to hear what I've got to say or not?' She frowned up at him.

He held his breath. What he wanted to do was yell

at her for putting herself in unnecessary danger *again*. She seemed to think she so lacked desirability that she was safe from male predators, but she couldn't be more wrong. Yes, she didn't dress well and her hairstyle was suitable for a much older lady, but she had wide, beautifully intriguing eyes and full sensuous lips and underneath her shabby clothes was a slim, feminine figure. He couldn't have been the only man to notice that she really was very desirable despite her attempts to hide it.

'Well?' she asked when he didn't respond to her question.

'Please tell me what you saw, Mistress Leofric, and then promise me you will not be so cavalier with your safety in future.'

'I will make no such promises about what I will or will not do. You are not my brother or my husband and therefore you have no authority over me.'

Her matter-of-fact statement shouldn't hurt, but it did.

'Maybe I don't have any say over your actions, but I'm sure your brother won't be pleased to know that you wander around alone at night.'

She gasped. 'You wouldn't dare tell him.'

'Why wouldn't I?'

'Because I am about to help you,' she said quietly. 'And to tell him would betray my trust in you.'

He sighed. She had a way of disarming him when he least expected it, 'Very well, Mistress Leofric. I won't tell Sir Braedan about your night-time wanderings.' He made no such promise not to mention it to her brother's wife. Someone ought to keep an eye on Katherine. It appeared no one did at the moment and they should because she obviously didn't think about her own safety. 'Please do tell me what it is that you witnessed.'

She nodded, but didn't speak, twisting her fingers together.

'What is it, Mistress Leofric?' he said gently.

'You won't like it,' she said.

He bit back a groan of frustration, 'Try me.'

'I saw Erik Ward.' She glanced at him and then away again, focusing on the water near her feet.

'Erik! Doing what?' Of all the things he was expecting her to say that wasn't one of them.

'He was hiding in the shadows.'

'I think you need to start from the beginning. How do you know he was hiding and not merely out taking the air, not unlike yourself?'

'He was moving in the same way as me. That is to say, he was hiding in the shadows, close to the wall, walking slowly and not striding about as if he was meant to be there. When one of the guards shouted out he flattened himself deeper against the wall. Then he waited for a bit and a short man, who was completely covered from head to toe in a large, dark cloak, appeared. They spoke for a moment and the man gave him a package. Then they went their separate ways. After they parted Erik began walking normally again, as if he didn't have a care in the world.'

Jarin stopped as they reached the river and Braith began to drink deeply. Katherine stood next to him, a small frown marring her forehead; her fingers still tightly entwined.

'That does sound strange,' he said slowly. 'But it doesn't follow that his behaviour has anything to do with the men we saw last night. I'd know Erik's voice anywhere; he wasn't one of them.'

'I know,' she said quietly. 'I'm not trying to drive a wedge between you and your friend. It's only…'

'It's only?'

'It was odd. That's all. I thought you should know.'

He paused. It was strange behaviour and part of him didn't like that Erik was clearly hiding something from him. He knew nothing about packages or meeting strange men after dark. But Erik was his own man and what he did in his free time was nothing to do with Jarin. Still, it was worth looking into…

'Thank you for telling me. I will speak to Erik and ask him what he was up to.'

She gasped. 'You can't do that. He'll know I saw him and…'

'I'm not going to tell him you were watching him. What do you take me for?' His anger at her actions blazed up once more; she needed to think more of her own safety. Was there no one around her who cared what she was up to? It would appear not and it shook him a little that he increasingly wanted to be the person did. 'If word got out that you were prone to night-time wanderings, I dread to think who would be lying in wait next time you venture out. It would put you in danger. I will say that one of my men saw him and mentioned it to me.'

She nodded, ignoring his angry outburst. 'Thank you and I'm sorry if I've caused you unnecessary worry.'

He turned to look at her, surprised she had recognised her foolhardy behaviour so quickly. 'Well, as long as you promise not to do it again. Wandering around alone at night is very dangerous.'

'I didn't mean about me,' she said sharply. 'I'm not of your concern. I meant about Erik.'

'I can take care of Erik. It's you and your unhealthy disregard for your own safety that concerns me.'

'And I told you last night: I'm not feminine enough for you to worry about in that way.'

Two high spots of colour appeared on her cheeks.

'And I told you,' he ground out, 'that regardless of what you think you look every inch a woman.'

They stood glaring at each other, neither of them backing down an inch. A soft breeze pushed her braids away from her face, revealing her long, graceful neck. Even as his body thrummed with anger he still had to fight the urge to lean down and run his lips along the skin beneath her ear to her collarbone. It appeared that was becoming something of an obsession.

'I'll take Braith to get some food,' he said eventually.

She nodded briskly and turned her attention to the stream, clearly dismissing him. While the rest of the world treated him with respect because of his position, she seemed to consider him little more than a newly sworn-in page with nothing better to do than wait on her.

What irritated him more than anything was that he seemed to do what she wanted. Last night, instead of marching her back to her room as he should have done, he'd ended up showing her the stars. He'd been pleased she was interested in knowing about the Roman god. He'd spent an inordinately long time today wondering if she would be interested in learning more. He should have been dwelling on more important things, such as what was awaiting him at Borwyn. It was as he'd feared all along. Desire for her was playing with his mind and she didn't even like him. What was wrong with him?

A sharp tug on the reins caused Braith to snort and toss her head. He murmured sweet nothings to her as he walked, trying to calm his irritation. What was Katherine thinking, walking around by herself at night? Anything could happen to her and no one would blame the man who took her body as his plaything. It would be her fault for wilfully putting herself in danger. How could she not see it? Despite his promise not to mention it to her brother he resolved to do so. If he had a sister, he would expect the same courtesy.

He handed Braith to his master of horses and strode towards Erik.

'We're not making good time,' said his friend as he approached.

'No, we're not.'

'I'll ride ahead if you like. I can take a few of the men.'

Jarin frowned. It would make more sense for him to ride ahead rather than Erik. It was his home under threat and Erik should know that. Was Erik offering because he had something to hide or was Jarin reading too much into it after what Katherine had told him? Jarin had been tasked with keeping the Leofric sisters safe, so perhaps Erik was keeping that in mind rather than plotting against him. He rubbed his forehead to relieve the headache that was building up behind his skull. It made no difference and the pounding continued unabated.

'I'd prefer not to separate,' said Jarin eventually.

'Very well,' said Erik briskly. 'I'll speak with William and see whether he has any thoughts on a quicker route.'

Jarin watched Erik stride away from him and then shook his head. Erik had been his closest companion for many years. They'd grown up together and when Jarin's father and older brothers had laughed and jeered at him, it had been Erik he'd turned to. It was Erik who had shown him how to get away from the fortress whenever his father's temper had turned to fists. The two of them had hunted in the nearby forest for days until heading back once they'd deemed it enough time for his father's temper to have cooled. It was Erik who had helped him when his older brothers had died, leaving him as the sole heir to the vast Borwyn estate, much to his father's disgust. Whatever Erik was hiding, it was nothing to do with Jarin. He trusted his oldest friend.

Jarin's stomach rumbled, reminding him he'd not eaten today. He made his way over to Alban, who was handing out some oatcakes to those who wanted them.

He hadn't got very far when screams erupted from the river bank.

It all happened so quickly. Katherine was staring into the depths of the riverbed, trying to control her swirling emotions—Jarin Ashdown was such a contradiction. One minute he was treating her with care and compassion and the next he was growling at her and implying she was an idiot. And was that care and compassion because he hoped to use her for Ogmore's dowry or because he really was a good person?

She was just trying to convince herself that she

hadn't enjoyed his strong arms helping her down from Braith when several riders on horseback burst out of the woods nearby. There was no time to stop them as they swept through the rough gathering of Jarin's unsuspecting men.

One man rode so close to her his knee brushed against her back and she smelt the damp sweat of his mount. She slipped and gasped in surprise as one of her feet became submerged in icy water. The rider didn't spare her a glance as she scrambled back on to the bank.

'No,' she screamed as she realised their intent. 'Stop! Get away from her.'

She stumbled towards Linota, but it was too late. One rider leaned down and grabbed her sister, dumping her across the front of his horse as if she weighed nothing, and urging the beast on with a sharp kick of his heels.

Katherine's heart pounded as she scrambled after Linota. 'Put her down! Leave her alone!' she screamed, her lungs burning. But it was to no avail. The riders kept going and very quickly disappeared out of sight.

Katherine continued to run, slipping and sliding on the muddy shores of the river bank. She didn't realise she was still screaming until firm arms grabbed her around the waist.

'Let go of me!' she shouted, pummelling the arms that held her with her fists. 'I need to get her.'

'You're not going to catch up with her on foot,' came Jarin's voice, calm over steel. 'Some of my riders are already following her. They'll catch up with them quickly.'

'I need to… I need…'

'I know, come on.' He raced over to his own horse,

tugging her in his wake and shouting his instructions to his men to follow the direction of the riders. Those on faster mounts were to go first. If they were separated, they would reconvene at the nearest town, Ickleston.

It took two attempts for Katherine to climb on to Braith. Her arms were shaking so much she couldn't pull herself on to the saddle. Jarin came up behind her and flung her into the seat. She didn't wait to thank him before she set off in pursuit.

Fear coated every breath as she kicked Braith into a canter, urging the placid mount to go faster than she'd ever moved before. The docile horse began to run and Katherine gasped as she was jolted from side to side. This was even worse than riding at a trot. Nothing felt steady or secure, but it didn't matter.

All that mattered was Linota. Dear, sweet Linota, who was so beautiful and innocent. What would those men do to her when they got her alone? That must not happen.

Katherine rounded a bend in the road and started to slip from her saddle.

'Not now,' she muttered, deeply regretting not paying more attention when Jarin had tried to help her with her riding. He was right; she was dreadful. Her stubbornness meant her sister was paying for it when it mattered most.

She managed to right herself only to find herself falling to the other side. Beneath her the saddle shifted.

'What?' she said out loud.

'Is everything all right, Mistress Leofric?' yelled Jarin from close by.

'The saddle,' she gasped, as her seat moved beneath her once more.

In her fright, she tightened her legs on her horse. Braith took this as a sign to go faster and she screamed as the air began to rush past her face. She pulled on the reins, but Braith was galloping now, perhaps sensing Katherine's fear, and the two of them began to careen towards the woodland lining the rough path.

'Please,' she whimpered as she began to tilt towards the ground.

But nobody answered her prayers. Braith continued to hurtle towards the trees. In a blinding moment of panic she realised what was about to happen and she tried to save herself, raising her arms above her head. But she was too late. The world exploded in pain and then went black.

Chapter Eight

She came round to gentle fingers probing her head, a soft, yet firm pillow beneath her.

'Mistress Leofric,' came a deep voice. 'Are you awake?'

She scrunched her eyes tightly. She didn't want to wake. Everything ached, especially her head. The beating from Mother must have been particularly bad this time. She didn't normally lose consciousness. She wanted to go back to her dream of being held and stroked by strong, capable hands.

'I'm sorry, Katherine, but you really must wake up.'

She rolled over on to her side and buried herself deeply into the pillow. It was firm but comfortable.

There was the sound of a long breath being released and the warm fingers were back, stroking her hair away from the nape of her neck in a soft, soothing gesture. Fingers grazed the back of her neck, sending tingles down her spine. She arched into the sensation, but kept her eyes firmly closed, grateful that Linota was close by and taking such good care of her. She normally tried to hide how badly she was hurt from her sister, but she was so tired today. Perhaps she could close her eyes and rest for just a little bit longer.

A breath whispered across her face and she frowned. That didn't feel like Linota. It was heavier somehow with a faint scent of recently drunk ale. The fingers that were now rubbing her back in a wide, comforting arc were too strong to belong to her sister.

She forced her eyes to open.

She was not in her bed at Ogmore's castle and her head was not resting on a comfortable pillow, but on Jarin Ashdown's thighs.

She gasped and tried to push herself into an upright position. Her head swam and bile rose in her throat.

'Careful,' came Jarin's warning as he held her in place. 'You've had a nasty encounter with a tree. I want to check that nothing's broken before you get up.'

'Linota!' she gasped, as the recollection about what had happened to her sister hit her with full force.

'Hush, stay still. It's going to be all right.'

'She's been found?'

'Not yet, but I've got my best men heading after them. I'm sure they'll find her very soon.'

Katherine pushed herself off him and staggered to her feet. The world tilted alarmingly and she clutched Jarin's strong shoulder for support, his muscles bunched under her fingers.

'I told you to be careful,' he growled.

She snatched her hand back and stepped away from him. It was imperative that she get back on Braith.

'Where is everyone else?' she asked as she took in

their surroundings. There was no sign of any of the rest of Jarin's men.

'They've carried on after your sister. I'm afraid we've had to abandon the cart and our belongings. It was slowing us down'

'It doesn't matter,' Katherine waved her hand. It wasn't as if she had anything of value anyway. 'I have to go after her. When I think what might be happening to her right now…' She convulsed at the thought of those grubby hands on her sister.

'We will catch up with them before anything happens to her.'

'How do you know that? Can you really trust all your men?' she demanded.

'Of course I trust them,' he snapped as he got to his feet.

'Really? Then have you had an explanation from Erik as to what he was doing creeping around at night?'

'Not yet, but I fail to see how that relates to those men appearing out of the woods like that.'

'Someone is planning something against you and they have taken my sister as part of it.'

Jarin frowned. 'I really don't think so. They were opportunists who must have been watching us from the woods. They saw us stop and took the easiest person they could. They are probably planning on ransoming her. It can't have been personal; your sister is nothing to me.'

'Oh, don't I just know it,' said Katherine, fear turning to misplaced anger. 'You couldn't care less if she was left to rot amongst the trees. I know that to you she is practically worthless, but not to me. To me she is everything.' Tears burned the back of her eyes and she dashed them away before they could fall down her face.

She turned blindly away from him, searching for Braith. She took a step and tripped over something solid. She would have fallen if strong arms hadn't come around her once more.

'Be careful,' roared Jarin, his temper finally erupting. 'Your recklessness keeps getting you into trouble over and over again. You are thoughtless and rude and insulting and you pay no attention to the hazards around you.'

Jarin settled her on her feet and stormed away from her. She glanced down at what she'd nearly fallen over and discovered her saddle lying on the ground.

She hefted it into her arms. She needed to get it back on Braith, but she was not going to ask Jarin for help.

'You won't be able to use that,' he said curtly as she tried to carry it towards her horse. 'It's damaged.'

Jarin was glaring at her from beside his own horse. 'We'll both have to ride on Eira.'

She shook her head. 'No, I'm not riding with you.'

To be so close to him would be torture when the slightest brush of his fingers caused her body to tingle in a way that was strangely pleasurable. There had to be another way.

'You can walk, then,' said Jarin, preparing to mount his horse. 'The nearest town is about a day's walk in that direction. I'll have one of my men wait for you there.'

'You can't leave me here.'

He stopped with one foot in the stirrup.

'Make up your mind, Katherine. Your options are to walk or to share Eira, but as I'm sure you're aware, time is pressing and we need to get to your sister as soon as possible.'

'You don't need to remind me. Hey, what are you doing?'

'I'm getting on my horse. I don't need to listen to any more of your time-wasting lectures.'

'You don't care about—'

'So you keep telling me. But for someone who professes to care so much, you aren't making any sacrifices to find her.'

A hundred excuses flew into her mind, but Jarin was right; she was wasting time by arguing with him and by not getting on Eira. She would have to control her body's reaction and hope that he didn't notice. It would be humiliating if he knew how much his body called to her. She didn't want to be like all the other ladies she'd witnessed clamouring for his attention.

'Fine, I will ride with you.'

She heard Jarin mutter something about her lack of graciousness, but she ignored him as he hauled her into the saddle in front of him.

'You're going to have to sit more upright,' said Jarin as Eira began to move beneath them.

His large hands moved about her body, shaping her into the position he required. She forced herself to ignore him even though her skin burned in the wake of his touch. The shape of the saddle meant that her thighs were pressed against his and with his arms around her to hold the reins, it felt as though he was everywhere, filling her senses and making it difficult to think about anything else.

Eira moved on to the path.

'What about Braith?' she asked as they set off at a brisk pace.

'I'm hoping she will follow us or make her own way back to Borwyn. She's travelled the route many times so I'm sure she will find it. If not, a lucky farmer will find a free horse,' came his curt response as he kicked Eira into a faster movement.

She twisted in the saddle to see if Braith was following and breathed a sigh of relief at the sight of the mare plodding placidly behind them. Katherine knew she wasn't the best of riders, but she had grown fond of the animal and the thought of leaving her to fend for herself made her feel sick.

The sun began its slow descent and there was still no sign of Linota or any of Jarin's men. The silence stretched so tight between her and Jarin that it was almost deafening. Guilt started to coil in her stomach. She had been hard with him when he had been nothing but considerate. He'd sent men after Linota as soon as she'd been taken. He'd been calm and reasoned when she had panicked. She needed to apologise, but the words stuck in her throat.

'What makes you think I don't care about what happens to your sister?' asked Jarin as the sun began to disappear behind the trees.

'It's not something I think. It's something I know,' said Katherine, her voice cracking.

'What do you mean by that?'

'I heard you talking to Erik. I know of Ogmore's suggestion that you marry either me or Linota and I know how you feel about that. You said something about sullying the Borwyn lineage. My father's treason and my mother's rumoured insanity make us repellent to you.'

She felt him flinch and she closed her eyes. Confronting him with the truth didn't make her feel as good as she'd thought she would whenever she'd imagined it. There was complete silence from behind her and she wondered what he was thinking.

Darkness descended and the temperature dropped. Her boot still hadn't dried out from her earlier dip in the river and she started to shiver in earnest.

Without saying anything, Jarin untied his cloak and threw it around them both, tugging her backwards into the warmth of his body. She tried not to sigh in relief as some of his heat began to transfer to her.

'I am sorry,' he said after they had covered some distance. 'You should not have had to hear what I said about you and your sister. It is unforgivable, but for what it is worth, I am very sorry.'

'Sorry about what you said or sorry that I heard it?' It was mean to press him during what must be a difficult apology, but she wanted to know the truth; the answer was important when it came to making up her mind about him.

She felt him laugh against her back, the movement doing strange things to her body.

'You aren't going to make this easy for me, are you, Mistress Leofric? I am sorry about both. I did not know you when I made a judgement against your character without any evidence to support what I said. That you had to hear such a slur against you fills me with shame. For what it's worth, my opinion of you both has changed greatly since I have come to know you over the last few days. I think any man would be proud to call either you or Linota his wife, although I am sure that probably doesn't make amends as far as you are concerned. I can only offer my deepest apologies and hope that in time you can forgive me for my abhorrent words.'

They rode in silence while Katherine thought about what he'd said. She knew from experience it was difficult to offer an apology even when you knew yourself to be in the wrong and she was impressed that such a high and mighty man had the humility to do so. She didn't doubt from the tone of his voice that he was sorry and embarrassed. His behaviour since then had been exemplary and he had never treated Linota with anything other than complete respect. Even when he was wrongly being rude and overbearing with her, it was usually with good intentions.

'Thank you for your apology. I accept it,' she said eventually. She felt him nod against her hair and the movement sent tingles over her scalp. 'Now that you've got to know me, I expect you find me worse than you had imagined,' she added.

He laughed and the tension between them broke.

'I find you to be brave and headstrong and, when you're not doing madly irresponsible things, I do like you,' he said.

Her heart swelled strangely at his words though she didn't know why. It was hardly a declaration of love. He'd only said he liked her and that some nameless man would be proud to be her husband, which he was almost obliged to say as part of his apology. She noticed he hadn't said that *he* would be proud, but nevertheless his statement made her feel happy.

Then it hit her again that she had no right to feel like that. Her sister was probably out of her mind with fright and despair and here she was, enjoying the company of the very man she had sworn never to forgive. Perhaps it was time for her to let go of her hurt now. He'd proven himself to be an honourable man and she was depending on him to get her out of this disaster.

'How soon before we reach the town?' she asked.

'Not soon enough. I fear it is still some way ahead.'

'Will we make it before night sets in?'

'No, I'm afraid not.'

An owl hooted from high in the branches above them and Katherine felt a tear trickle down her face. She tried to stop others following it, but it was too hard. She held her body still, trying not to let the sobs shake her.

'Oh, Katherine,' said Jarin, slipping an arm around her waist. Even through her misery she noticed the use of her first name and decided she liked the sound of it from his lips. The thought only made her feel worse.

'Please don't cry,' he said.

'I'm sorry,' she mumbled through her tears. 'If I wasn't such a bad rider, we'd still be with the others. I should have listened to you at the beginning of the journey. If I had I might have made some improvement, but instead I rushed headlong into that tree.'

Jarin cleared his throat. 'I don't think it was your fault you hit that tree.'

'What do you mean? I was slipping and sliding all over the place. If only I'd learnt how to hold on properly.'

'It wasn't your riding that was the problem. The saddle was broken. A strap snapped, which meant it was loose, and that's why you fell. I will be having words with Jay, my master of horses, when this is all over. He's meant to check each saddle thoroughly before it is used. It is because of his negligence that you fell and, as he is under my charge, I owe you yet another apology.'

'But that can't be right,' said Katherine, her tears stopping in her puzzlement. 'I was with Jay earlier this morning as he checked over my saddle, he was showing me how I could do it myself. I saw with my own eyes that all the straps were in good working order.'

Jarin's arm turned rigid against her stomach.

'Are you sure?' he asked.

'Yes, I'm very sure.'

The sound of Eira's heavy footsteps seemed louder as night began to draw in. In the darkness of the night Katherine couldn't see whether Braith was still following them. She hoped so. No one should be alone in a strange forest. As the silence between them continued, her mind began to focus on Linota. Her stomach twisted as if live snakes had taken up residence inside her. Linota was all that was good and pure—how would this terrible experience change her?

'If you're sure about the straps, then your saddle must have been tampered with,' said Jarin into the silence.

'What?' she exclaimed, her mind so far away from her own troubles that she'd almost forgotten about her encounter with the tree.

'I wish I'd brought the saddle with me so I could check. At the time I was thinking mostly about you and praying that you'd wake up and didn't pay close attention to your saddle, but if the straps were broken by the time you fell then someone must have cut them.'

A cold, icy dread slipped down Katherine's spine. 'That means you can't trust all your men after all.'

Silence and then, 'No. It seems I can't.'

'Erik...'

'I gave Braith to Jay and then spoke directly to Erik. He then went to speak to William about our journey to Borwyn. He can't have had time to tamper with your saddle before the horsemen took Linota.'

'Would it have taken long?'

Behind her Jarin held himself tightly. 'No,' he said after a long silence. 'It would not have taken long, but I still don't see how he would have had the opportunity. Neither I nor William were anywhere near the horses. It can't have been him.'

Katherine had her doubts. She'd seen Erik acting suspiciously and then something like this had happened. It made sense for him to be involved, but she had to admit she couldn't see why. There was nothing Erik would gain from her getting hurt. For that matter, there was nothing anyone could gain. She was the most expendable out of the whole group. In the whole world only Linota truly cared for her.

'I can't see what Erik would gain from cutting the straps of your saddle,' said Jarin in an echo of her own thoughts.

'I can't either. I can't see what anyone would gain. I'm not important.'

Jarin's arm tightened around her momentarily.

'I suppose whoever did it meant to slow me down, but I'm not the fastest rider anyway so...'

'Until we know where this is leading I guess we

won't find out. When we do, you can rest assured that the perpetrator will be punished.'

Katherine shuddered at the steel in his voice.

'What will…?'

Jarin brought Eira to an abrupt halt. 'Can you hear that?' he whispered harshly.

'Hear what?'

'Listen.'

At first all Katherine could hear was Eira's heavy breathing, but as she listened carefully she caught the sound of several things moving in the undergrowth in front of them.

She shrank back against Jarin, the hairs on her neck standing up on end.

'What is it?' she whispered, her heart hammering painfully in her chest.

'It's an ambush.'

Chapter Nine

The urge to flee and protect Katherine warred with Jarin's need to slay each one of the men who dared to creep through the forest to threaten her. Later he would question why her safety was so important to him, but right now only one thing was paramount: Katherine.

He tugged on Eira's reins. It was better to live another day to protect Katherine than die fighting and leave her to the mercy of the group of savages. Eira turned quickly and he squeezed her flank, urging her to fly faster. But before they could take a step, Eira reared in fright. Men poured out from behind and in front of them. Katherine screamed and the shrill sound pierced his heart. He held her tightly as Eira bucked, kicking her legs in terror.

A rough hand grabbed Eira's reins. Jarin whipped his dagger from his boot and thrust it into the grasping fingers. There was a howl of pain, but more hands were pawing at Katherine and tugging on her cloak in an effort to pull her from the horse. He stabbed wildly, causing more yelps and curses, but he knew it was only a matter of time until they were overpowered. In front of him, Katherine's breath was coming in frightened pants and then she was gone from in front of him as she was pulled to the ground, screaming his name as she fell.

He jumped down after her and punched her assailant full in the face. The force of his rage sent the man to the ground and Katherine staggered back into his arms as he pulled her away from Eira. There was no telling what damage the panicked horse would do if she accidentally kicked Katherine's slight body.

'Calm that horse,' growled a voice full of authority.

Jarin winced as Eira's reins were sharply tugged. A burly man tried to subdue his horse through force, but even though it went against his instincts, Jarin didn't try to intervene. Katherine was his priority now.

'Get that mule away from here,' the same authoritative voice commanded.

Eira was pulled away, her head tossing angrily in her effort to pull herself free.

Jarin used the distraction to tug Katherine towards the safety of the forest.

The rasp of a sword being pulled from its scabbard made him freeze.

'I can see you're a smart man, your lordship,' said the voice of the man who had been barking out orders. 'There is no way for you to fight us all so it is best you surrender.'

Jarin thrust Katherine behind him. When she got the chance, he hoped she would run. He could not protect her against this many opponents, no matter how skilled a swordsman he was. Instead of inching away, as he hoped she would, he could feel her slender fingers clinging to his back. She really was the most foolhardy person he knew.

'What do you want?' he asked.

'Everything you have of value, starting with your magnificent horse and the pouch of money I can see dangling from your belt.'

Jarin swallowed. He'd been expecting worse, much worse. As long as they didn't strip the clothes from his body—or, more importantly, Katherine's body—he could cope with the loss of a few coins.

'And the girl,' piped up another voice and the crowd of men jeered.

Katherine whimpered, her small frame curling closer to him.

'Not the girl,' Jarin said firmly. He would die before he allowed that to happen.

'I don't think you're in a position to argue,' said the leader.

'I can't fight you all,' said Jarin, his voice steady, 'but I can fight some of you. I'll definitely be able to kill a few and, if I get lucky, even more. Is she really worth your lives?' He paused, waiting for his threat to sink in. 'If you leave her alone, you can have everything else I have without a protest.'

'I say we take the risk and get the girl,' said one of the men.

There was a murmur of laughter among the crowd, but it wasn't as loud as the jeering earlier.

The leader watched him closely. Jarin stood very still, breathing evenly.

'Very well,' said the leader at last. 'We'll take everything you have, but leave the girl.'

Jarin nodded, silently thanking God that the leader had accepted he was a credible threat. As much as he abhorred violence, he would have killed every one of them if they had tried to take Katherine from him.

He cut the pouch of money from his belt. He threw it and his dagger at his assailant, who caught it with one hand.

'Your cloak and your sword.'

Jarin hesitated. Without his sword he'd be defenceless, excepting his size and that he knew how to use his fists.

'You wouldn't be going back on your word now, would you?' asked the leader slyly.

Jarin unclasped his cloak and threw it to the man who caught it and passed it back to someone standing behind him.

Removing his sword was harder. He didn't want to part with it. He'd been given it by his sword master when he'd finally deemed Jarin a worthy opponent and it had served him well over the years. But he'd given his word and so he untied the scabbard and held it out to his opponent.

Jarin saw a flash of teeth as the man grinned and his fists curled as the man ran his fingers over the jewelled exterior.

'Now the girl's money.'

'She doesn't have any.'

'Do you really expect me to believe that?'

'It's true. She has no money or jewellery to give you. She has nothing but the clothes she is wearing.'

'We'll take those, then,' said the man who was very

keen to get his hands on Katherine and whom Jarin was itching to beat with his bare fists.

'Silence,' said the leader. 'We are not barbarians. We will not leave the lady to freeze. Lady, show me your belt.'

Jarin could feel Katherine trembling against him, but he felt a surge of pride when she didn't hesitate to step forward and pull her cloak apart so the leader could see that she wasn't wearing fine clothes or jewellery.

'Very well, we'll leave you here,' said the leader. 'It was a pleasure to meet you.'

The men laughed and began to make their way back into the forest. This time there was no need for them to move quietly and the sounds of wood snapping underfoot followed them into the night.

Jarin pulled Katherine's trembling body into his arms. She buried her head into his chest and he threaded one hand through her braids, whispering nonsense words of comfort. His other arm clasped her tightly to him.

Even though their situation was dire, he still noticed how well her body fitted against his. Her slender frame nestled into his arms as if she belonged there. His body tightened and he cursed himself for feeling the stirrings of desire. This was not the time or the place, but it seemed his body was once again not listening to his mind.

Gradually her body stilled and he reluctantly released her.

'Are you hurt?' he asked.

'No, at least I don't think so. Everything feels

strange, as if my body isn't my own.' She looked up at him. 'Are you?'

'No. We had a lucky escape.'

'Why didn't you fight them?'

He barked out a bitter laugh. Anger at their situation flared. 'Fight them! There were fifteen men that I could see, maybe more hiding in the darkness. I'm good with a sword, but not against those odds. I'd have been skewered before I could cut down more than two. What do you think would have happened to you once they'd left my bleeding corpse on the road? Did they not make it clear enough what they wanted you for? Those men were not the type to mind sharing a woman. Do you understand what that means?'

She gasped and he knew he had gone too far, but he was suddenly too furious to care. What could he do to make her see how vulnerable she was? Why did she always question him? He stepped off the track and began to move into the shadow of the trees, not stopping to see if she would follow him.

'Where are you going?' she asked, scurrying after him, her light tread barely making a sound. 'I thought we needed to follow the path to get to the nearest town.'

'We're following the men.'

She paused, but when he didn't slow she hurried after him again 'Why are we doing that? I thought you said you couldn't fight them.'

The track the men had made as they travelled through the forest was easy to spot even in the darkness. Believing they had Jarin cowed had made them careless and they'd made no effort to cover their tracks.

'I can't fight them as a group, but that doesn't mean I can't pick them off one at a time.'

Jarin was going to find the imbecile who had made those remarks about taking Katherine from him and he was going to make damned sure the man regretted ever opening his mouth.

'I thought we were nearing the town. If we go there, we could meet your men and get reinforcements if you really want to get Eira and your money back. They may have already caught up with Linota.' When he didn't slow she added softly, 'Please, my lord. I need to see my sister. I'm sure my brother will repay any money you may have lost in protecting me.'

He slowed to a stop and let out a long breath. 'I'm sorry, Katherine. I'm angry, furious even, but I'm not chasing after these men for petty revenge. This is not about the money I lost. Did you notice anything about them?'

'Only that they were impertinent. For the most part I was hiding behind you like a coward.'

He snorted. 'That's the first rational thing you've done since I've known you. I was pleased you stayed behind me, believe me, although next time you should run. No, the reason we are following them into the woods is because some of those men—and, before you start questioning me, I'm absolutely sure about this—were part of the gang who took your sister.'

She queried him anyway. 'Are you sure?'

'Yes.'

Katherine stopped and he braced himself for an onslaught of questions, but she surprised him by catching on quickly. 'So that wasn't a random ambush?'

'No. At least I don't think so.'

'What makes you think that way?' she asked.

He should have known she wouldn't keep quiet while he thought the incident through. He stepped over a fallen log and turned to help her. Their fingers briefly touched, hers cold against his. He wanted to link fingers with her again, but he dropped them instead. This mad desire for her had to stop. Not only did she clearly not feel the same in return, but it went against everything he was striving to achieve. A life without uncontrollable lust was a calm one.

'In the beginning the leader called me "your lordship" as though he knew who I was,' he continued as they carried on walking. 'I noticed he was careful not to make the same mistake again during the encounter. He also didn't insist when I said you didn't have any money. I know he went through the motions of checking, but his heart wasn't in it. It felt to me as if he already knew you'd be without.'

He walked in silence for a moment, trying to keep a hold on the tenuous thoughts that were flitting through his brain.

'Tonight wasn't about money or taking our goods. I think you were right when you suggested that this has been about slowing me down so that I'm kept away from whatever is happening at Borwyn in two days' time.'

Behind him, Katherine made a strange sound.

'What was that?' he asked.

Katherine's response was so long in coming he thought she wasn't going to answer.

Eventually she said, 'I'm surprised you are prepared to accept you're wrong. Most people I meet—and admittedly I haven't met many—would rather cut off their arm than confess someone else might be right. I know that I am one of them.'

Jarin laughed. 'So have I redeemed myself in your eyes at all?'

She was silent again. He guessed not. He tried not to feel disappointed.

'If we're right, then Linota might not be in as much danger as we thought,' said Katherine, changing the subject.

'I think it's a possibility, but we mustn't discount other ideas until we know what's happening, which is why we are going to catch up with those men and demand some answers.'

Jarin's fists clenched at the thought of what he would like to do if he got his hands on their leader.

'They might even take us to her.' Jarin's heart went out to her at the hopeful note in her voice. He would never say this to Katherine, but he thought it might be kinder to Linota if she were dead. He'd seen what a group of men could do to a woman if their blood was up. If she had suffered that at the hands of her abductors, then she would never recover.

'Let's hope so,' he murmured instead.

Her footsteps became lighter at his words and he cursed himself. It was unlikely Linota was with the men in the woods and part of him was regretting not following his original idea of heading to Ickleston. Those men he'd recognised, though, were the first lead he'd had since this bizarre turn of events had started.

'Are you cold?' she asked after a while.

'No.' Despite the coolness of the night air, the anger

coursing through him burned brightly, heating him from within.

'Are you sure? I can lend you my cloak for a bit if you'd like.'

He glanced back at her. She was already unfastening the clip at her throat as if ready to lend the small garment to him. It would barely cover his back, let alone his body, but his heart clenched at such a sweet gesture.

'Thank you, but please keep your cloak on. I really am fine.'

He remembered the way she'd trembled with cold against him earlier. He'd wanted to share his warmth with her and so he'd thrown his cloak around them both. He'd revelled in the way her slender frame had curled into his and how victorious he'd felt when her shivering had stopped.

She was a strange one, his Katherine. He would swear she didn't actually like him very much, but despite the fact that she definitely wasn't warm herself she had enough kindness in her to lend him her cloak on this cold winter's night. And when had he started to think of her as *his*? She wasn't and never would belong to him. He'd made sure of that when he'd denigrated her family, accusing them of being traitorous and insane.

His whole body cringed when he remembered his conversation with Erik where he'd brutally discussed her unsuitability. He'd thought no one was around to hear him, but that was no excuse. He should never have said those things about Katherine and her sister. He was ashamed by his behaviour and was disappointed that he'd been lessened in her eyes. No wonder she couldn't look at him without frowning.

He almost groaned out loud as he remembered Erik calling Katherine 'the plain one'. How that must have hurt her to hear those words. It wasn't even true. Her face was so full of expression, so constantly animated that it was impossible to call her plain. Her eyes were always different, sometimes a light brown, fading into green, sometimes nearly yellow like a cat. He could watch her face for hours and never get bored by the many different expressions that crossed its surface. But even if he did overlook her family's background and offered her marriage, she would never accept. He had slighted her family in the worst way possible and she would never forgive him.

He was acting like the boy he'd been when he was first smitten with Viola. As if he would take any crumb she was willing to throw him as long as she didn't hate him. Perhaps he was the idiot his father had called him. He seemed to be forming a habit of being attracted to women who were wholly unsuitable. Although Katherine herself was nothing like his first wife—there didn't seem to be even a hint of treachery in her whole body. The raging desire still felt the same and he had to keep remembering that chasing lust in the past had left him in a living hell.

'They haven't hidden their tracks well,' said Katherine quietly, pulling him back to the present.

'They obviously think I wouldn't dare follow them without my sword,' said Jarin wryly.

'How *are* you going get answers without it?'

'There are more ways out of a situation than fighting,' he said tersely. This was an old argument he'd had many a time with the male members of his family.

Their answer to anything was to take up arms and beat their opponent into submission. His father had openly mocked him to his other sons because Jarin believed in thinking through a problem. If he could negotiate his way out of a situation, then he would. That was not going to be an option here.

When he'd succeeded as Earl he'd vowed, not only to his mother but also to himself, to be a fair ruler. He'd wanted the Borwyn name to stand for honour and justice. He rubbed his brow. If he didn't act soon, then the Borwyn name would only be acquainted with failure; *he* would be remembered as a failure.

'I'm not suggesting you fight,' said Katherine once again breaking into his thoughts. 'I only want to know what the plan is.'

'I...'

Jarin stopped. Up ahead he could hear men shouting and laughing; his quarry had finally stopped moving. They were probably settling down for an evening of celebrating their success.

'I think we've found them,' he said quietly. 'Is it too much to ask that you stay here safely while I investigate?'

'Yes.'

'Yes, you will stay here?'

'No. Yes, it's too much to ask,' she clarified.

He sighed. Of course she wasn't going to be sensible and stay hidden in the darkness where she would be safe.

'Fine, but you must do as I say. If I say fall back, then that's what you do.'

'Mmm.'

'Katherine,' he warned. He was in no mood for her to put herself at more risk. If he had to march her back out of the forest he would, answers be damned. He waited in silence for her reply.

This time it was her turn to sigh. 'Very well, I will do as you say.'

'If you break your word to me on this, you will be sorry.'

Guilt flickered inside as he caught the widening of her eyes in the darkness. It was better she was afraid of him than that she get herself caught by one of the men by the campfire. He shuddered to think what they would do to her if that happened.

She nodded in acceptance of his decree. He would have to be happy with that.

Although the sounds coming from the makeshift camp were rowdy, Jarin still crept the remaining distance through the forest, watching where he put his feet.

Katherine stayed right behind him and, although he would rather she was far away from this place, preferably safe in his fortress, deep in his keep, he was glad she had refused to stay behind. He would only have worried that she was getting into trouble elsewhere. She seemed to bring it on herself.

He stopped at the edge of a small clearing. Through the trees he could see the men sitting around a large fire. A water skin was being handed round, but from the way the men were hungrily grabbing at it, it clearly contained something a lot stronger. One young man was already slumped over, probably knocked out by whatever they were drinking. Jarin counted quickly;

he'd been correct in his estimate of fifteen men and one was down already.

'Can you see Linota?' Katherine whispered at his back.

'She's not there, unless they have her tied up away from the fire.'

'We should check,' said Katherine, moving away from him as if to circle the camp.

He grabbed her arm. 'I'll go first,' he said.

He let out a long breath he hadn't realised he was holding when she immediately did as he asked.

The chances of Linota being here were slim. The gang would have had to leave her here when they set off to intercept Jarin earlier. They wouldn't leave such a prize lying around unattended in the forest, unless the worst had happened and the girl was already dead. He didn't want to suggest either option to Katherine just yet.

He and Katherine slowly made their way around the camp until they came across Eira tied up with several other horses. She nickered in recognition at their approach. He rubbed her nose gently, 'Hello, old girl,' he murmured. 'We're going to get you out of here.'

Eira was only loosely tied up so it wouldn't take much to unhook her and lead her away, but Jarin wanted answers so he left her where she was for now. He began to move faster to continue his search.

'My lord,' said Katherine, urgently grabbing his arm. 'Somebody is coming.'

Chapter Ten

Katherine wanted to run. Run so far and so fast that no one would ever catch up with her. The only thing holding her to the ground right now was that the man heading towards them, oblivious to their presence, might know the whereabouts of Linota.

Nothing, not even her father's brutal execution, had prepared her for the bone-chilling terror of today. She would never forget the horror of her sister being snatched away in front of her eyes. Her throat still burned with her screams. Every moment that passed without knowing whether Linota was safe or not seemed like an eternity.

In this new world where the ground appeared to be shifting under her feet, Jarin was her rock. His solid presence lent her confidence. She tried not to think about that too much. Every time she thought she might be softening towards him, she conjured up the memory of him talking to Erik about her family. But even with his callous words ringing in her ears, it was getting harder to hold on to her anger in the face of his persistent care towards her.

She pushed the thought to one side. The priority now was to stay alive and rescue Linota, not to puzzle over her muddled feelings.

'What are we going to do?' she whispered as the stranger got closer.

'I am going to do this,' Jarin whispered back.

Moving swiftly, he grabbed the man as he stepped out of the safety of the clearing. The man had no time to react as Jarin wrapped one arm around his neck, holding his other hand across his mouth.

'We're going to move quietly away,' Jarin said with a voice like steel. 'You're not going to utter a word or else I will snap your neck. Is that clear?'

Wide-eyed, the man nodded.

Jarin pushed the man in front of him and Katherine followed, trembling with the knowledge of Jarin's strength. Would he carry out his terrible threat? She didn't doubt that he could. Gone was the sophisticated man he normally showed to people, replaced with a dangerous warrior. When she'd first seen him, she'd thought him a beautiful man, but with his title she'd assumed his broad shoulders and muscular body was all for show. She'd fleetingly thought he might even pad his shirt, although having leant against him she knew he was all muscle. She hadn't imagined he would know how to handle himself in a real fight. Now she was not so sure. He clearly knew how to subdue a man, but would he really kill him? Could she trust him with her safety if he did?

When they were far enough away from the clearing,

Jarin shoved the man against a tree and held him in position with his body.

'Where's the lady Linota Leofric?' he demanded.

Katherine's heart stuttered. She hadn't thought Jarin would begin with that. She'd thought he'd want to start with finding out about the plot against him.

'I don't know,' said the man.

'Not good enough.'

In the darkness, Katherine missed what Jarin did next, but there was a grunt of pain and then the man wheezed.

'Try again,' growled Jarin.

The man gasped, 'I know she's been taken on ahead of us, but I swear I don't know where exactly.'

'Is she hurt?' Katherine demanded, her heart racing.

'No,' the man said quickly before Jarin could move again. 'The men who have her have been given strict instructions not to hurt her in any way.'

Katherine's whole body sagged and she leant against a tree. The rough bark bit into her back. She didn't care, her knees were no longer able to hold her up. Linota wasn't hurt. She might be frightened and alone, but she wasn't in pain.

'Why take her if she's to be kept safe?' Jarin demanded.

'I don't know.' There was another grunt of pain and then, 'Somebody doesn't like you. They're paying us well to make your life difficult, but we're not murderers. Nobody's going to come to any harm.'

'Apart from you,' growled Jarin menacingly and the man whimpered. 'Who doesn't like me?' Jarin demanded.

'I don't know. No, please don't…my family…we need to eat. I only wanted to get paid. I promise you I'm telling the truth. I don't know. We've got to slow you down, that's all. I just do as I'm told.'

'Then you're of no more use to me,' said Jarin coldly.

The man's eyes went wide.

'Please don't kill him,' Katherine cried out.

'Keep out of this, Katherine.'

'No, I will not. Please don't…'

Jarin hit the man on the side of the head, sending him to the ground.

There was a silence as they both stared at the fallen man. Katherine could see the rise and fall of his chest and she let out a shaky breath. She'd been so sure…

'I'm not a murderer, Katherine,' Jarin ground out, picking up the man and flinging him over his shoulder as if he were a sack of cloth.

She followed after him as he headed back to the clearing, her heart racing. She'd been so sure Jarin was going to end the man's life and her body still trembled from residual fear. He'd been so different from the Jarin Ashdown she'd witnessed ever since she'd first spied him from her chamber window. Gone was the sophisticated nobleman who charmed all those who met him and in his place was a cold-hearted warrior.

They reached the clearing. Jarin carefully lowered the body to the floor and began to cover him with loose undergrowth.

'Are you hiding the body?' Katherine whispered.

'That and keeping him warm. I don't want him to die of frostbite.'

And here was another side to Jarin. This man was his

enemy, yet he was still taking the time to make sure he lived. Just when she thought she had the Earl figured out he changed again. Who was the real Jarin Ashdown?

'What do we do now?' she asked as Jarin straightened.

'Now we take Eira and go.'

'Don't you want to get your sword back?'

He hesitated. 'Yes, I want it back.'

He strode over to Eira and murmured softly into her ear all the while stroking her neck. After a while he gently untied her from the tree. The noise from the gathering was louder than before and no one appeared to notice they were down one man.

'I thought you wanted your sword,' said Katherine quietly as they moved further away.

'I can hardly storm into the centre of those men and take it back, can I?' he said impatiently.

'We could have waited and then…' Katherine paused '…and then when they've all had too much to drink you could walk among them and take it back. I don't think they're too far away from that stage now.'

'It's too risky,' said Jarin firmly.

'You don't strike me as a coward.'

He stopped mid-stride and rolled his shoulders.

'Thank you,' he said wryly. 'I don't like to think of myself as a coward either, but if your daring plan went wrong then you would be alone in the forest. Do you know how to get to Ickleston, or Borwyn for that matter?'

'No,' she admitted after a few steps.

'I didn't think so.'

'But you wouldn't have failed, would you? You're

much stronger than you make out. I really believed you had it in you to kill that man.'

Jarin surprised her by laughing softly. 'You, Katherine Leofric, are terrible at giving compliments. I look like a lily-livered man, but inside I'm a killer. Perhaps I'll have the Borwyn motto changed to reflect that statement.'

'I didn't mean it like that,' she said crossly. 'You certainly don't have the shoulders of someone lily-livered. I just didn't think of you as someone who could take a man's life.'

'It's not something I would do on a whim and without extreme provocation,' said Jarin, all trace of humour gone from his voice. 'I've only killed men during battles, when there is no other choice. It is not something I take enjoyment in and would prefer to avoid it at all costs. Give me a wide, open space and a horse and I'd be happy.'

He'd surprised her again. From the little she'd seen of him before and the rumours that had swirled around Ogmore's fortress, she would have imagined he'd be happiest in the mix of intrigue, beautiful women trailing after him and men hanging on his every word.

She opened her mouth to ask him more, but from behind them came the distant sound of shouting.

'I think we've been discovered,' said Jarin, coming to an abrupt halt. 'I thought we'd have more time. Those horses of theirs didn't look up to much, but we can't underestimate desperate men.'

He threw her up on to Eira's saddle and vaulted up behind her.

'Hold on,' he said as he kicked Eira into action.

Katherine gasped as the horse began to move through the trees. She was riding faster than she ever had before and every muscle screamed in protest. Just as she thought she'd collide with another tree, Jarin used his skilled horsemanship to avoid it.

'Move with me,' Jarin yelled.

'I can't,' she shouted back. 'I don't know how.'

Jarin yanked her back in the saddle until she was sitting flush against his thighs. She gasped at the contact and the strange tingly feeling she kept having every time they touched started up again. This time it swept through her whole body. She tried to pull away from him; she shouldn't be feeling like this right now.

'Now isn't the time to be modest,' he said into her ear, his breath whispering across her skin. He pulled her even tighter against him. 'Follow my movements and we'll ride faster.'

Katherine's stomach fell away as Eira leapt over a fallen log, but she wasn't jolted by the action. Her whole body was now pressed against Jarin. It was much easier to ride when he took over their movement. His strong arms surrounded her, protecting her from the world around.

They burst out of the forest and back on to the path.

'How...?' She wanted to ask him how he'd known where they were, but her words were lost on the wind rushing past them.

At least the light from the moon and stars could reach them and it was easier to see where they were going. She closed her eyes tightly. Actually, maybe it was best not to see the ground disappearing beneath them as Eira ate up the distance.

She couldn't hear the sound of the men chasing them, but that didn't mean they weren't. She knew she should be frightened. She was expendable, not central to anyone's plans. No one needed her to live and those men wouldn't care if she died as they tried to get to Jarin. But she wasn't scared and that was all because of the man sitting behind her. No matter what they'd been faced with, he'd remained practical and in control. Not once had he panicked, even when she'd thought her knees would give way in terror. Of course Jarin's relationship with Ogmore would suffer if he lost both of the Leofric sisters on the same day, but Jarin had never given her the impression that she was an obligation. It was as if he actually cared about her as a person.

Or perhaps she was reading too much into it.

Maybe her head was being turned by his strong jaw and full lips. She'd wanted to like him from the off; it was only his harsh words about her family that had turned her against him. Now she seemed in danger of liking him too much. There was nothing to be gained from developing feelings for him—only pain lay in that direction. He'd made it abundantly clear he wasn't interested in marrying into the Leofric family, but even if he put those prejudices to one side he still wouldn't want the *plain* Leofric sister. Her heart shouldn't hurt at that thought.

Eira's hooves continued to pound along the track.

'What if there are men waiting for us at Ickleston?' she asked.

'What was that?' yelled Jarin.

She turned her head and her lips brushed against the

stubble of his jaw. 'I was thinking there might be an ambush in Ickleston,' she said close to his ear.

She really should turn back away from his warmth, but this close she couldn't seem to look away from the fullness of his mouth. What would it be like to have those lips pressed against hers? Would they be soft or firm and demanding? She shivered and this time it had nothing to do with the cold night air.

Jarin slowed Eira to a walk.

'That's a very good point,' he said softly.

'What was?' asked Katherine, her gaze still on his mouth.

He squinted down at her, a slight frown across his forehead. 'A possible ambush at Ickleston. I would have rushed straight into one.'

He led Eira off the track and into the darkness of the trees.

'We can't stay out here all night. You've not got a cloak.' Katherine bit her lip. She didn't know why she'd said something so inane. Jarin getting cold was the least of their worries.

'We'll approach the town from the side. I know someone who will put us up for the night.'

'Don't you think we should keep going?' she asked, panic clawing at her throat. If they didn't keep going, Linota could be lost to her forever.

'I know you want to find your sister, but we're riding around in the dark. We could be going in the wrong direction for all we know. We don't know what's going on and we have no idea if blundering on will put your sister in more danger. I think it's best we head to Rowan's residence and ask him to make enquiries on our behalf. We also need to sleep. We can't help Linota if we're half-dead with exhaustion.'

Now that he'd mentioned it, Katherine realised she was bone-numbingly tired, every muscle ached and her back throbbed from trying to sit upright. Her eyelids fluttered closed and she tried to force them back open. She slumped against Jarin and then jerked away again.

'Don't fight it, Katherine,' murmured Jarin. 'You can lean on me if you need to.'

What frightened her, more than strange men chasing them through the night, was the knowledge that she wanted to lean against him, to feel his strong chest supporting her. Her eyes fluttered shut again and her head drooped. She forced them open once again, but she very quickly lost the battle and the world became black.

She awoke briefly as she was gently lowered from Eira. She struggled as unfamiliar arms grasped her.

'Shush, it's all right. I'm here.' She was lifted from the stranger by a familiar pair of strong arms and she settled against Jarin's broad chest, his smell familiar to her now.

There was a brief rumble of male voices talking above her head and then she was moving again, still cocooned in Jarin's arms and still half-asleep.

The creak of a door sounded, waking her slightly.

'Is this it?' asked Jarin as he came to a stop.

'I don't have as many rooms as ye, your lordship,' came the amused response. 'You're lucky this room is free at all. It was full of wood until a few days ago, but I've been busy this last week and I've used up all of my supplies.'

Jarin snorted. 'I'm not sure Mistress Leofric will want to be so close to me.'

'I don't know about that. The lasses seem to like that pretty face of yours.'

'This one thinks I'm an idiot.'

'Ah, she's got you figured out, then. I'll fetch ye both some blankets and then head to the inn. If anyone knows anything about all this, it will be old Terrin. Nothing goes on in this town without his knowledge.'

'Thanks, Rowan.'

'Don't mention it.'

And then the creak of the door again.

Jarin slowly lowered himself to the floor, making sure he didn't jostle her. She knew she should let him know she was awake, but it was lovely to be cosseted and cared for. No one had ever done that for her before. He settled with his back against the wall and moved her head to the crook of his arm.

She sighed. She really should move off him; she was in his arms under false pretences.

'Where are we?' she murmured.

'Ah, you're awake. Is your head hurting from where you hit it earlier?'

He didn't seem to be releasing her even though she'd let him know she was no longer asleep. She took advantage of his lapse by snuggling closer to his warmth. He responded by tightening his grip. Maybe he was cold as well.

'My head is a bit tender, but it's not too bad.'

'Good…' He paused. 'Rowan is a friend of mine. He was an apprentice carpenter when my father was alive. I used to enjoy watching him work when I was a child.

He works for himself now. We're in his house. He's a gruff man, but he's kind. He's going to ask around for sightings of your sister while we wait here. I'm afraid...'

Katherine waited, but he didn't go on.

'What are you afraid of?' she asked quietly.

Just when she thought he wouldn't answer, he said, 'I'm afraid there's not a separate chamber for you to sleep in. We'll have to stay here together. I think it's safest for us not to be parted anyway.'

Her heart stuttered at the thought of spending the night with Jarin. Would he expect her to lie with him? No, he wouldn't want her. Despite his assertions that she was obviously a woman, he had never given her any indication that she was an attractive one. She was far too plain for the likes of him.

A strange sensation settled around her heart. She tried to reassure herself it was relief, but it felt all too much like disappointment.

Chapter Eleven

Jarin tensed as the door creaked open again. There was little he could do if the person entering was hostile.

He relaxed as Rowan stepped back into the room. 'I'm afraid I don't have much in the way of spare blankets.' He held out a small bundle of thin material and a candle with the wax almost completely gone. 'Is the wee lass still asleep?'

'Yes,' said Jarin, looking down at Katherine's face in the flickering candlelight. She was sleeping deeply now and hadn't stirred when the door opened.

'Ye don't have to keep holding on to her. The wee lass won't float away.'

'You always were funny, Rowan,' said Jarin wryly. 'She had a nasty head injury today. I'm worried about her.'

'Aye, I'm sure that's why you're holding on to her so tightly.'

Jarin was glad for the darkness. It would hide the heat creeping up his face at Rowan's jest.

Rowan handed Jarin the blankets and he arranged

them around Katherine, tucking them tightly around her so that no cold air could get through, not caring if Rowan saw him do it. Katherine deserved someone to take care of her for once.

'I'll go for ye now and see what I can find out. I'll leave ye this.' He set the candle down on the rough stone floor.

'Thanks, Rowan.'

'You're welcome, lad. It's a bad business, this. I can't imagine who'd be behind such a thing against ye. It's generally thought that ye are an improvement on the old Earl.'

Rowan closed the door on them both, leaving Jarin alone with his thoughts. How had he not noticed there was someone intent on doing him harm? What signs had he missed? His father had despised him because he wasn't like his older brothers, but the man was long since dead. Besides, the late Earl of Borwyn had been so proud of his lineage he wouldn't make trouble for the only surviving heir, no matter what he thought of him.

And why take Linota? Despite his words to Katherine, he didn't think she'd been taken randomly. The riders had swept past Katherine and made straight for her sister. Unless Ogmore had talked, and that was entirely possible, then the only person who knew about his offer of a generous dowry for the two girls was Erik.

Erik had made his thoughts clear on which sister he thought the most attractive. Jarin had never shared his preference for Katherine with Erik and so his friend wouldn't have realised that Katherine was more precious to him than Linota.

He shifted his legs, trying to find a comfortable position. He'd rather not think about Linota at all. Guilt that she'd been taken from his protection almost swamped him. He could never make amends to her family if she'd been killed because he'd failed to protect her.

If she was still alive, then his honour dictated that he make reparations. He closed his eyes tightly. Really, there was only one way to make it up to Linota and that was to offer her marriage. Becoming his Countess would protect her from a lifetime of being shunned for something that was not her fault. It would restore his honour in the eyes of her family and he would get the dowry he'd been promised and so badly needed. Linota was the practical choice if he had to pick one of the sisters. He felt no raging desire for her; he wouldn't be driven by lust around her. He could marry her, receive the dowry and rebuild the Borwyn fortune. Unlike Viola, there would be no treachery, no screaming rows and no tortuous one-sided longing as he waited like a stray dog for a bit of attention from his wife.

He swallowed as bile rose in his throat. Could he really contemplate getting Linota pregnant? He felt no desire for her, not even a flicker, and while his mind argued that this was a good thing his body protested vociferously.

Despite his efforts to think rationally about his future, his gaze kept being pulled back to Katherine's sleeping face. Her long lashes cast a shadow on her cheekbones and her lips looked plump and inviting. His fingers itched with the desire to unbind her hair and run his fingers through the thick tresses. In his arms he could feel how thin she was, almost painfully so. She couldn't have had access to Ogmore's generous tables and the thought filled him with a simmering anger. Ogmore was rich and powerful enough to have taken care of Katherine. If he had decreed she must be treated with respect, everyone would have done so in fear of falling out of his favour. She should never have been kept locked away. It wasn't her fault her father was a traitor to the king.

He leaned his head back against the wall and closed his eyes. He needed sleep.

Despite the cramped, uncomfortable conditions he must have fallen asleep because he was woken by a cry. His eyes snapped open, but he and Katherine were still alone in the room. The noise came again and he realised it was coming from Katherine. The candle was guttering now, nearly gone out, but he could just discern that her eyes were still closed.

She twisted and cried out, 'No, please. I promise I won't…'

She cringed and brought her hands to her face, 'Please, Mother. I…'

'Katherine, you're dreaming,' he said, bringing a hand to her face; her skin was soft under his callused fingers. 'Please don't worry, you're safe now.'

'No!' she screamed and her eyes flew open. 'Where am I?' she panted, twisting in his arms as if to escape. 'What's happening?'

'You're safe,' he repeated. 'You're with me, Jarin.' It felt right to use his given name instead of Borwyn. Nobody else used it, only his mother, but the intimacy they found themselves in now had no precedence. He touched the skin of her forehead to check for a temperature. 'Do you remember?'

Her eyes were wide, her breathing erratic, but she wasn't overly hot and so he suspected she was disorientated rather than feverish.

'Linota,' she gasped, struggling with the blankets. 'I need to get to her.'

He rubbed her back soothingly. 'I know you're desperate to see her, but it's the early hours of the morning. There is not much we can do.'

Her breathing slowed and gradually the tension left her body. He continued to stroke her back, marvelling at how small she was under his hands.

'What if she's hurt? I always look after her. She'll be frightened without me,' Katherine's voice cracked.

Jarin didn't know what to say to that. The chances were that Linota was hurt and very frightened and his heart filled with shame again at not being able to protect her.

The flame gave one last frantic flicker and then guttered out, plunging them into darkness.

'Linota's so beautiful and kind,' said Katherine, her voice cracking in the darkness. 'She'd never hurt a soul. Why didn't this happen to me instead of her?'

Jarin's heart twisted at the thought. He would kill any man who tried to take Katherine from him.

'It was random,' said Jarin, even though he was starting not to believe that himself. 'They took her because she was easiest to grab. It was not your fault. Try and remember what the man said in the woods earlier. They are under instructions not to hurt her.'

Katherine took a deep breath and exhaled slowly. 'I hope that's true.'

So did Jarin, but he didn't say it. It was best Katherine believed her sister was going to come out of this well. It would help to keep Katherine going over the coming days.

'I've always...'

'You've always what?' prompted Jarin.

'Linota is six years younger than me. She's always been such a gentle soul and after our father was...' His hands tightened involuntarily.

Jarin had never thought about her father's execution outside of the scandal. To witness such a brutal act must have been horrific for the young girls. It shamed him to think that he was like everyone else, condemning the girls for their father's crime before getting to know them. And Katherine had borne the brunt of everything; she was the one who did the caring. There had been no one to do the same for her. She had only ever faced ridicule and censor and it shamed him that he had done the same.

'After our father died,' continued Katherine, 'I wanted to make sure that Linota stayed innocent. It's been hard. Our mother is a difficult woman, but I think I succeeded. Linota has always been happy and now this has happened and it's my fault.'

Jarin frowned. 'How is it your fault?'

Katherine paused and he felt her shift restlessly on his lap. Parts of him, parts that he'd begun to suspect were dead, woke up and took an interest in the way her body rubbed against his. He shifted her slightly so that his inappropriate reaction to her nearness didn't become apparent. She wouldn't want to know about his attraction to her and would probably be disgusted by his response.

'It's my fault because you would have taken us straight to our brother's castle and I made you change your mind because I'm selfish,' she said in a rush.

'I don't understand.'

She shifted again and he groaned.

'I'm sorry, you must be so uncomfortable,' said Katherine, struggling to sit upright and making matters a lot worse. 'Perhaps we should both lie down.'

Jarin didn't want to let go of her, but to insist would look odd; there was no good reason to keep her in his arms other than that he liked her being there.

She began to slide off his lap and he missed the contact immediately. She wriggled around in the space, trying to give him room to stretch out. He turned and tried to straighten his legs, but his feet hit a solid wall before he could fully lie down.

'Is that better?' murmured Katherine. 'Here, we'll have to share the covers.'

She threw half of the blanket over him and rolled slightly closer. Now nothing separated them apart from their clothes and a hair's breadth of air. His cock strained towards her and he shifted closer despite himself.

'Are you warm?' he murmured.

'No.' She half laughed. 'I've never been so cold and uncomfortable.'

He snorted. 'Here, rest your head on me.'

She hesitated and then moved closer still and laid her head on his shoulder. The top of her hair tickled his chin and he brought a hand up to smooth it down. He wanted to continue to run his fingers over her braid and down her slender neck. He wanted to trace his fingers over her collarbone and dip down into the valley between her breasts. He dropped his hand instead.

'You were telling me why you thought you were selfish in suggesting we go to *my* castle to sort out *my* problem. You realise that's insane,' he said.

'I told you not to call me that,' she said quickly.

He was pleased to hear the argumentative tone back in her voice. He wanted her back to normal, arguing with him and being opinionated. The defeated voice seemed so unlike her. 'You'll have to convince me, then,' he said, deliberately provoking her.

She sighed softly, the fight going out of her almost immediately. 'I didn't want the journey to end too quickly.'

'Really? You looked so uncomfortable riding on Braith I thought you would be pleased to get to Castle Swein.

She was silent for so long he thought she'd fallen asleep again. 'I've been virtually locked up for years,' she said quietly. 'You can't imagine what a difference it makes to be out in the countryside and to be able to see so far into the distance. I felt free for the first time in my life. I didn't want it to be over and because of that my sister has been taken. I'm being punished for wanting something more. I should have been content with gaining a new home. It's more than I ever dreamed possible for myself.'

Jarin's fingers stole back into her hair as if he couldn't help himself. The tight braids stopped him from running his fingers down the length of it, but he gently began to massage her scalp, careful to stay away from the spot where she'd hit the tree yesterday. A dark bruise had formed in her hairline and he knew it must be causing her considerable discomfort but, as always, she didn't complain. She didn't appear to object to him touching her and so he carried on.

'You are not to blame,' he said. 'The men who took Linota are guilty. Not you.'

'You're kind to say so, but it's not true.'

'I'm never kind.'

'Now that really isn't true. You are one of the kindest men I have ever met. You always have a good or encouraging word to say to people. The respect your men have for you is obvious.'

Jarin's heart stopped. He hadn't believed she thought one good thing about him.

'I thought I was a rude and obnoxious boor in your eyes,' he said.

There was a long pause. 'Yes, you are that, too, my lord.'

He laughed and felt her responding giggle vibrate through her.

'Please call me Jarin,' he said. '"My lord" seems too formal in the circumstances.'

There was a long pause and he thought she was going to refuse.

'Thank you, Jarin,' she said eventually and his heart swelled.

'We should try and get some sleep,' he said gruffly.

'Yes, tomorrow is going to be long and difficult. Do you want me to move off you?'

'No, you're fine where you are.' The last thing he wanted was for her to move away from him.

Gradually her body became heavy and she dropped back into sleep. He envied her. His mind and body refused to switch off. His brain swirled with thoughts, racing between a desire to know what was going on and a desperate need to find out more about Katherine, about what made her tick and what made her sad.

He wanted to close the tiny gap that separated them and to press the full length of his body against hers. He wanted to taste the mouth that could be so generous towards him one moment and then make him laugh with her audacity the next.

He sighed; it was going to be a long night.

Rowan's central room smelled strongly of sawdust. Katherine sat at his table near the roaring fire, uneaten bread in front of her, her face pale. Jarin was too restless to sit. Every moment that passed with them not moving was a moment wasted.

Rowan hadn't been able to find out much last night. There were reports of unknown riders racing through the town, but those he'd spoken to weren't able to give many details and he'd be unable to find Terrin, the man he'd claimed knew everything. As soon as the sun had risen he'd gone back out to see what other information he could find. Jarin walked the length of the room. Stopped, turned around and walked back.

Sending Rowan out was the sensible option. If Jarin had enemies in town, then it was best he stay out of sight, but he was done with being rational. He wanted to storm out into the middle of the town and demand his adversaries face him like real men instead of hiding in the shadows.

'How much longer do you think he will be?' asked Katherine.

Jarin rubbed his forehead. 'I don't know. If feels as though he's been gone for several lifetimes.'

She nodded and broke off a bit of the bread. 'We should try and eat,' she commented, shredding the morsel between her fingers. The crumbs fell to the table, but she made no move to sweep them away.

He began pacing up and down again. It wasn't getting him anywhere, but it was better than standing still.

'My hair feels awful,' murmured Katherine, idly fiddling with the end of her braids.

He stopped mid-stride.

'I could redo it for you.'

'You!' exclaimed Katherine, open-mouthed.

He barked out a surprised laugh at her expression.

'I'm a man of many talents.'

She frowned. 'Is it a lover thing?'

He laughed again even as his heart rate increased. 'Not that I'm aware of.' She still didn't look convinced and he wasn't sure either. He'd been dying to get his hands on her hair since the first moment he saw her. Perhaps when it was over his desire would die and he would return to normal. It was worth a try. He looked across at her, wariness still clouding her eyes.

'I was very close to my mother and spent a lot more time with her than any of my brothers,' he explained. 'Once she became ill she couldn't bear for people to touch her hair—her scalp was too sensitive. I learned how to do it carefully so as not to hurt her. My father wasn't pleased when he found out.'

For a moment Jarin was back in the room, his mother screaming in terror as his father picked him up bodily and threw him against the wall, such was his anger at Jarin learning 'women's work'.

Katherine touched her head, a look passing across her face that Jarin couldn't read. Jarin held his breath. To have his hands in her hair, to finally be able to untie the ugly braids and run his fingers through the long tresses might be a mistake. If his body turned hard just at the thought of doing so, then he would be lost if he actually did. But to miss the opportunity to feel the silken locks would be worse.

'I would like it very much if you could redo my braid, thank you,' said Katherine, her gaze fluttering up to meet his and then away again.

He moved behind her quickly so as to hide his body's unwelcome reaction. She was an innocent who probably wouldn't know what the bulge under his clothes signified, but if she did…their hard-won accord would probably be over.

His fingers trembled as he tugged at the first ribbon. He let go and flexed them out, willing his body under control. This reaction was ridiculous. It was only hair he was touching, for goodness sake. He took a deep breath and began again.

As soon as she agreed to let Jarin touch her hair, Katherine regretted the impulse. It had been bad enough lying next to him all night as if they were lovers, but at least they could claim their time together had served a practical purpose. The thought of those strong fingers touching her hair was causing her breasts to tighten and her breathing to catch in her throat when he'd still been on the other side of the room.

He'd hesitated and she'd thought he was going to take back his offer, but then he strode towards her and without further comment pulled the ribbons from the end of her braid.

Suddenly, her body was alive with sensation. Her spine tingled as he separated the strands, pulling them apart and smoothing them out. His fingers brushed the sensitive skin at the back of her neck and she almost purred in delight.

'Your hair reminds me of fields of wheat in the summer sunshine,' he said softly.

She opened her mouth to deflect the compliment and then closed it again. It was probably the nicest thing anyone had ever said about the way she looked. She was going to take it and preserve the memory to she could take it out again when she was alone and Jarin's presence was a distant memory.

He quickly began to pull the hair away from her face, parting it in the middle with sure, confident fingers that sent shivers of sensation across her scalp. He began to thread an elaborate braid together.

'I don't normally wear it like this,' she said, reaching up to touch the braid he was beginning. 'This is a young girl's style.'

'You are a young girl, Katherine.'

'I'm twenty-four!'

'And I'm twenty-eight. I would say we were both a respectable age, but hardly in our dotage. Anyway, this is the style I know how to do so you'll just have to suffer through it today.'

She allowed herself to relax and think of nothing except the firm pull of his fingers as they worked through her hair. She almost giggled. If anyone had told her she would one day be sitting in a carpenter's abode while an earl acted as her maid, she would never have believed it. That the earl was Jarin Ashdown, one of the most eligible men in the country, made it even more ridiculous. She closed her eyes and gave herself up to the sensations running through her body as Jarin pulled and twisted the strands. It was the most pleasure she had ever experienced. As he continued she couldn't help but imagine his strong fingers following on from her hair and tracing the curve of her spine, tugging on the ties of her dress and pushing the material aside. She bit her lip and tried to think of something else, but the images kept coming as his hands pulled through her hair.

The door banged and Katherine jumped. Jarin calmly finished twisting the ends of her hair and tied the last of the ribbons in place.

Rowan raised his eyebrows at the scene before him, but made no comment. Heat rushed over her face at being caught in such an intimate act, but Jarin didn't flinch, calmly moving away from her as if the last few moments had not occurred.

'What news?' asked Jarin, when Rowan didn't begin talking immediately.

Rowan's gaze flicked between the two of them before he said, 'Several groups of riders were seen moving through the town yesterday. The first group did indeed have a woman among them. I've spoken to several witnesses, all of whom reported that the lady was not distressed. She was riding on a horse with a man, but she was not bound.'

'Perhaps it wasn't my sister.'

Rowan shrugged. 'There were no other women in the other groups. The second was only male riders. They stopped briefly to get refreshments, but moved on fairly quickly.'

'That second group has to be my men,' said Jarin firmly.

Rowan nodded. 'That's what I thought, although the description of the leader doesn't sound like Erik, more like that lad, William. It could be that Terrin's wrong, though.'

Jarin nodded. 'At least we have confirmation that my men were hot on Linota's trail.'

Katherine still had her reservations about Erik's innocence and now that it sounded as if he wasn't with the second group of men her suspicions were aroused even further. She kept quiet, though. She'd already said her piece and Jarin was convinced Erik was not involved. She had to trust his judgement.

'The third group arrived in town late last night. I'm guessing shortly after ye turned up here. According to several folk they were drunk and rowdy. They were looking for a man and a woman on horseback. Their leader wasn't happy when no one was able to say they'd seen ye. They wanted to stay overnight in the tavern, but the innkeeper wouldn't have them.'

'What did they do next?' asked Jarin, rubbing his chin.

'They bedded down in old Garrick's barn; he's never

one to miss the opportunity to make a bit of money,' Rowan laughed shortly. 'It's not the best place to spend the night. Anyway, by all accounts their leader split them into groups. Some headed back the way they had come, a couple have stayed in town and the majority have gone on ahead. Reckon ye did the best thing staying here the night.'

'They sound like our friends in the woods,' said Jarin. 'It's a blow that some of them have gone on ahead. It will make travelling on difficult.'

Katherine tapped the rough wooden table with her fingertips. 'Why would Linota not make any signal to the townsfolk that she had been kidnapped? It doesn't make any sense.'

'Perhaps she deemed it safer not to,' said Jarin absentmindedly. 'Are there any reports of any of my men staying in the town?'

'None.'

Jarin rubbed his chin thoughtfully and made his way back over to the fireplace.

'What is it?' Katherine asked.

'I gave instructions for my men to reconvene here. It is unusual for them not to follow my orders or at least to leave a message explaining why.'

'Are you always obeyed?' Katherine asked.

'As a rule,' he said drily. 'Only very occasionally do I meet someone who thinks they know better.'

His lips twitched and the look he sent her left her in no doubt he was referring to her.

'I suspect most people think they know better, but they are too overawed by the greatness of your title to point out otherwise,' she said tartly.

Rowan barked out a laugh. 'She's got ye there, lad.'

Jarin raised an eyebrow. 'I've never known you to show me any deference because of my title, Rowan.'

'Aye, well, I think ye have to earn respect. Ye are a good lad, Jarin, and ye have earned mine. Just don't go telling that to anyone else. Now, as much as I appreciate ye coming to visit, you can't stay here nattering all day. What are ye going to do next?'

'We have to get back to Borwyn,' said Jarin.

Katherine's heart skipped. 'But what about Linota?'

'I've not forgotten about her, but we need reinforcements and the only way we are going to get some is if I can get to my men.'

'Ye can't take the main road. It'll be being watched.'

Jarin nodded. 'We'll have to go through the woods. It'll take much longer, but it'll be safer.'

Katherine's chest became tight. 'But we don't have time to lose.'

The look Jarin gave her was filled with sympathy. 'I know, but we'll be of far more use to Linota if we manage to avoid getting caught than if we blunder into another trap. Goodness knows how long it will take us to extract ourselves from another incident.'

'Can ye remember the way?' asked Rowan.

'I could do it blindfolded,' said Jarin stiffly.

'Very well. Ye had best be on your way then.'

Jarin nodded, 'Are you ready, Katherine?'

Katherine stood. It was not as if she had to collect together her belongings. She'd had very little to begin with and now she had nothing at all. 'I'm ready.'

'Good.' Jarin nodded. 'Thank you, Rowan, for all you have done for us.'

'Ach, it was nothing, lad. Come and visit again when ye are settled.' He looked at Jarin, but nodded towards Katherine. Katherine frowned. What did Rowan mean by that?

Jarin gave him an odd twisted smile, but didn't respond to the hidden message.

Katherine ground her teeth as Eira picked her way slowly over fallen logs and around thick gnarled tree trunks that were packed densely together. Dull, grey cloud blanketed the forest, muffling the sounds of life among the vegetation. Occasionally a bird would burst from the leaves overhead, its beating wings the only sound other than Eira's hooves against the woodland floor.

The silence gave Katherine time to think.

Linota had now been missing for a whole day and night. Too many people knew about it for it to be ignored. Even if those men hadn't laid a finger on her, no one would believe it. Her chances of making a good marriage were very likely ruined. They'd been difficult enough with their background, but this would finish her off. All her loveliness couldn't make up for the fact that she would be regarded as a damaged woman and no decent man would take on a violated bride. Her abduction would be seen as her fault.

'You are very quiet,' murmured Jarin after a while.

Katherine managed a small nod.

'Are you worrying about Linota?'

Katherine swallowed past the lump in her throat. 'Yes.'

'We will find her,' said Jarin firmly. 'And when we do the men that took her will pay dearly.'

'But what of her person?' Katherine asked desperately. 'What if…?' She stuttered to a stop. She couldn't bring herself to voice her deepest fear.

Jarin shifted on the saddle behind her. 'Ogmore and I will stand by her. The weight of two such eminent earls will ensure she is not snubbed.'

Katherine twisted her fingers together. 'It is kind of you to say so, but ultimately, I'm afraid, your support will count for nothing. Ogmore's hasn't for the last eight years. Everywhere we go we are whispered about. No one wants to be our friend in case the taint of treason rubs off on them. It has been painful and lonely and Linota has had to live with that her whole life. Our father was executed before her eyes when she was only ten years old. Instead of treating her with the care she deserved, my mother kept her a virtual prisoner.' Tears began to fall in earnest now. She swiped them away, but didn't stop. 'At least I was sixteen when it happened. I knew what it's like to experience freedom. She has grown up almost completely confined to a tiny chamber.'

'I promise I will do all in my power to make it right,' said Jarin.

Katherine could hear the truth of his promise in his tone. 'Thank you for your kindness, but I don't know what you can ever do to redress the balance. Her good name has been stolen from her, first by our father and now by the person behind this attack. But that's not the worst of it. I'm terrified that she…'

Katherine still couldn't bear to voice the worst. Her

mind shied away from even thinking about what could have happened to her sister's body. Saying the words out loud made it seem more real. Everything that she had hoped for her sister was destroyed and it was all Katherine's fault for wanting a little more taste of freedom.

'Katherine.' Jarin lightly touched her arm. 'Katherine, hear me out.'

She pulled in a shuddering breath. 'I know you mean well, Jarin. But whatever you do, the outcome will still be the same.'

'I will marry her.'

Katherine's body stilled, apart from her heart which she could feel pulsing in her neck. 'You?'

'Yes.'

'Why?'

She felt Jarin inhale sharply. 'It's the logical conclusion to this whole thing. Surely you've already realised this. It is my fault she is in this predicament and my honour dictates that I must make amends. I will not let Linota suffer when I can do something about it.'

'I…you…but…' She took a deep breath, trying to collect her scattered thoughts. 'But what about Borwyn's lineage? If you were concerned about marrying one of us beforehand, then what's happened since then will make it much worse.'

Jarin groaned softly. 'I wish you would forget what I said before. I was a boorish idiot. I would be honoured to marry into your family.'

His words were stiffly formal; he didn't sound like a man who was happy at such a union, but neither did he sound forced.

He was a good man after all. It had only taken this tragedy for her to know for sure.

Katherine rested her hands on the pommel in front of her. Jarin was offering something extraordinary. Not only was he going to save Linota from ruin, he was also going to make her one of the highest-ranking women in the land. The union was all she had ever wanted for her sister and more. Why then did she feel so sick?

She would have time later to sort through her own feelings on the matter. Now the important thing was Linota's future. Katherine had the power to put things right, to secure Linota's fate.

'That is a very kind offer,' she said quietly. 'Thank you. I will accept on her behalf.'

Jarin's nod brushed against her head, but he didn't say any more.

Jarin had taken her by surprise with his proposal, which was why a lump of stone had formed in her stomach. When the news had sunk in, she would feel better, happy even. The marriage would be a triumph for Linota and for the Leofric family as a whole. Their family name would be more than restored when it was linked to two of the most important noblemen in the country. Yes, it was a good thing he'd offered, really good, and in no time at all she would feel all the positive emotions she ought to on finding out her sister was going to marry well.

Despite the good news, Katherine had had to fight to keep herself from crying. Jarin seemed to pick up on her mood because the rest of the day passed in unspoken silence.

'Katherine,' said Jarin eventually, 'I think we are going to have to stop for the night. It's getting too dark to keep going.'

Katherine glanced around her, shocked to realise that the grey day had nearly faded to black.

'But I thought we were near your fortress when we were at Ickleston.'

'We were, but unfortunately there is no direct path through the woods and I've had to take us a fair bit out of our way. I want to keep moving, but it's too dangerous in the pitch black.'

Katherine looked around her. Jarin was right; shortly it would be too dark to see anything. Something rustled in the undergrowth and she shrank back against him. 'How will we sleep?'

'To our right there looks to be some chimney smoke. I'm hoping it's from some sort of dwelling. We can offer the owner some of the money Rowan lent me for a place to bed down for the night.'

Katherine nodded; anything was preferable to spending the night out in the forest, although when she caught sight of the run-down crofter's cottage she began to doubt the wisdom of stopping.

'Wait with Eira,' said Jarin, dismounting with ease.

Only a week ago Katherine would have been terrified of being left alone with such a big animal, let alone left sitting astride it. Now she was grateful for the warmth of Eira's strong body as the coldness of dusk began to seep into her.

Katherine watched Jarin stride over the ground that led to the dwelling's front door. If it wasn't for the fact that smoke clearly rose from the chimney she would have said the place had been abandoned many years ago, such was the state of the disrepair.

A short figure answered Jarin's knock. Katherine was too far away to hear what was being said, but from the shaking of the man's head it didn't look promising. After a brief interchange the figure closed the door in Jarin's face. He turned and walked towards her.

'We can sleep with the animals,' he said once he was in earshot.

'The animals?' she asked, looking around. 'Does he mean out here?'

A faint smile crossed Jarin's lips. 'He's a she—a widowed woman who doesn't want strangers in her home, but is willing for them to sleep with her livestock. I would imagine there's a loft so we don't actually have to lie down among them.'

'That's fine, good even. The animals' heat will keep us warm.' She didn't mention the inevitable smell; she had to keep positive or she would start crying again and she didn't want to become an irritating burden, weeping all the time.

Jarin didn't comment. He led Eira to the other end of the dwelling and pushed open a rough, wooden gate. He stepped inside and Katherine heard the baaing of a few surprised sheep. His footsteps disappeared into the darkness before he re-emerged again.

'All is well,' he said calmly. 'There's enough space for Eira and there's a surprisingly sturdy ladder up into the loft. It will be all right for one night. Here, let me help you down.'

Jarin held up his hand and Katherine reluctantly took it. She didn't want to be touching him now. Not when the feel of his skin on the palm of her hand still sent tingles along her arm. These weren't sensations she should be having when she touched her sister's future husband. As if he could sense her thoughts, he dropped her hand as soon as her feet hit the ground, taking Eira's reins and leading the animal into the barn.

Katherine followed them in, standing just inside the entrance while her eyes took a moment to adjust to the darkness. Jarin settled Eira and then returned to place the wood back in the doorway. Without the light from the stars, Katherine could only see a little way in front of her.

'Put your hand in mine,' said Jarin, holding out his arm. 'I'll lead you to the ladder.'

She reached out and once again slipped her hand into his. His warm, sure fingers closed over hers and he pulled her gently away from her standing place.

'Here,' he said when they'd walked about ten steps into the building. 'Can you see the ladder?'

'Just about.'

'You go up first and I'll follow behind.'

He placed her hand on the edge of the ladder and let go. She instantly missed the contact and shook her head irritably. She should not want to touch Jarin at all, let alone feel bereft when that connection was over.

She began to climb, gaining in confidence as the ladder remained solid beneath her footsteps. She reached the top and heaved herself into the open space. She tried to stand, but there wasn't enough space and so she shuffled over on her hands and knees, feeling for the edges. Her hands hit the wall soon enough and she realised that the top was only a few wooden boards across, 'There's not much space,' said Katherine as Jarin joined her.

Jarin huffed out a laugh. 'I wasn't expecting a great deal. It's a fairly humble dwelling even by most standards.'

Katherine stretched out her legs and hit another wall. She was going to be able to lie down, but only just. Jarin was going to be in for a very uncomfortable night and there would be no escape from one another. They would be closer than when they'd shared a room in Rowan's cramped town house.

Katherine cursed her traitorous heart for being glad.

Chapter Twelve

Jarin lay on his side and stared into the darkness. He'd turned his back on Katherine as soon as they'd laid down to try and get some sleep. He didn't want to watch her as he had done the night before. If he looked at her, he'd be reminded of the promise he'd made today. His promise to marry a woman who wasn't Katherine.

Offering for Linota was the right thing to do. It was his fault she had been abducted and it was because of him that her good name was ruined. Marrying her would ensure she was protected and that his honour had been restored. And she was considered beautiful by most. She might not have Katherine's vitality or her mysterious eyes, but they could learn companionship. It would be a better match than his parents had endured, a couple who should never have entered the same room together, let alone shared a marriage bed.

He'd initially had reservations about the family's suitability, but the two girls had been too young to be involved in their father's treasonous plot. Katherine had shown herself to be a good, kind and thoughtful woman.

There was no reason to suspect that Linota would be any different. Katherine was incredibly fond of her and that counted for a lot.

The union also meant he would receive Ogmore's generous dowry. The money and status would help restore the Borwyn fortune, which was what he'd been working towards ever since he'd inherited the earldom. He'd be able to build on the foundation and before long his wealth would be true rather than illusionary. He was a lucky man and he knew he should be grateful for the fortune that was about to come his way, but a heavy weight had settled around his heart and he didn't seem to be able to shift it.

Behind him, Katherine whimpered.

He held his breath.

'No, Mother, please...'

She was having another nightmare.

'I'm sorry... I didn't mean...please, Mother.'

Jarin clenched his fists. Katherine's mother had clearly hurt her badly. He had to fight the urge to return to Ogmore and tear her limb from limb. The emotion surprised him because it went against everything he stood for. He had always favoured rational discussion over using his fists, but there was something about Katherine that brought out his protective side. Someone should take care of her and it seemed he had decided it should be him.

He snorted quietly; she didn't think she needed his safekeeping. She didn't want him full stop. His name was useful for her beloved sister, but as a man she didn't seem to think much of him. But it didn't matter how she felt, he seemed to have placed himself in the role of her protector anyway.

Katherine moaned, low and deep, and the sound was so full of terror that he turned towards her.

'Katherine, you're dreaming.' Instinctively, he slipped his arm around her and rubbed her back.

She gasped at the contact and her eyes flew open. 'What's happening?'

'We're in a barn on the way to Borwyn. You're quite safe with me.'

He continued with his slow-moving strokes across her back, ignoring the way his body flared to life with this innocent touch. He swallowed and subtly shifted his body, once again hiding his reaction to her. This was getting worse than ridiculous. She wasn't the first woman he'd held in his arms, yet his body was acting as if she were. This unwanted desire had to stop. Now that he'd proposed marriage to her sister she was out of bounds.

Gradually her breathing returned to normal.

'Oh, yes. Of course.' She rubbed her eyes. 'I'm sorry, did I wake you?'

'I wasn't asleep.'

'Oh.'

There was a beat of silence.

'What were you dreaming about?' he asked.

He heard her swallow.

'My mother.'

'I gathered, but what did she do to you that frightens you so much?'

There was a pause. 'She isn't mad.'

'Katherine, I've promised to marry your sister. I'm

not going to go back on that.' As much as he might want to. 'There is nothing to fear from telling me the truth.'

The silence was so long he didn't think she was going to talk.

'She really isn't insane—at least, I don't think so. I think, in a way, that's what makes it worse. My mother, she changed after my father…after my father died. She was never particularly loving before that, but she didn't hate us. Actually, maybe she doesn't hate us now. Only me. I look most like my father, you see, and the way I act, she says, reminds her of him.'

He continued to stroke her back as she talked, her spine so delicate under his broad hands. He was offering her comfort. That was all. It was an innocent gesture.

'I didn't want her to take her anger out on Linota. Linota is the best person I have in my life. I couldn't bear it if she got hurt.' Katherine cringed against him and he had to flex his fingers to stop them curling into fists.

'So you take all the beatings,' said Jarin, rage sweeping over him. How could her mother hit someone as defenceless as Katherine? Katherine might have the heart of a lion, but she had the body of a woodland nymph. She could no more protect herself than stop the wind from blowing. How could her warrior brother let her mother get away with treating her this badly for so long?

'It is not that Linota lets me take them for her,' said Katherine, quick to defend the sister she so adored and in doing so admitting that she was indeed the one who was beaten. 'I just make sure that if Linota upsets her, I upset her more. That way it is me who takes the punishment. It's the right thing to do; I'm the oldest.'

'Your brother is older,' said Jarin coldly.

'My brother has done all he can to keep us safe,' she said, leaping to Braedan's defence also. 'Without him we'd have had no roof over our heads after our father's disgrace. He had to go on bended knee to Ogmore and beg him to take us in. As soon as he was able, he has given us a home away from our mother. Life has not been easy for him either.'

Jarin disagreed; it was her brother's job to protect her. 'It might not have been easy, but it has been worse for you, I think. He has had the freedom to go where he wants. He could have taken you anywhere, but he chose to take you to Ogmore's where you have been kept a virtual prisoner.'

'It is hard for you to imagine with your life of privilege, but we don't all have luxurious fortresses to escape to when the going gets tough.'

He reared back as if she'd hit him, striking his head on the wooden ledge and biting his tongue to stop the curse that rose to his lips. 'You know nothing of my life,' he growled, hurt at her accusation. 'Don't assume that things are true based only on what you think you see.'

'What I see is a man quick to judge and to condemn.' Her spine became taut under his fingers and he took his hand away. She clearly didn't want or need his comfort. 'I've seen you from my chamber window,' she continued. 'Your days are filled with pleasant pursuits, a little bit of hunting, a little bit of riding; there is nothing stopping you from doing what you want, when you want. So don't censure my family when you have no experience of the hardships we've faced. Whatever we've done, we've done it to survive.'

Jarin sat up abruptly. 'Don't speak to me about judgement or condemnation when you have already made your mind up about me without knowing any of the facts. Yes, I was rude about your family, but that seems to have damned me for eternity in your eyes.'

'Then tell me, your lordship, what hardships have you had to endure? Was the mattress you once slept on too hard, or perhaps the blankets that covered you were a little too soft?'

Her voice was laden with scorn and he curled his fists. Heaven help him, but he wanted to tell her, tell her everything about himself so that she would see him for the man he really was, not the one he showed to everyone else. But once she knew everything there would be no going back. She would not forget and he would know that there was someone out there who knew the truth behind the mask he always showed to the world. She would know he was a lesser man than the one he pretended to be.

The silence stretched between them and then he felt a soft touch on his arm.

Her voice was much quieter when she spoke. 'I am sorry, Jarin. Sometimes…after the dreams, I am angry. Angry because of what happened to me and angry at the way my mother acted. That was no excuse to take it out on you. You have been nothing but kind and considerate to me. Please forgive me.'

He grunted, not quite ready to relent so quickly, but her hand stayed on his sleeve, silently pleading with him.

'Please, Jarin. I feel awful. I don't want to ruin our friendship. It has become so important to me.'

After a long moment he raised his own hand to cover hers and he heard her little sigh. His own body gave a jolt of lust at the sound. He imagined it was just the noise she would make as he slowly ran his hands over her body, finding all her secret places which brought her pleasure. This was not the time for such thoughts. She had made it clear that they were friends and he had to honour that, much like he had to honour the promise to marry her sister. A promise he had made because he wanted to be the man who solved Katherine's problems. A promise that made his heart feel like a lump of stone.

Now she wanted to know about his past and, God damn him for a fool, he was going to tell her.

The truth might reduce him as a man in her eyes, but it might also make her trust his motives a bit more. Besides, she was stroking small circles on his bicep and he hoped she would continue if he carried on talking.

'I understand more than you think about what it is like to live in fear of a parent,' he said quietly.

Her fingers moved along his arm, sending goose pimples over his skin.

'Tell me,' she said.

Jarin lay back down, cushioning his head under one arm.

'My father had three sons. The two older ones were the image of him: they lived for the hunt, whether that was animals, enemies or women, it didn't really matter. Perhaps without my father's influence my brothers might have been decent men, but he indulged them in their excesses and they became boorish brutes.'

'Then there was you,' she said quietly.

He huffed out a laugh; maybe her opinion of him wasn't too bad after all.

'Aye, I was fifteen years younger than my next brother. A late surprise for my mother. From the beginning I was different from either of them, taking after my mother rather than my father. I enjoyed reading and learning and found fighting pointless and futile. My father was not pleased with me and he made that very clear from the start, but it didn't bother me. My early years were happy. I spent them with my mother and didn't have to see much of the other males in my family. That changed when I was eight.'

He squeezed his eyes shut at the memory of being sent away from Borwyn to begin his knight's training. It was what boys of his rank did. He'd known it was expected of him, but unlike other boys his age he hadn't looked forward to it; instead, he'd been terrified. Not that he would admit that bit to Katherine. Bile rose in his throat as he remembered how loudly he'd screamed as his father had taken him from his mother; her dress had torn under his strong grip, but it hadn't made a difference. He'd been taken from her despite his protests and her quiet sobbing.

'My father didn't take my reluctance to undergo knight's training well,' he said.

He rolled his shoulder, remembering the beating he'd received for acting in a way which had disgraced the Borwyn name in the eyes of his father. He'd not been able to walk for several days afterwards and his brothers had mocked him as weak despite the fact that they'd never received such treatment.

'Did he hurt you?' Katherine asked softly.

Jarin nodded and then, realising she couldn't see him, said, 'Aye, he beat me then and continued to do so whenever we met, until I reached a height and weight that could easily dominate him. Then he stopped.'

At heart, his father had been a coward, but Jarin hadn't realised that until it was too late.

'Did you ever hit him back?'

'No. Contrary to how I acted yesterday, I abhor violence. Hurting people seems pointless if you can achieve your aims through rational discussion. If my father and I had ever sat down and had a conversation, then maybe we would have dealt much better together. As it was, he despised me for being his… I was going to say weaker son, but that's not true. I grew to be bigger and stronger than my older brothers, so it wasn't that I had less strength than them. No, they despised me because I didn't want to use my physical strength to dominate others around me. I've always believed talking through a problem is better and violence should only be used if all other options have failed.'

'You are a diplomat. That seems sensible to me.'

He smiled into the darkness at her pert tone. She might not want to admit it, but it sounded rather like she was defending him. 'Aye, I am…sensible.' He grinned. Sensible wasn't quite the way he'd like her to describe him. He'd prefer courageous and strong but sensible was better than 'boorish oaf', which seemed to have been her opinion up until now. 'But being that way only served to infuriate my father more. He believed that real men were hot-blooded and always acted on the spur of the moment.'

Below him the sheep baaed at random intervals,

joined occasionally by Eira's snort of disapproval. It was a strange place to stay the night. He'd not had many that were this uncomfortable, but for some strange reason he felt remarkably content. Maybe it was because he was finally telling someone the truth about his past. Not even Erik, his closest confidant, knew all the details.

'Did you reconcile with your brothers before they died?' Katherine asked.

'No. I hadn't seen my brothers in the two years before their deaths. I'd been banished from Borwyn—not that he admitted that publicly; it would have brought too much shame on the Borwyn name to confess he thought his youngest son an embarrassment. My father called it a training exercise in the north, but I think really he was hoping the cold would finish me off. Instead, it was my brothers who caught a fever. They were both dead within a few days of each other. That's when I returned.'

'What happened then?'

He rubbed his brow. 'Perhaps we should leave that story for another time; suffice to say, it wasn't a happy time.'

'Tell me,' she said quietly.

She knew the worst of his past so he figured she might as well hear the rest. Jarin let out a slow exhale. 'My father could no longer beat me. My time in the north had honed my battle skills. I was bigger and better at fighting than anyone in my father's fortress. You would think that would win my father's favour, but, no, his hatred was too entrenched by then and he made my life hell in other ways.' He swallowed. 'As the heir, I had to learn how to manage the estate. And…' he laughed softly '…my father didn't like it that I was cleverer than him. He would deliberately mislead me about certain facts, sending me on wild goose chases that would sometimes last for weeks. It was frustrating and petty and totally pointless.'

Katherine's fingers continued to stroke his arm. He supposed the gesture was meant to be comforting, but every sweep sent a sensation straight to his groin. He sucked in a breath and closed his eyes tightly.

'To cut a long story short, I met a woman, thought I was in love and married her against my father's wishes. Now that I'm older, I see that her being forbidden to me was part of her attraction; it was certainly an angle she played to great effect. I was…blinded by desire. So lost in it that I didn't see the woman she was behind her beautiful face.

'I realised my mistake too late. My error compounded my father's opinion that I was unfit to be the Earl of Borwyn. Life got worse…' He petered off as he remembered the months of living hell his marriage had been. He cleared his throat. 'Then my wife died and despite everything, I swore to the old man, on his death bed, that I wouldn't disgrace the Borwyn name again. I wanted him to die proud of me, but that was too much to hope for. My mother died not long after. I promised her…' He cleared his throat. 'I promised her when I was growing up that I would be nothing like my father and brothers. That I would make the name of Borwyn stand for honour, peace and prosperity. Every day I try to live up to those values.' He smiled bleakly into the darkness. 'Obviously I don't always manage it.'

He'd said enough. He didn't want to revisit the past

any more. His wife and father were dead and that meant they no longer had the power to torture him.

'And now you've promised to marry my sister and link the Borwyn name to the treasonous Leofric family.'

He opened his mouth to protest, but she stopped him. 'You don't have to deny it. I know the truth. This marriage will go against your oath to both your mother and your father, although I don't believe your father deserves the respect of someone as good as you. I would release you from the promise if it hadn't been made to save my sister.'

His heart swelled at her words. She did think well of him. It was a shame he'd had to engage himself to her sister to prove it.

'I will keep my promise,' he said firmly. That was one principle he would never turn from. If he made an oath he would stick to it, no matter whether it was something he wanted or not, even more so now that Katherine believed him to be a good man.

Katherine shifted on the ground next to him and her hand brushed against the skin of his knuckles. Despite his words, he wanted to capture her hand and trace the length of her fingers. He heard her soft inhale and before she could ask him another question he said, 'We need to get some sleep. Tomorrow will be another long day.' He didn't want to talk any more. He'd buried the pain and humiliation of his past deep inside.

He turned on his side away from her and forced his breathing to become soft and even. Behind him she stretched out her legs, gently brushing the back of his knees with the toe of her shoes. His body tightened and he burned to turn around and bring his mouth down on hers, but that would make a mockery of everything he had just said.

The tension in his body did not dissipate, no matter how long he stared into the distance. Behind him, Katherine's breathing eventually slid into deep sleep, her limbs twitching as she fell under. He still could not relax. When he was sure she slept soundly, he turned on to his other side and looked at her. He could not make out her delicate features in the darkness, but he was content to watch the rise and fall of her chest as she breathed deeply through the night; this was the only time he would be allowed to do so. Tomorrow they would be back at Borwyn and life would return to normal.

He must have finally dozed off because he awoke to find he had taken Katherine into his arms at some point in the night. He kept his eyes tightly shut as the bundle he was holding released a sigh and pressed into him. Was she aware of what she was doing? Her rhythmic breathing suggested not. His body tightened as she moaned in her sleep. This was exquisite torture.

Despite his best resolutions his hand slowly traced the length of her spine. She moved closer still, bringing her face near to his, her breath warm across his lips. He opened his eyes. Early morning light came in through a gap in the roof. This close, Jarin could make out a faint smattering of freckles across her cheekbones.

'Katherine,' he murmured. 'Are you awake?'

'Mmm-hmm,' was the unintelligible reply.

Her lips were gently parted, her soft breath continued to whisper over his skin.

'Oh, Katherine,' he murmured, as desire, hot and thick, raced through him.

Gently he placed his lips against hers, stealing the softest of kisses before moving away. Her mouth followed his, capturing a kiss of her own. He couldn't stop the groan of desire that escaped him. Her eyes flickered open and in the weak morning light her eyes were liquid gold.

Before he could think too much he reached over and traced the length of her delicate jaw with his fingertips. The tip of her tongue licked her upper lip and he was lost. He closed the gap between them and pressed his mouth to hers. After the briefest of pauses, her mouth began to move under his.

His fingers stole into her hair at the nape of her neck as he began to kiss her properly, fighting to keep his movements light while his body roared to consume her completely. Slowly, she relaxed into him, her body becoming flush with his. This time he didn't move away to hide his body's reaction as his cock pressed against her stomach. He scrambled to remember she *was* innocent, but it was hard when his body was clamouring for him to remove the clothes that separated them and to feel her soft skin against his.

She gasped at the first sweep of his tongue, but she quickly caught on and reacted with a passion that swept him away.

The hard, dirty floor melted away as his world became lips and tongues. He growled as her hand swept into his hair and held him tightly in place. His fingers stole back from the nape of her neck and gently traced the curve of her collarbone.

It had been so long since he'd had a woman in his arms, so long since he'd felt even the slightest stirrings of desire. Despite all his high-handed resolutions he missed it. Missed the way it made him feel alive.

He heard her whimper as his hand moved down the front of her dress to caress her breast. She arched into his touch and through the fabric he brushed her pert nipple with his thumb. She was making incoherent noises at the back of her throat and he tugged at the edge of her dress, desperate to feel the peaked flesh without the barrier of fabric.

How had he lived without this for so long? This was what he had been born for: to make love to this woman, to hold her in his arms and worship her body with his. Everything had been leading to this moment.

Through the haze of his lust he heard Eira pawing the barn floor, impatient to get back out into the open. The reason he was crushed into the hayloft came flooding back to him and his fingers froze.

Linota! How could he have forgotten? He'd offered marriage to one woman and now he was pawing at her innocent sister like a lust-crazed beast. He was a monster. One minute claiming to be a rational man, but as soon as the opportunity presented itself he was like his old self, swept away by uncontrollable lust. With great reluctance he lifted his head and gazed down at Katherine.

Her lips were swollen, her eyes were unfocused. Everything inside him screamed at him to reclaim her mouth. His fingers rested on the swell of her breasts and it would only take a small movement to reveal the whole. He was sure she would not resist if he continued his exploration, but it would be wrong. She was an innocent and he was taking advantage. His fingers shook as he tugged the edge of her dress up to cover her skin and he mentally cursed himself for having been turned into a callow youth just by a simple kiss.

Her breathing was slowly returning to normal and he risked a look at her face. She was still dazed. Her tongue flickered out and licked her lips and he bit back a groan as desire rushed over him.

'I'm sorry,' he said huskily. 'I did not mean to do that.'

Hearing his voice seemed to snap her out of her trance and she gasped, rearing back from him quickly and hitting her head on the wall behind.

'Careful,' he said, his voice still not his own.

'I... I...'

Her eyes were wide now, her lips parted, no longer in desire but in horror. His stomach twisted and he moved his gaze, staring at the wall behind her shoulder because he couldn't bear to see the repulsion in her look.

'We seem to have got a little carried away while we were both half-asleep,' he said formally. 'I apologise if my actions caused you any distress. You can rest assured that you are safe with me and nothing of this nature will happen again.'

There was silence, broken only by the baaing of the sheep below.

'Thank you,' she said shakily. 'I would be grateful to put this incident behind us.'

His stomach swooped with disappointment. Of course she didn't want to continue now that she knew who'd she'd been kissing. It was only he who was consumed by this all-encompassing desire that had him breaking so many vows it made his head hurt.

He nodded briskly. 'Then we are agreed.'

He sat up and swung his legs over the edge of the hayloft. 'We need to carry on our journey.'

He quickly climbed down the ladder and waited as he heard her rustling movements ahead. She was probably rearranging her clothes after their encounter and the thought did nothing to relieve his aching lust.

He cleared his throat. 'Do you need help getting down the ladder?'

'No, I'm fine, thank you.'

Despite her reassurance he stayed where he was. He didn't want her to fall and hurt herself through sheer stubbornness.

After an age, one dainty foot appeared on the top rung of the ladder. He waited as the second one followed. It waved precariously around for a moment before it, too, found the rung. He began to move away; now all she had to do was climb down and that was a simple enough matter. She wouldn't appreciate him hanging around waiting for her. The disgust on her face when she realised she'd been locked in an embrace with him spoke volumes. She still hadn't forgiven him for his harsh words about her family and she probably never would now that he had taken advantage of her innocence and been disloyal to his promise to marry her sister.

It shouldn't matter. They were in agreement that they shouldn't be kissing and, even if he hadn't promised to marry Linota, Katherine was bad for him. Just like his reaction to Viola, Katherine's presence made him act unlike himself. Nevertheless, a dull ache had settled between his ribs.

There was a yelp and a ripping noise and he instinctively turned back, catching her just before she hit the ground.

'How on earth did you manage to fall?' he growled, irritated that the desire he'd been getting under control roared back to life by the simple act of holding her in his arms.

'I missed a step and I'd have been perfectly all right without you acting the hero. It wasn't a big drop.'

'Fine. Next time I'll let you fall.' The unabated lust was making him irritable.

'Good,' she said, her eyes sparking with anger.

Despite their heated words, he didn't let her go and she didn't struggle for release. Her mouth was dangerously close to his and he found his head was dipping closer.

Chapter Thirteen

He was going to kiss her again and her traitorous body was going to let him. The air between them stilled. His breath brushed against her skin. She leaned towards him and his hands drifted down her arms until his long fingers curled with hers. Her pulse pounded in her throat.

Eira snorted impatiently to their right and the mood was broken. She stepped back quickly. What was she doing? The man before her had promised to marry her sister. Linota was Katherine's everything and yet she was about to betray her and all because her body craved Jarin's touch. She was a dreadful human being. She was more her father's daughter than she'd wanted to believe. No wonder her mother hated her.

They didn't speak as Jarin led Eira outside. A frost had settled while they slept and the muddy ground was frozen solid. Katherine hugged her cloak to her as the cold air bit into her skin.

'We'll be home soon,' said Jarin, keeping his eyes fixed on Eira's flank. 'You'll soon be warm.'

Katherine didn't comment. Jarin's home wasn't hers

and now that she knew how his lips felt against hers it never would be. She could not trust herself to live with Linota and her husband. She would always know what it was like to be held in his arms and she would always want to return there like the traitor she was.

Jarin helped her up on to the saddle. 'I'll lead her,' he said, remaining on the ground. 'It will be easier that way.'

Katherine nodded and stared into the mass of trees ahead. She couldn't bring herself to look at him as tears pricked her eyes.

'About what happened this morning…' Jarin said as Eira started to move.

Katherine held up her hand. 'I would prefer not to talk about it,' she said, pleased that her voice came out calmly. Years of living with her mother had given her plenty of practice at hiding her emotions and Jarin would never know that she was near to tears.

Jarin cleared his throat. 'I feel that we must.'

'There is nothing to say. We were both befuddled by sleep. It won't happen again and no one needs to know about it.' That was paramount in Katherine's mind. It was one thing for her to know about her traitorous body, but no one else must ever find out, especially Linota.

'Very well,' said Jarin stiffly and he quickened the pace, moving purposefully through the trees.

Katherine tried to watch where they were going, but her gaze kept returning to the back of Jarin's head. In the weak light of the early morning sun his hair appeared almost golden. She longed to reach out and touch it. She knew now that it was as soft and as thick as it looked.

She closed her eyes tightly. She needed to banish this morning's memory from her mind. She didn't pretend to herself that she was anything special. Jarin had been half-asleep when he'd kissed her. He was probably used to waking up with a different woman in his arms. As soon as he'd realised who she was he'd stopped abruptly and his words afterwards had confirmed that he'd made a mistake. He'd obviously imagined he was with a different woman—perhaps that widow she'd seen him with the night of her brother's wedding. She'd certainly acted like someone else.

Heat crept over her face; she knew she should have been shocked when his hand had brushed her breast, but she'd only cursed the material of her dress for being in the way. She'd thought for a moment that he would push her dress aside and run his fingers over her flesh and her body had come alive with need.

A small voice in her mind protested that he'd been about to kiss her again after he'd caught her at the bottom of the ladder. He hadn't been half-asleep then. They'd been in the middle of another argument when the atmosphere had changed, becoming charged in a way she hadn't known was possible. The way his hands had touched hers had been tender, as if he really did care about her. Sometimes she caught him looking at her as if she *was* beautiful. No one had ever looked at her like that before and she wanted to treasure it, to be able to bring it out as a golden memory in years to come, untarnished by the reality of these latest doubts.

She pushed the thought aside. Jarin was marrying Linota because he was an honourable man and that was the end of it, and if her eyes were stinging with unshed tears at the thought then it served her right for being a fool.

They plodded on. The light around them became brighter, although Katherine couldn't see the sun through the denseness of the branches about them. She guessed it was nearing midday and her stomach rumbled, reminding her that she had not eaten since the day before.

She pressed her hand over the noise, but obviously she didn't muffle it enough.

Jarin brought Eira to a stop and rummaged around in a saddlebag.

'Here,' he said, thrusting an apple towards her.

'Thank you,' she said, taking the green fruit from him.

She bit into the crisp flesh and juice flowed down her chin. She wiped it away with the back of her hand and licked her fingers. She flushed when she realised Jarin was watching her, a slight frown between his brows.

He turned away without comment and they carried on with their journey.

Gradually the dense tangle of trees thinned and they emerged on to a wide riverbed almost devoid of water.

'The tide's out of the estuary,' said Jarin, not looking at her. 'We should be able to cross on horseback.' He hesitated. 'I'll join you.'

He vaulted on to the saddle behind her and she inhaled sharply as he gathered up the reins and kicked Eira into a trot.

Before this morning, she'd found an innocent sort

of pleasure riding in front of Jarin. Now it was a form of torture. His arms were only around her to guide the horse. They were not there to caress her or to hold her tenderly, but that didn't stop her body longing for him, longing to turn around and press her lips to his once more.

Her chest was tight and breathing was difficult. She wanted to get away from him so she could think, but he was everywhere. His arms engulfed her body and his scent filled the air around her.

A fine trembling started up throughout her body and, although she mentally scolded herself, she could not get herself under control.

'You have nothing to fear from me,' said Jarin, mistaking her shivers for fear. 'I will not hurt you or force my attentions on you again.'

Tears pricked her eyes; of course he wouldn't kiss her again. He'd promised to marry her sister and she was a horrible, traitorous fool to wish any different. She was more than grateful that he put her trembling down to fear rather than desire.

Eira splashed through a stretch of water. She was cantering for home now and didn't seem to need much direction from Jarin. They must be close.

They rounded a sharp bend in the estuary and there it was: the grand Borwyn fortress, rising above the edge of a high riverbank on one side and facing a cliff edge on the other. The sight took her breath away.

'It's beautiful,' said Katherine softly, taking in the grand edifice and the craggy rocks below.

Jarin snorted. 'Trust you to be contrary. It's supposed to be intimidating.'

'Well, yes, I suppose beautiful is the wrong word. It is striking. All that blue, the sky, the river and the sea against the stone. Do you know I've never seen the sea before? It's so big.'

Katherine put her hand up to her forehead to shield her eyes from the glare of the sun. She looked out over the vast expanse of water that was becoming clearer with every step. It stretched on forever, disappearing into the horizon, and she felt a pang of longing for places she would never see. The world was so big and she'd mostly seen the inside of the same four walls for years and years.

'I'll make sure you get a room with a view of the beach,' said Jarin gruffly. 'No two days look exactly the same.'

Katherine turned her gaze back to the fortress. It was only then that it hit her that Jarin was the master of this vast building and all those that lived within its walls and that, through marriage, her sister would become its mistress. It was difficult to equate its awe-inspiring grandness with Jarin the man.

The Earl of Ogmore's fortress was not nearly so magnificent, but he ruled with an iron fist. She had never once seen him display the levels of kindness and consideration that Jarin had shown her.

Eira began to climb, following a narrow path that was cut into the mud and which took them to the edge of the stone fortress. Jarin turned Eira to the east and began to walk her along the wall.

'This is odd,' muttered Jarin as they carried on.

'What is?'

'There should be guards stationed every twenty paces along this wall. Where is everybody?'

Hair's stood up on the back of Katherine's neck. 'Do you think we should…?'

They rounded a bend in the fortress's walls. A man stood in front of them barring their way. At first Katherine took him for a soldier, but as they drew closer she realised he wasn't wearing chainmail.

'Jarin,' she said, clutching his arm tightly.

'I've seen him,' he growled. 'I'm afraid it's our friend from the woods.'

Katherine's heart beat painfully in her chest and she instinctively grabbed Jarin's arm.

'Here we are again,' said the same oily voice that had hounded her nightmares. 'Last time we met I was polite and courteous. I could have taken your girl from you easily, but I didn't. I could have taken the clothes from your back, but I didn't want you to freeze. This time things are going to go a little differently.'

Katherine could feel Jarin shifting in the saddle behind her. She wondered whether he would have a better chance of surviving this scene if she removed herself from the saddle. As it was, she was blocking him from getting to the gang's leader. She knew he didn't have a sword but she'd seen him use his fists and she had no doubt he could beat his opponent if she wasn't in the way. She made to move, but, as if sensing her intention, Jarin gripped her tightly, his arms like steel against her waist.

'You can't defeat me by yourself,' said Jarin coldly.

'I'm not alone,' said the leader and Katherine jumped as a hand curled around her calf. She turned and saw more men appearing from behind the bend in the castle wall. They must have been following them at a discreet distance because she hadn't sensed their approach.

She kicked out and connected with her assailant's nose. The man cried out as blood spurted from his face and he let go of her abruptly.

'Hold on,' Jarin growled to her as he began to push Eira forward.

Katherine looked around her; there weren't as many men as there had been in the forest—maybe five—but it wasn't any less frightening despite being in broad daylight and so close to safety.

The leader grabbed hold of Eira's mane and started to tug on it, sending the horse wild with fright. Eira bucked and Katherine screamed. Jarin held on to her tightly.

Another hand grabbed her ankle and this time she couldn't kick out.

'Jarin,' she screamed, as a knife slid up inside the skirts of her dress and against the skin of her calf. 'There's a knife.'

'Stop trying to fight us,' said the leader of the group. 'Or your girl will be cut. Who knows, she might even bleed to death.'

Eira was still panicking. With every desperate move that the horse made, the blade dug deeper into Katherine's skin. A bead of blood trickled down her leg and she whimpered.

'Stop pulling at Eira,' commanded Jarin, 'and I will stop trying to fight you.'

The leader stood back and Jarin soothed his horse through whispers and stroking until she stilled beneath them. Katherine wished she could be so easily calmed.

'Leave the lady alone,' said Jarin. 'Let her ride on to the fortress entrance and I will come quietly.'

'I don't think so,' sneered the leader. 'Threatening the girl seems to be the only way to keep you under control. Get down from the horse.'

When Jarin didn't move to comply, the leader nodded to the man with the knife. Katherine cried out as the blade was pressed into her skin, pain sweeping the length of her leg.

Jarin gave her one last tight squeeze and swung down from the horse.

Instead of moving towards the leader, however, he punched her assailant hard and fast, sending him flying into the castle wall. There was a sickening crunch and the man crumpled to the ground, his blade falling from his lifeless fingers.

Before Katherine could even draw in a gasp Jarin had taken out another man, leaving only three left. He was moving fluidly now, throwing punches at their attackers who were immediately overwhelmed by Jarin's superior strength and skill. He was awe-inspiring to watch. Within the space of a few heartbeats only Jarin and the leader were left standing.

The leader waved his sword about and Katherine recognised it as Jarin's. The man smiled. 'I've orders not to kill you, but this is personal between us now. Once you are dead, I will take the girl for myself. When I've finished with her, I will share her among my men. Know that she will die cursing your name.'

Jarin merely laughed, a mad sound that Katherine did not recognise, and moved towards his attacker.

Katherine's heart stilled as she watched Jarin approach a man who held a sword aloft while he was unarmed.

'No,' she screamed as the leader swung his sword arm down towards Jarin's head.

But Jarin was too fast for him. Years of training clearly more than made up for his lack of weapon. Before Katherine could draw breath, the leader was doubled up in pain from a punch to the gut. Jarin easily took his own sword from the man, before punching him in the face, knocking him unconscious.

Jarin stood, breathing heavily, his shoulders rigid.

Katherine jumped down from Eira and ran to him. He caught her in his arms and she buried her head in his chest.

'I thought he was going to kill you,' she said against his skin.

'I told you I couldn't fight fifteen men when we were in the woods. But five, here...' he shrugged '...that was easy.'

She laughed but didn't release her tight grip.

For several moments Jarin held her against him. She could feel the strength of his heartbeat against her cheek. She never wanted to let go; with him she felt safe...and another emotion she didn't know how to name.

'We need to move,' said Jarin eventually. 'There could be more men coming up behind them.'

Reluctantly she let her arms drop to her sides. Jarin made no move towards Eira. She looked up at him. Once again the expression on his face held her captive. She glanced at his lips and then back to his blue eyes. She licked her lips and Jarin's head bent towards her.

She held her breath, both longing for his mouth to brush hers and knowing that it was beyond wrong for it to happen. Behind Jarin, one of the fallen men groaned, breaking whatever was occurring between them.

'We need to get back to the keep,' said Jarin.

Jarin retrieved his sword and scabbard from the fallen leader and then vaulted up behind her, kicking Eira into a gallop. The horse was only too happy to oblige and soon they were flying along the narrow path.

The gate, when they reached it, was surrounded by fierce guards all armed to the teeth. Their unfriendly demeanour sent a shiver down Katherine's spine. How could she and Jarin tell who was their friend or foe? If more than one person was acting against Jarin, then how could he protect them both from a whole battalion of armed men?

'My lord,' said the nearest man, 'welcome home.'

Katherine sagged in relief at this friendly tone. Behind her, Jarin's body remained rigid. She looked around. None of the men looked happy to see their lord, but none of them were outwardly aggressive either.

'Why aren't there men on the south walls?' Jarin demanded. 'There should be one every twenty paces, but instead I find you all here. What is the meaning of this?'

The man coloured. 'We received your orders to draw back and protect the gate.'

'Who gave you those orders?' growled Jarin.

'They came as a written order, my lord, with your seal on it.'

'My seal is in my bag and I have given no such commands,' growled Jarin. 'I was attacked by a group of men who were lying in wait for me, while you all stood here doing nothing. Send reinforcements out and collect the men, who are in various states of consciousness. Have them thrown in the dungeons and alert me when they awaken. Have the guards along all the walls been called back in?'

'Aye, my lord,' said the soldier.

Jarin snarled, 'Send the men out as usual. An attack is being planned and I want everyone to be extra-vigilant. I want you to report to me at the end of your shift. I especially want to know about anything out of the ordinary, however small it may seem.'

'Yes, my lord,' said the man, who was visibly sweating.

Jarin made to move on, but stopped. 'Has Erik arrived back?'

'Aye, yesterday.'

'Was there a woman with him?'

The guard frowned. 'No, sir.'

Katherine's stomach dived. Even though she hadn't been expecting her sister to be here when they arrived, the confirmation of it was a blow.

Jarin nodded. 'Send a message to Erik that I want to see him in the Hall. I'll be there directly.'

The guard nodded and Jarin nudged Eira into a movement again. They passed the silent, staring soldiers as they made their way through the thick entrance without incident and emerged into a bustling courtyard.

Before they could dismount, a stable boy appeared with a step for Katherine. All around people were rushing, untying the bags and removing Eira's saddle—yet another reminder of Jarin's status, which was far greater than her own even before her father's execution.

'Come,' said Jarin and, without checking to see if she was following, he strode off in the direction of the keep.

She scurried after him, trying to ignore the pointed stares that were thrown her way once Jarin's back was turned. She was used to being the object of curiosity so it shouldn't bother her that once again people were looking at her and making a judgement. It hadn't occurred to her that arriving alone in Jarin's company would set tongues wagging. Not that it mattered, she was used to it, after all, but it would have been pleasant to arrive somewhere without the taint of scandal following her.

The great door to the keep was flung open as they arrived and Jarin strode on through without pausing. Katherine threw a grateful smile at the attendant, but there was no answering flicker in the man's eyes.

Jarin's pace increased and Katherine had to skip every few steps to catch up. As they walked, people sprang into action, holding doors open or bowing towards Jarin, but there was no welcoming smile or friendly word for him.

At last he ground to a halt in front of a tall, thin middle-aged woman whose hair was severely pulled back and hidden under a wimple.

'Ah, Mistress Sutton, there you are. This is Mistress Leofric. Please take her up to a guest chamber, one that looks towards the bay, and make sure she has every comfort. She has a wound on her leg. Have someone provide an adequate dressing for that. A bath and some clean clothes would also be desirable.'

Katherine looked down at her travel-stained dress and tried to smooth out the wrinkles. She hadn't realised how dishevelled she looked. Heat raced across her face at the thought that Jarin had. Even so, she refused to be banished to her rooms to be kept away from what was happening.

'Jarin,' she said as he began to turn away from her, 'I need to know what's going on.'

She realised her mistake in the widening of the servant's eyes.

'I mean, my lord. I need, I mean I…'

A flicker of amusement crossed Jarin's eyes, but his tone remained calm and even. 'I will send for you as soon as I have news. Please make yourself comfortable while you wait.'

He turned and strode away from her, the tall servant blocking her when she tried to follow.

'My lord has asked that I show you to your room, Mistress Leofric, if you'll follow me.'

Chasing after Jarin would do no good. He'd already disappeared from sight and she could be wandering for days in this vast, stone castle before she found him again. She had to hope that he would keep his word and come and get her as soon as there was news.

She traipsed up a narrow, spiral staircase, her heart sinking lower with every step. Despite the promise of a guest chamber, the route was reminiscent of her journey to her room at Ogmore's castle—the chamber where she'd been kept a virtual prisoner for so long. She folded her arms across her chest to keep her fingers from trembling. She would give Jarin until tomorrow morning, but if he hadn't sent for her by then she would take matters into her own hands.

Chapter Fourteen

The chamber proved to be far larger than the route had suggested. She could easily have fitted both her old room and her mother's into the space with more to spare. Mistress Sutton had surprised her by organising warm water to be brought up to the room straight away so that she could bathe.

The water had been beautifully spiced with sweet-smelling herbs and she sank into it, her aching limbs grateful for the relaxing warmth. Her wound stung a little, but she was relieved to see it was not as deep as she'd feared. She stayed in the water until it cooled, revelling in her first ever bath. Before now she'd had to make do with washing standing up with cold water that her mother had left over from her own ablutions, lavender soap her only luxury and something she hid from her mother's prying eyes.

When her skin had a fine layer of goose pimples over it, she climbed out to find clean clothes had been arranged on the bed, along with some white cloth for the cut on her leg. She bound it and then dressed quickly, tightening the strings on the red dress so it didn't flap around her figure. It was still too large for her, but it was better than her own clothes, which looked as though they'd been dragged through a thorn bush in comparison. She folded the clothes—though they looked nothing better than rags—and left them on top of a chest. She would probably need to throw them away, but as they were currently her only clothes in the whole world she was reluctant to do that straight away.

A table stood in one corner of the room. She wandered over and picked up a brush, running it over her hair in long soothing strokes. The gesture made her think of Jarin braiding her hair. For the first time in her life someone had made her feel beautiful. She held her hair up to the light, trying to see it in the way Jarin had described. Although it wasn't the stunning, pale blonde of Linota's, its different shades did make it interesting.

She went to braid it as normal, but then decided to try the style Jarin had used. It had felt better to wear her hair away from her face, especially when she'd been riding since the braids hadn't continually hit her in the face. The braid might be a style for a younger woman, but Jarin had thought it was appropriate and this was his castle. She quickly pushed away the thought that she was dressing to please a man who would never be hers. It wasn't about that. The new style made her feel good and why shouldn't she feel attractive for the first time? Whatever happened in the future, she would always be grateful to Jarin for that.

When she was finished she took the trencher of food that had been left for her over to the window. Several large cushions had been arranged for guests to sit on.

She curled up on one and gazed out on the landscape below.

A wide stretch of yellow swept in a long arc, disappearing into the distance. The expanse was empty apart from small black dots. She squinted and eventually realised they were birds standing at the water's edge. The sea rippled, sometimes deep blue, sometimes silver, and high in the sky white birds circled, calling to one another. This was a view she could watch for days without the slightest tug of boredom.

She was startled by an abrupt knock on her door, causing her to spill a seed cake she hadn't got round to finishing. She stood and brushed the crumbs off her dress.

'Enter,' she called.

Mistress Sutton stepped inside, no hint of a smile on her face. 'The master requires your presence in the solar.'

Katherine's heart leapt. She'd expected him to keep her waiting until at least tomorrow, but she hadn't been by herself for very long at all. She hoped this meant he had good news to tell her.

Katherine followed Mistress Sutton in silence, trying to memorise every twist and turn in the complex labyrinth of corridors, but she soon became lost. She wondered if this was the lady's objective. If Katherine didn't know where she was going, then she was dependent on someone showing her the way every time she wanted to get anywhere. A befuddled guest was a guest who wasn't plotting against the lord of the manor.

She entered the solar by a side door and took a minute to look around. Knights and their ladies stood dotted around the space, talking amongst themselves, occasionally flicking glances up at the raised dais. Up above them, Jarin sat in an ornate chair, his head resting on his closed fist as he listened to Erik speak.

He looked up as she approached and a smile touched his eyes, although his lips remained solemn.

'Mistress Leofric,' said Erik, bowing to her as she got near. 'I trust you have recovered from your nasty encounter with a tree.'

Katherine's jaw clenched. 'I have, thank you. What news is there of my sister?'

Jarin shifted on his seat. 'We've had a message.'

For the first time she noticed the parchment resting on his leg.

Her heart leapt. 'What does it say?'

He held it out to her, but she didn't take it. 'I can't read,' she said quietly, a wash of heat rushing over her cheeks.

She fixed her gaze upon Jarin's shoulder rather than see the look on his face. She knew it wasn't unusual for women of her class not to be able to read, but Katherine had always felt the lack of her ability. When her father had been alive she'd asked if she could learn, but he had only laughed, saying there was no need and that her future husband would be able to undertake that task for her. Now that she knew she would never marry, she hoped she could find someone who would teach her. Perhaps Jarin... But, no, of course not. Her heart constricted; she wasn't going to be spending time with him once Linota was found.

Jarin cleared his throat. 'The note assures us that

Linota is being well looked after, but her captors have asked for money for her safe return.'

Katherine's gaze flew up to his. 'But I haven't got any.'

'The message is addressed to me. I will pay.' He broke eye contact and turned to his steward. 'Erik, write my response and follow their instructions. We'll agree to their terms.'

Erik made a swift bow and retreated from the room. Many a woman stopped to watch him saunter past. He had a fine figure, similar to Jarin's, tall and muscular. But whereas Katherine found it difficult to take her eyes off Jarin, there was something about Erik that made the hairs on the back of Katherine's neck stand to attention.

She turned her attention back to Jarin who was watching her, a slight frown crossing his features once more. She raised her hand to her braid and smoothed it out. She hadn't managed to accomplish the tight knots he'd achieved, but she'd thought it looked all right and the dress she was wearing now was clean, if not a little loose. His intense scrutiny suggested she hadn't done a good job.

'Have you been fed?' he asked abruptly.

She nodded as her stomach constricted. Only this morning she'd called him by his given name as he'd lain next to her. His hands had been on her body, his mouth claiming hers. She knew she would have given herself to him if he hadn't come to his senses. Now it was as if a great chasm had opened up between them and she didn't know if she would be able to cross it, or even whether she should try.

'Is everything all right, my lord?' she asked quietly.

'Things are…' He shook his head and glanced at the groups of people within the Great Hall. His lips thinned, 'We can't talk here. Much as I hate you walking about without a proper guard to accompany you, I think we need to meet elsewhere.'

She nodded quickly, her heart thumping.

'Return to your chamber with Mistress Sutton. Once she has left, leave the room and turn left. Climb the stairs until you are at the top. I will meet you on the ramparts.'

Without waiting for a response, he nodded to Mistress Sutton who immediately came over. It seemed Jarin expected Katherine to obey him like everyone else. She couldn't help thinking it would do him some good to have someone question his dictates once in a while.

It must be strange, mused Katherine as she followed the servant in silence once again, to have every whim obeyed without question and yet have no real friends to turn to. Jarin must be lonely without someone to challenge him now and again. Katherine might have lived almost as a prisoner for a large part of her life, but at least she'd had Linota to turn to and keep her company. Jarin had Erik, but it wasn't the same. Erik was a retainer just like everyone else in this castle. Jarin must have questioned whether Erik stayed with him out of loyalty or because he had to.

'I will return before the evening meal to take you back down to the solar,' said Mistress Sutton once they had returned to Katherine's chamber.

'Very well,' said Katherine, making as if to resume her seat by the window.

Mistress Sutton nodded stiffly and then withdrew. Katherine wondered whether the lady was as starchy with everyone or whether her disapproval stemmed from the unusual circumstances of Katherine's arrival at Borwyn. Perhaps she thought that Katherine was Jarin's mistress. Katherine shook her head; no one would think that if they saw them together.

His beauty was almost godlike whereas she could blend into the background and no one would notice whether she was around or not—well, Linota would notice and...was it presumptuous to think that Jarin would notice, too? She remembered that half-smile in his eyes and thought that perhaps he would. They were becoming unlikely friends in all this. Her heart swelled at the thought. She'd never had a friend before and she found she rather liked having one now, even if her feelings for him weren't entirely pure.

She stood and ran her fingers over the embroidered coverlet that lay on top of the bed. It was more beautiful and intricate than anything she'd ever owned and yet it had been carelessly thrown over a bed kept for guests. How wonderful to have such wealth, but also what a responsibility. All the people she'd seen today along with hundreds of others worked to keep things running, and they all depended on Jarin for their security. If he failed, then so did they. She didn't know if she could endure such pressure and remain sane.

She moved over to the doorway and pulled it open a crack. Peering through, she saw that Mistress Sutton had disappeared and she slipped out into the corridor.

It was easy to follow Jarin's directions and she soon found herself stepping outside. She was so high she almost touched the clouds. A laugh escaped her as strong winds lifted the edge of her dress, making it billow out like a tent.

'Katherine,' said a deep voice from behind her.

'Oh,' she said, turning quickly. 'I didn't realise you were already out here, my lord.'

She debated dropping a quick curtsy, but quickly dismissed the idea. The time they had spent together surely meant that she could dispense with such formalities, especially when they were alone.

'Please carry on calling me Jarin,' he said, stepping towards her. 'No one does any more apart from Erik and I hadn't realised how much I missed it.'

Her heart trilled as she nodded. It would appear they were friends after all. 'Of course, thank you, I'd be honoured to call you Jarin.

He smiled. 'And may I continue to call you Katherine?'

She smiled back. 'Of course. What did you want to see me about?'

The wind took her braids and began to whip them around her head. She held her hands up to hold them down, but it had little effect.

'Let's sit,' suggested Jarin. 'It will provide us with a bit of shelter, although I brought you up here because I thought you might enjoy the view and you won't be able to see it from down here.' He nodded at the stone floor.

She turned and looked out towards the sea. 'It's magnificent, but it is better that we speak.'

He nodded and sat down with his back against the wall of the castle. After a moment she joined him, carefully allowing a decent space between them.

'I'm sure you are right about Erik,' said Jarin.

Katherine's heart leapt. 'What makes you think so?'

Jarin rubbed his forehead. 'It's obvious. I don't know how I've taken so long to come round to the idea. I hope it's because I trusted him and not because I am as stupid as he obviously thinks. He might as well have been standing in front of me telling me he was guilty. Perhaps he has so little regard for my intelligence, although what I've done to deserve such condemnation from him I don't know.' Jarin leaned his head back against the wall, his eyes tired. 'I expressly told him to wait in Ickleston, but he didn't. He's apologetic, saying that he must not have heard in the chaos of the moment, but my man-at-arms was with him when I questioned them both and there was something off in the way he was standing.'

'What do you mean?'

Jarin shrugged. 'He wouldn't look at me, which isn't unusual. A lot of my dependants find it hard to make eye contact with me since I succeeded my father to the title. It's as if they are expecting me to be as vile as my father now that I have all that was his. But… Waldon is not normally like that. He's known me since I was a child and has always spoken his mind before. I think he knew Erik was lying to me, but didn't want to cause trouble.'

'What else?' asked Katherine. It wasn't enough to condemn a man on a funny look—even she thought that.

Jarin grimaced. 'Erik was not far behind Linota and he was riding on a fast horse. He's a skilled soldier and should have caught up with the abductors quickly.' He rubbed his forehead again. 'Then there's the note.'

Jarin faded into silence and crossed his ankles.

'What about the note?' Katherine prompted.

Jarin bent his knees and rested his elbows against them. It was a surprisingly boyish gesture from the big man and Katherine had to fight the urge to run her fingers through his hair, which was still blowing wildly in the wind.

'Well, firstly, paper is not exactly common; even I find it an expensive luxury. The abductors must have access to some wealth to start with, but it's not only that...' He tailed off and stared into the distance. 'Can I trust you, Katherine?' he asked slowly and he turned his head to look directly at her.

The shock of his eyes, startlingly blue in the bright light, made her pulse race.

'Of course,' she croaked.

'Because I'm about to tell you things I want no one else to know. I can't stress enough how important this is.'

Katherine swallowed, trapped in his intense gaze. 'I swear to you, on my sister's life, that I will not reveal what you tell me to a single soul.'

He held eye contact for a long moment. Whatever he saw in the depths of her eyes seemed to reassure him. He straightened out his legs and turned his head away from her again.

'I told you that my father and I didn't see eye to eye and that I was sent to our northernmost border for training.'

'Yes.'

He pushed his hand through his hair, but the wind whipped it back as soon as he let go. 'Well, I was there for several years. In some ways it was a good time; the life was tough, but at least I was away from the male members of my family. Even at that distance I was aware of the wealth of the Borwyn name—reference was made to it often enough.' His lips twisted bitterly. 'I had virtually no allowance, but that didn't stop people befriending me, particularly for any coins they thought I might hand out.'

Katherine's fingers twitched. She wanted to reach out and put a soothing hand on his, but she kept twisting her fingers on her lap instead, unsure whether he would accept her sympathy. She'd thought him lonely before, but now she knew for sure. He'd been unwanted by his own family and he couldn't trust anyone who tried to become his friend. For all his wealth and freedom, his life had been as lonely as hers.

He took a deep breath. 'After my brothers' deaths I was trained to take over from my father, but he didn't want me near him any more than I wanted to be near him, so although I was given reason to believe the Borwyn family was still wealthy I never saw any evidence of it. I should have demanded to be more involved, but I didn't. Back then, I would do almost anything to keep away from my father.' He shook his head, a look of disgust crossing his face. 'Of all the things I thought would be waiting for me after I inherited, financial ruin wasn't one of them.'

He half smiled and turned to look at her again. 'The reason the note is odd is that the abductors are asking for the exact amount of coins I have left. The only person who knows that detail is Erik.'

Katherine sank back against the wall, her mind reeling. 'But how...?'

'How am I still carrying on as normal? Or how has it got so bad?' he concluded for her. He inhaled deeply. 'There was more when I inherited. It was a lot less than I was expecting, but the situation wasn't dire and I was confident I could turn things around within six months, but...' He paused, running his hand through his hair again. 'There have been skirmishes on my borders—more than when my father was alive. I thought that was natural: neighbouring lords were testing me to see if I have the same strength as my ancestors. But now I wonder if someone is deliberately causing the unrest. Stupidly, I sent Erik to all of my borders to investigate. I've had to pay for more soldiers and bigger, stronger defences. My reserves have dwindled to almost nothing. Tithes are coming in, of course, but almost everything goes straight back out. I'm treading water and praying that nothing goes wrong, otherwise I will drown.'

'That's why you approached Ogmore. You hoped to make a strong alliance. Were you hoping to marry my brother's wife before he did?'

His gaze flicked to her and then away again. 'Yes.'

'I see.' She rubbed the spot above her heart. It shouldn't hurt that he had considered marrying another woman. That was before he knew her and now he was going to marry Linota after all, but her foolish heart ached anyway.

'And then Ogmore offered my sister as a replacement,' she said briskly. 'Was it a similar dowry?'

Jarin winced, but continued honestly, 'Ogmore offered either you or your sister and he did promise a similar settlement, yes.'

Katherine nodded slowly. 'Who else knows?'

'Only Erik.'

'And Erik would think you would choose the pretty sister rather than the plain one.'

'That's not—'

Katherine held her hand up to stop Jarin carrying on, but he spoke anyway. 'Erik did seem particularly taken with your sister, yes. But I never gave him any reason to suspect that I thought she was more beautiful than you. Not once.'

Katherine's heart started to pound as his steady gaze held hers. Somehow, although it seemed incredible to her, Jarin did not think of her as the *plain* Leofric sister. The knowledge fizzed through her veins and caused her to smile despite the seriousness of the situation.

She turned away from him before he could see how happy he had made her. She rubbed her thumbnail with her forefinger. 'Erik would think you would choose Linota over me and that's why he's taken her. He'll know how valuable she is to you. Because of Ogmore's settlement, that is,' she clarified.

Jarin let out a long breath and leaned his head against the wall. 'It all sounds feasible, but I have to keep coming back to the one argument against the whole thing. Why would he do it? We are like brothers. Better than brothers even. I certainly like him more than I did my real ones, whose company I couldn't stand.'

Katherine shook her head and stood. She leaned her arms against the edge of the parapet and looked out to sea, its constant rolling motion similar to her swirling emotions.

On the one hand she was relieved. If Linota had been taken as part of some kind of power play, then she was less likely to have been hurt than if it was a random attack. That was reassuring and it was a belief she wanted to cling to with both hands. On the other hand were her growing feelings for Jarin, feelings that she was desperately trying to ignore, but which kept flaring up, demanding she take notice of them.

She couldn't deny the attraction she felt for him and it was getting worse every time he made her feel special. She was starting to care for him as a person—no, she had to be honest with herself. She *already* cared for him as a person, far too much for a man who was going to marry her sister.

She'd thought him too proud when she'd heard him talking to Erik about her family, but now she understood what was at stake for him. His was an old and proud title—having to make sacrifices to keep it going must be hard for the man she had come to know and respect. He was strong and capable, firm yet kind. She knew she was in danger of thinking about him too much, of coming to care for him much more than she should. The more time she was spending with him, the more strongly she felt for him; it was like a constant craving to be in his company and to have his intense gaze resting on her.

She stared out to sea in silence.

'What's that?' she asked, pointing to a shape far in the distance.

Jarin came and stood next to her, his forearms resting close to hers. 'It's a boat.'

'A boat,' repeated Katherine, lacing her fingers tightly together to stop her moving her arm closer to his, to feel his strength and his warmth. She'd never seen such a large boat before, not one that could go out to sea. 'Where's it going?'

'I don't know for sure, but probably to France.'

The wind buffeted Katherine from every angle as she watched the tiny boat bob about on the sea's surface.

'Perhaps I shall cut my hair,' she said without thinking.

'What? Why would you do that?'

Katherine felt heat creep up the back of her neck. She hadn't meant to say that out loud, but now that she had... She turned to face him. 'Because if my hair was short people would easily believe that I am a boy and I would be free to travel the world.' She pointed to the horizon. 'I want to see, Jarin. I want to know what the world is like beyond the four walls of my chamber. I want to know what it feels like to stand on a boat and to feel the world move beneath my feet, but more than anything I want to be free.'

He turned to face her during her impassioned speech. They were so close she could see that his blue eyes were tinged with green towards the top and were surrounded by thick lashes.

'I keep telling you,' he said softly, 'you are unmistakably a woman.'

His breath mingled with hers and despite herself she swayed towards him. His gaze flicked to her mouth and she held her breath.

He slowly lowered his head, but before his mouth could touch hers she remembered why they were there on the battlements. 'But before I am free I must find my sister,' she said.

He closed his eyes and stepped away from her. She missed the shelter of his body as the wind rushed in once more and her lips longed for the kiss that hadn't come.

'And so we're back to Erik,' said Jarin. 'I'm still struggling to see his motive in all this.'

'He'll have your ransom money.'

Jarin's mouth twisted. 'That's what makes it so suspicious. The ransom is too small to have an impact on men who would be desperate enough to abduct a young woman. It is not much for a man like Erik. It would purchase but a few items of luxurious clothing and I cannot see that Erik wants for anything. He's been my right-hand man ever since I knew I was going to inherit the title. He lives here for free and is paid for his time. Unless he's been an amazing actor, ever since he was a very young lad, he's always cared for people over material things.'

Katherine tapped her fingers against the edge of the parapet. 'Was he in love with your late wife?'

Jarin snorted. 'Viola! I wouldn't have thought so, but I suppose it's possible. She had a way of twisting a man so he was inside out.' Katherine's heart hurt at the look on Jarin's face; she could never be a woman to inspire such passion in a man. 'I never thought they spent any time together, but she told so many lies that I suppose they could have been lovers. Hell, he may even have been the father of her child.' He grimaced. 'That would be reason enough to hate me.'

Everything inside Katherine stilled. 'You have a child?'

'No.' The pain in Jarin's eyes tore at Katherine's heart. 'Viola died in childbirth. Her daughter only lived for a day. I don't know if the girl was mine or not, but I… I still loved her. She was tiny and perfect. She died in my arms.'

Without thinking, Katherine reached out and placed her hand on his arm; he covered it with his own, the warmth of his strong fingers seeping into hers. The strange tingling she always felt when she touched him started up again. She knew she should take her hand away, but she couldn't summon up the willpower.

'It's all in the past now,' he said, giving her hand a quick squeeze and then letting go. She managed to pull her fingers away from his arm and let her arm fall to her side. 'But it does give us a possible motive for his actions.'

'Did you ever have a suspicion that they were…?' Katherine trailed off, aware she had been about to utter the word 'lovers'. Heat raced across her skin and she kept her eyes fixed on the horizon.

Beside her Jarin huffed out a laugh. 'No. I would have said he couldn't stand her. He tried to warn me that she was manipulative before I married her, but I was so blinded by what I thought was love I wouldn't listen. But then, I'm not the best judge of character, am I? First my wife betrays me and then my best friend.' He shook his head. 'I promised my mother, I swore to her, that I would be a better man than my father, but I've failed to live up to the oath in every way.'

Katherine's heart wrenched. 'That's not true.'

'Isn't it?' Jarin turned to her and the look in his eyes made her throat thick. She swallowed, trying to dislodge the sensation.

'If course it isn't true,' she said. 'You're a good man.'

His lips twisted into a half-smile. 'That's not enough, though, is it? The truth is that I've blindly allowed myself to be brought to the brink of ruin because, once again, I trusted the wrong person. This can't all be Erik's doing either. He must have had help and support from others among my men. And—'

Katherine reached out and touched Jarin's sleeve 'Do you know what I see when I look at you?'

'The man who rudely dismissed you and your sister on no evidence whatsoever?' Jarin's eyes were pained and Katherine squeezed his arm.

'I see a man who's survived a violent father, ignorant brothers, the death of his mother, wife and child. I see someone who's been let down by people who should only have loved and supported him, but despite all that has become a man with strong principles. A man who cares about the people who depend on him. You won't let this beat you because that is the type of man you are.'

For a long moment Jarin only looked down at her. As the silence stretched between them she feared she had overstepped the mark. Eventually he reached up and gently caressed her cheek as he tucked a strand of hair behind her ear.

'Thank you, Katherine,' he said at last. 'Now, you'd better go back inside. I'll send Mistress Sutton to get you as soon as the abductors make their next move. I don't think it will be long now. If it is Erik behind this, he won't want your brother getting wind of Linota's disappearance. No one would want The Beast on their tail.' He smiled slightly at the name given to her fearsome brother.

Recognising that Jarin wanted to be alone with his thoughts, Katherine nodded. 'Do you promise you will let me know as soon as something happens?'

'I promise.' She began to move towards the staircase that would take her back down to her chamber. 'Oh, and Katherine…' she stopped '…don't cut your hair; that would be a travesty.'

For a long moment she held his hypnotic gaze. Then, before she could act on her urge to fling herself into his arms, she turned and fled.

Chapter Fifteen

Jarin pulled the ribbon through his fingers, twisting it around and letting it out again, then he threw it down in disgust. He was acting like a young boy with his first crush. Sitting in his room gazing at a ribbon that had once been in Katherine's hair was a ridiculous waste of time. That he had kept it at all was a sign of just how stupid he really was.

She had made it clear over and over again she wasn't interested in him, going as far as to ensure he married her sister. Yet his heart leapt every time he saw her and he'd trusted her with his deepest secret. He was a fool. He hardly knew her. Her innocence could be a carefully constructed façade—his experience with Erik and his late wife only reminded him that he should trust no one. But then he had told Katherine his deepest secret, which meant that, despite all his careful rationalisations, he trusted her on instinct alone.

He groaned and stretched out his legs towards the fire, picking up his spiced wine as he did so. Even now, when his mind should be focusing on why his closest friend was acting against him, all he could think about was Katherine. He swirled around the dark liquid and contemplated going to bed.

Although it was only early evening, he was bone tired. His eyes burned with the need to sleep, but he couldn't rouse himself to get up and cross the room.

For the last two nights he'd slept with Katherine in his arms and his empty bed no longer held any appeal. For better or worse he wanted her with him.

He imagined her on his mattress, her hair unbound and spread across the covers. She would look up at him with those unusual eyes and he would be lost in their depths. She was an innocent so he wouldn't rush her. He would take his time to savour her lips, slowly awakening the passion he knew resided just beneath her skin.

When she was pliant in his arms he would slowly remove her clothes, taking care to run his fingers gently over the soft skin of her legs. Her breasts were small, but perfectly formed. He would spend time worshipping each one with his mouth. Only when she was insensible with desire would he move between her legs, tasting her first and then touching her hot, wet centre with his fingers. When she was calling his name, he would finally make her his and his alone.

He rubbed his eyes. He'd made his cock throb with unfulfilled desire for a woman who would never join him in his bed, let alone sigh his name while he pleasured her.

He leaned back against his chair and willed his body under control. But it was no good—his mind turned back to thoughts of Katherine straight away.

He wondered if Katherine had nightmares every

night. Did Linota wake and comfort her or did she have to soothe herself? Knowing Katherine, she probably didn't wake her sister or confide in her that she was frightened. It was always Katherine who did the caring, not the other way around.

He wanted to be the one who held her when she was frightened. He wanted to be the one who soothed away her worries, but that was impossible. He had offered to marry Linota because it was the honourable thing to do, even more so now that it looked as though Erik had abducted her because of Jarin. He could not and would not renege on his promise, but that didn't mean he was pleased about it.

A knock on the door finally roused him from his thoughts.

'Enter,' he called.

Erik stepped into the room and Jarin's skin crawled. He forced his posture to remain relaxed despite the urge to lunge from his chair and thump his former friend until he got answers.

'What news?' he asked as Erik crossed the room and took the seat opposite him, acting as he had done on many an evening.

'The abductors have responded that they will exchange the girl for the money tomorrow evening after dark.'

Jarin nodded. 'Where?'

'They will send instructions at dusk. They probably don't want to give us enough time to set a trap.'

Jarin nodded again. 'We'll set an ambush anyway. These men can't be allowed to get away with this.'

Erik's hand twitched. 'Of course we will. Although we don't want anything to endanger the girl, do we?'

Jarin watched his friend closely. Was this because he didn't want his accomplices caught or because he genuinely cared for Linota's safety? It was impossible to tell from Erik's expression. Jarin decided to poke the nest a little.

'Obviously it would be better if Linota remained unharmed, but it's of paramount importance to me that the men behind this are caught.'

Erik looked at him sharply. 'I thought…'

'What did you think?' asked Jarin, calmly taking a sip of his wine.

Erik swallowed. 'What of Ogmore's settlement on the girl?'

'The settlement applies to both sisters.'

Erik's nose wrinkled. 'You would tie yourself to the other sister? She has the body of a young boy.'

Jarin's fingers tightened on the glass, but he forced himself to remain calm and take another sip of his drink before answering. 'What does it matter what she looks like? I married for lust once and you saw where it got me. It's the dowry that's important. As you know, I am sunk without it.'

Erik shifted in his seat. 'Yes, but I think it would be foolish to put the girl in danger.'

'Why? She is nothing to me. These men have tried to shame the Borwyn name and they must be taught a lesson. I cannot be seen to be weak. I'll be plagued by abductors and petty thieves for the rest of my life.'

Erik paled and for the first time Jarin was utterly

convinced of his old friend's guilt. His heart sank. Erik should be just as keen to catch the perpetrators as Jarin.

'Very well,' said Erik after a long pause. 'I will give the orders to your men that they must capture the abductors at any cost.'

Jarin nodded. 'Good.'

He stared into the fire. Now their business was done he wanted Erik to leave him alone, but he could feel the weight of Erik's stare even though he couldn't bring himself to look at his steward.

'So you would consider marrying the older sister?' asked Erik.

Jarin froze in the act of bringing his drink to his mouth. What had he done? The last thing he wanted was for Erik to turn his attention to Katherine. Katherine, whose tiny body could not take any more rough treatment, would have to be protected from Erik at all costs.

Realising he was acting strangely, he forced himself to take another sip of spiced wine. He almost choked on the liquid as he forced it down.

He shrugged, hoping the gesture looked natural. 'I don't have a burning desire to marry either of them.'

'But you need the dowry,' Erik protested. 'And the added protection Ogmore's name will bring you. With your two names linked, your enemies will think twice about attacking you. Our borders will be safer and your coffers will be fuller.'

Jarin shifted in his seat. 'If word gets out that I allowed Linota Leofric to be taken from me before my very eyes, I doubt Ogmore will be keen to promote our alliance.'

'Ogmore's a man of his word,' said Erik, leaning forward on his knees and staring intently at Jarin.

Jarin watched the flames flicker in the hearth. He knew that if he turned to Erik, his steward would be able to read the truth in his eyes. Jarin had never been able to lie to Erik, even as a young boy. It turned out the ability was not mutual.

Instead Jarin nodded tightly. He wanted, *needed* this conversation to end. The more he spoke, the more he risked placing Katherine in danger. 'Let's see what tomorrow brings, shall we?' he said vaguely. 'For now I need some rest. The last two days have been draining.'

'Of course,' said Erik, standing. 'I expect both you and the lady Katherine are exhausted. Where did you say you slept last night?'

'I didn't,' said Jarin. When Erik didn't move to go he added, 'We stayed at a farm with an older woman there to look after her. It was all perfectly safe. I'm not worried about being forced into marriage to her by her angry brother, if that's what you're thinking about.'

Erik laughed, although it sounded forced to Jarin. 'Of course not. I know how you manage to get out of anything you don't like and, despite your protests, I know you don't want to be tied to a plain spinster. I'll leave you to get some rest.'

Jarin's hand tightened on his glass. What had Erik meant by Jarin being able to get out of things he didn't like? Jarin almost never got out of doing things he didn't enjoy. His father had seen to that when he was alive and the demands of the earldom were seeing to it after his death. But if Jarin could figure out what Erik meant, would he come to know why his friend plotted against him?

The door closed quietly behind Erik and Jarin stood abruptly, his heart thumping wildly. What if he hadn't said enough to convince Erik he had no intention of marrying Katherine? Katherine could be in danger right now...

He dropped his drink on to a table and raced to the door. Keeping a safe distance from her be damned; he needed to see for himself that she was safe in her room.

He took the stairs two at a time, his heart racing as he knocked on the chamber door.

There was no response.

He knocked again. Nothing.

He mustn't panic. He never panicked. He brushed away the beads of sweat that were forming on his forehead.

If he opened the door and she was in a state of undress, then she might never forgive him, but if he walked away now and something had happened to her then he would never forgive himself.

'Katherine,' he called, 'It's me, Jarin.'

Still no response. Damn it. Her safety was more his concern than sparing her blushes. He pushed open the door and stepped inside.

The room was empty.

He stood, frozen for a minute, ice filling his veins. How had Erik got to her so quickly? Did he have an accomplice who had taken her while he and Erik were talking?

He paced around the room. Nothing was disturbed. Katherine's old dress was folded neatly and he picked it up. Without thinking he inhaled her scent before dropping the garment back down on the chest.

Katherine wouldn't have gone anywhere with Erik without putting up a fight. He was sure of it. The room looked as if she had just stepped out to take some air.

He groaned in realisation. She had probably taken herself off for one of her dangerous night wanderings. The little fool!

Suddenly, he stopped in the centre of the room. He knew where she was. He turned and ran.

Chapter Sixteen

The moon sparkled across the darkness of the sea. Katherine rested her arms against the walls of the battlements, her thoughts in turmoil.

'I can't even find it in myself to be angry with you,' said a deep voice from behind her.

Katherine's pulse quickened, the hairs on the back of her neck standing to attention. She'd been so self-absorbed she hadn't heard anyone approach.

She heard Jarin's footsteps as he walked slowly towards her, but she didn't turn to look at him. If she did, she might do something foolish. She'd both longed for him to join her, up here on the ramparts, and also dreaded it happening.

She'd had to escape the confines of her guest chamber; despite its luxurious furnishings, the walls had still closed in on her. She needed to be outside again to think freely. And so she'd left the safety the room provided and climbed up to the top of the fortress. In the darkness she'd been acutely aware of the salty tang of the sea air and of the night-time calling of the birds.

Being outside in the cold night air had soothed her soul, but it hadn't helped distract her from her thoughts. Worry for Linota's safety warred with her overwhelming desire to be with Jarin.

Although she knew it was wrong, she was almost out of her mind wondering what would have happened if she had let him kiss her earlier. Her blood sang at the memory of his tongue mingling with hers and the way his firm hands had moved across her back. She wanted to know what it would feel like to have his fingertips trail across her skin.

She hated herself for the craving and now that he was here her body was rejoicing just as her mind was wishing he was elsewhere.

The swift breeze of this afternoon had died down and now only the cold night air brushed against her skin, gently lifting her unbound hair and pushing wispy strands across her face.

'There is no need to be angry with me,' she said, keeping her eyes on the shimmering water.

He was close enough to her now that she heard his sigh. 'I went to your room and found you were gone. How do you think that made me feel?'

Everything in Katherine stilled. What had prompted him to visit her bedchamber? Did he want *her* or was there news? Her skin tingled at the thought of them alone in the room with the large bed at its centre.

'I thought something had happened to you,' continued Jarin when she didn't answer. 'But, no, you were roaming around outside again, without a thought for your safety. It's as though you have no concept of how much danger you are in!'

'Why did you come to my room?' she asked. She had to know the answer.

There was a long silence. Her heart raced.

'I was worried.'

She turned to face him. The moon only lit one side of his face; the other was cast in shadow. Even in the half-light he was still so beautiful it hurt to look at him. Would she ever be free of this unwanted attraction?

'What were you worried about?'

He leant against the castle wall and ran a hand through his hair. 'Erik came to see me. He was asking questions about you. After he left I convinced myself he was going to try and take you. I was wrong, evidently.' Jarin pushed himself upright again. 'It feels as though I'm standing on shifting sands and nothing makes sense. One moment I'm sure of Erik's guilt and the next I'm not.'

'All evidence suggests that he is guilty,' said Katherine softly.

Jarin nodded briskly. 'It does, but I still don't understand why.'

'Once we know that, everything will fall into place.'

A gust of wind lifted Katherine's hair and spun it around her face. She smoothed it back into position and blinked. In that instant Jarin's stance had changed and now he was frozen in place, looking at her with an expression she couldn't read.

'Your hair is unbound.' His voice was rough, as if his throat was suddenly dry.

Katherine stilled as he reached out and caught a strand between his fingers. The soft touch sent tingles racing across her scalp.

'I prefer it down,' she said, trying to ignore the sensation. 'It feels freer.'

'It's the colour of sun on an autumn day,' he said, turning it over in his hand.

Even in her innocence there was no mistaking the desire in his voice. Her knees trembled and she reached out a steadying hand, coming to rest on the parapet wall. Nobody had ever said anything so complimentary about her before. She was in grave danger here and it didn't come from the abductors. It came from the man standing in front of her, who with a single compliment had her falling even harder for him. It would cause her unimaginable pain to see him marry Linota, but it was necessary to save her sister from ruin. With that thought forefront in her mind, she stepped away from him, pulling her hair from his grip as she did so. She turned to face the sea.

'How are you?' Jarin asked. 'Is your leg…does your leg…?' He cleared his throat.

'The cut is not as bad as I feared. I will live and I don't think it will scar.'

'Good. I would hate to think that you were badly hurt because of me.'

She nodded tightly and kept her gaze on the distant horizon. 'It would not be your fault even if I had died during the encounter. It would have been the man whose knife was against my skin. You must not take on everyone's burdens. It will only wear you down.'

There was a long pause. She could feel the weight of his stare against her skin, but still she didn't turn to him.

'What's our next move?' she asked eventually.

Jarin cleared his throat and came to stand beside her,

mimicking the way they'd stood earlier in the day. 'I've thought about this from every angle, but as far as I can see I am going to have to pay the ransom.'

Katherine gasped and glanced across at him. 'But it's all you have left. Surely there must be something else we can do.'

This time he was the one who kept his gaze out towards the sea. She studied his profile, his strong nose and chin and his high cheekbones. Within a day or two she would never be as close to him again so she committed every angle to memory.

'The problem is, I don't know who I can trust,' he said. 'If I cannot depend on my right-hand man, then that throws everyone under suspicion.'

'Can't you have Erik watched?' Katherine suggested. 'He might lead us straight to Linota. Or we could watch him ourselves.'

'But who can I trust to watch him? They could all be in league with him. That could make him aware I know what he's done and put Linota in danger. I can't keep watch on him myself because, believe it or not, I'm fairly well known around here and it's not as if I can do much sneaking around,' he said drily. 'And before you ask, you are not doing it either.'

'But—'

'No. And don't even start with that nonsense about looking like a boy again. I don't want you finding out how wrong you are about that on my watch.'

'But—'

A hand on her arm stopped her from saying any more.

'Can you see that?' Jarin's gaze had been caught by something far below where they were standing.

'What?' asked Katherine, peering over the edge of the parapet and trying to see what had caught his attention.

'There's movement below and I think…yes, it must be, but where is he going?'

'Who? Where?'

No matter how much she squinted into the darkness, Katherine couldn't make out what had caught Jarin's attention.

'Quickly,' said Jarin. 'We need to get you back down to your chamber.'

'Wait, what is it you've seen?'

'Erik's on the move,' said Jarin, heading towards the entrance to the castle. 'At least I think it's him. He's one of the few people who knows about the hidden access to the beach.'

Katherine ran to catch up with him. 'I'm coming with you.'

'No, you are not,' Jarin said as they started down the stairs.

'You can waste valuable time arguing about this or we can just get on with it. I'm coming. This is my sister we're talking about.'

'I could tie you to a chair,' muttered Jarin.

Katherine didn't comment. They'd passed the entrance to her floor without stopping and she knew she had won the argument.

They raced down the spiral steps, their darkness seemingly never-ending.

'Where are we going?' gasped Katherine. Her ears popped and she wondered if they were now beneath the castle's lowest floor.

'We can't go out through the front gates,' said Jarin, sounding annoyingly as if the speed they were racing at was having no effect on him. 'I'll have to take guards and by the time that's sorted out Erik will be long gone. We're going to have to take the same exit as Erik.'

The stairs finally petered out and they emerged into a cavernous darkness.

'Let's hope I can remember the way,' said Jarin, his voice echoing.

'You sound almost cheerful,' said Katherine accusingly.

'It's been a long time since I've been down here. It used to be my route to freedom.'

Katherine didn't ask what he had been escaping from and then they stepped into the darkness. His earlier years hadn't been as rosy as she'd believed. Her heart broke a little as she imagined a small boy crawling through this darkness, probably bruised and broken, trying to find safety. How alone he must have been. How much she wished she could have spared him from such pain.

Their footsteps crunched on the uneven floor.

'What are we stepping on?' asked Katherine, visions of dead spiders piled high filling her mind; she forced herself to keep going even as her feet recoiled.

'Shingle.'

'Shingle? What's that?' It didn't sound like dried bones, but that didn't stop goose pimples rushing across her skin.

'It's a mixture of sand and stone. We're way beneath the castle now in an old cellar that's long been forgotten about.'

Her foot hit something and she stumbled. A strong hand grabbed hold of her before she fell to the ground.

'Are you all right?' he asked.

'Yes,' she said, heat rushing through her at his touch.

'There's still time for you to head back,' Jarin suggested, his hand still holding her arm.

'No, I'm coming. Erik could lead us to Linota.'

His hand slid down her arm until it reached her hand and then his long fingers curled around hers. Her breath caught in her throat. For a moment neither of them moved.

In the dark she could hear his even breathing. She wondered if he could hear her thundering heart. She hoped not. She didn't want him to know what a simple touch from him did to her.

'It's this way,' said Jarin quietly.

They began to move again. Jarin didn't let go of her hand and she didn't take it back. *It's because it's so dark*, she reassured herself. As soon as they were out in the moonlight she would let go.

Jarin slowed to a stop. 'We're at the bottom of some steps. Can you feel where they start?'

She put her foot out and slowly tapped the area in front of her until she felt a stone step. 'Yes,' she said.

They began to climb. It didn't take long before Jarin stopped and muttered a curse, then, 'I've found the exit.'

Katherine's heart thudded. 'What's wrong?'

'Ah, nothing. Only that it was my head that found it.'

Katherine surprised herself by giggling.

Jarin's fingers tightened on hers. 'I'm glad you find my pain amusing.'

Although she couldn't see his face she could tell by the tone of his voice that he wasn't angry with her.

'What now?' she asked.

'I've just got to…' She felt him stretch next to her and then there was a creak as if wood was moving on a hinge.

Katherine was sure that whatever he was doing would be easier with two hands, but he seemed as reluctant to let go of her as she was of him.

Cold air rushed over them as whatever Jarin was doing was successful. He tugged her up the remaining steps and helped her climb out.

'Where are we?' she asked.

The darkness was absolute. The smell of the sea was even stronger here than up on the battlements and it sounded as if water was running all around them. She flinched when an icy drip landed on her forehead.

'We're in a cave,' said Jarin. 'It's this way.'

'Erik's going to be long gone,' said Katherine, despondent at not being on the beach already.

'We're moving more quickly than him. He doesn't know he's being followed,' said Jarin. 'Come on.'

He tugged on her hand and they hurried along. The roof of the cave lowered and soon even Katherine had to hunch to keep going.

'We're going to need to crawl,' said Jarin after a moment. 'This was easier when I was a boy. You go first; I'll be right behind you.'

Despite his words he held on to her hand for a moment longer. A soft sigh escaped her as his fingers slowly fell away from hers.

He cleared his throat. 'Can you see where we have to go?'

She crouched down and could just make out a patch of silvery light ahead of her.

'Yes,' she said and dropped to her hands and knees.

She began to crawl towards the light and after a moment she heard Jarin crawling after her. The passage was narrow and at one point she had to drop to her stomach to pull herself through. As the tunnel narrowed, her breathing quickened, the walls starting to close in on her.

'Keep going, Katherine. You can do it.'

Katherine held on to the sound of Jarin's voice as sweat beaded across her forehead.

She wasn't convinced she could continue, but with one last pull she managed to get free from the confined space. She rolled over on to her back and sucked in large lungfuls of air.

'Katherine, are you all right?' Jarin pulled himself free and hurried over to her side, dropping on to his knees in the soft sand.

'I'm sorry, it's the enclosed space, I don't like them. I'm all right.'

She tried to stand, but her shaky legs wouldn't support her.

'Take your time,' said Jarin softly. She wanted to hold him, to nestle her head in the space above his shoulder, but time was passing and Erik was getting away.

'I'm fine,' she said again and this time she almost believed it.

Jarin stood and then leaned down to pull her to her feet.

She couldn't say who instigated it, but somehow she found herself holding hands with him once more as they set off down the beach. She didn't let go; neither did he.

The sand was soft underfoot and it was difficult to get purchase on its surface as they half-ran, half-stumbled across it.

'He could have come off the beach anywhere,' she panted.

'There's only one way off if he's heading into the town,' said Jarin.

'How will we know where he's gone when we get there?'

'Someone will have seen him, it's not that big a place.'

Despite the moonlight guiding their way, Katherine didn't notice the rough path cutting through the sandy dunes until Jarin steered her away from the beach.

'Even your town is walled,' commented Katherine as they approached.

'Attacks from the sea are common around here. I had the wall built not long after I inherited the title,' Jarin said, pulling her up a sandbank. 'Life has been safer since the defences were built. Here's the only door into the settlement from this side. It's kept locked at night, but Erik must have come this way, so I'm hoping… Ah, yes, it is unlocked, which can mean only one thing.'

Jarin pushed through the thick wooden door and held it open for Katherine to follow. He dropped her hand as he did so and she rubbed her skin where his fingers had been.

Taking a few steps, Jarin stopped almost immediately. Katherine jumped as he banged loudly on the front door of a thin cottage. It opened almost immediately.

'Oh, it's you,' said the man whose face was made up mainly of beard.

'Aye,' said Jarin coldly. 'Where's Erik?'

The man swallowed and glanced at Katherine. 'I don't know what you're talking about, my lord.'

'I don't have time for this, Maldwyn. Tell me where Erik is and I'll overlook the fact that the door wasn't locked this evening, when keeping it locked is exactly what I pay you for.'

The man looked down at his feet and then back to Jarin. 'He's visiting his lady friend,' said the man quietly.

Jarin's eyebrows shot up. 'His lady friend?'

'She lives above the baker's,' said Maldwyn, clearly not willing to risk his job defending Erik's secrets.

Jarin nodded briskly. 'Lock the door, Maldwyn, and don't let me find it open again.'

He strode away with Katherine in his wake.

He stopped abruptly for her to catch up and she ploughed into him. He caught her around the waist, his fingers resting just above her hips. She leaned towards him and breathed in his scent. She heard him inhale softly and she took a step back. Once again, she was getting distracted by the feel of Jarin's body near hers. His hand found hers once more and she didn't pull away.

'Will you really let him keep his job?' asked Katherine as they walked down a narrow alley lined with shops.

'No,' said Jarin. 'If he's leaving the door unlocked for

Erik, who's to say he's not letting through the very people he's paid to keep out. It seems I can't trust anybody.'

They rounded another corner; the only sound in the cold night air was their feet on the worn cobblestones. Katherine stepped even closer to Jarin and he squeezed her hand tightly.

'We're nearly there,' said Jarin quietly.

'What will we do when we arrive?' she asked.

Jarin was quiet for a moment. 'Although it goes against the grain, I think we wait until Erik emerges before going in. He has to come back to the castle this evening or his absence will be noted.'

'What if she's not there?'

'Then we will get her back tomorrow,' said Jarin confidently.

'But what about your money?'

'Don't worry, I'll get it back.' He sounded so sure that Katherine almost believed him. It was only the memory of his face when he'd talked about his problems that made her doubt him. She had to remind herself that his wealth, or lack thereof, was not her problem. Linota was her concern. But it was difficult when she knew how few people Jarin could count on. The thought of leaving him to deal with his problems on his own was not something she wanted to contemplate. He needed someone on his side as much as she did.

'Ah, here we are,' said Jarin, stopping in front of a narrow building.

The bakery in front of them was locked up, but Katherine could make out the flickering light of several candles burning in the room above the shop front.

'Do you think they're in there?' she whispered.

'Yes, I do.' He pulled her deeper into the shadows. 'Now we wait.'

It didn't take long for the cold to seep into her bones once they stopped moving. She clenched her teeth together to stop them from chattering, but she must have made some sign of distress because Jarin tugged her towards him and wrapped his cloak around them both. She stepped closer to him, careful to leave a tiny gap between his body and hers. Even so, she could feel his warmth across the space.

'I told you not to come,' he said, rubbing his cheek against her hair and sending tingles across her scalp.

'It's fine,' she stuttered.

'Then why are you shaking like a leaf?'

'Nerves.'

Jarin snorted. 'Do you possess any?'

Katherine thought about her reaction to the enclosed tunnel. 'Yes, I do.'

She gave into temptation and leaned her head against his chest. She heard his sharp inhale and her nipples tightened in response. *It's only for the warmth*, she assured herself. *I'm so cold and all that's happening is he's warming me up.*

He rested his back against the wall of the house and it seemed like the most natural thing in the world to bring her body flush with his. His hand slipped around to her back and he began to rub her spine in slow, gentle, rhythmic strokes while the thumb on the hand that held hers began to mimic the strokes on the palm of her hand.

She could no longer pretend to herself that this was all about warmth. Something else was happening here, something far too scary to think about. She should step away and put some distance between them, but her body was weak. It craved his touch and welcomed the tingling that the swirl of his thumb was creating.

'Katherine.' Her name on his lips was like a plea.

She looked up at him; his face was bent towards hers. His lips so close. His gaze locked with hers and she couldn't have moved away even if she'd wanted to.

The first brush of his lips was soft and gentle. The second was firmer. She stretched up into the kiss and his mouth moved across hers. A moan escaped her and Jarin's hand slipped from her back and into her hair.

Her pulse beat wildly in her throat as his movements became urgent. She opened her mouth and he swept in his tongue. He groaned as she responded, tentatively at first, but with increasing confidence as his hand tightened on hers.

'Katherine,' he murmured again as his lips traced the length of her jaw, his rough stubble brushing against the soft skin of her cheek.

'Jarin,' she said back, arching into him.

His mouth returned to hers and the world slid away. Gone was the bone-numbing cold and the constant fear that had plagued her for days. Nothing mattered but this moment. Nothing mattered but him.

In another world, a door opened and closed and footsteps clipped along the cobblestones. Jarin raised his head and said the only thing that could register in this moment, 'Erik.'

Katherine blinked, her senses taking a moment to remember where she was. 'Are you sure?'

'Yes.'

She turned in his arms and saw a figure stride into

the distance. If she hadn't been standing with her arms around him, she would have mistaken the person for Jarin. They had the same width and height, even the same confident stride.

'Are we going in now?' she asked.

Jarin nodded, but didn't release her. She could feel his heart thudding against her cheek.

'Jarin?' she said eventually, when he didn't move.

He let out a long breath. 'I don't suppose I could get you to stay out here?'

She didn't answer. He read her answer in her silence.

'I thought not. Come on, then, let's go and see whether I'm about to violate my closest friend's privacy or find out whether he's betrayed me.'

Katherine pulled away from Jarin and shivered as the cold air rushed in to take his place.

He reached for her hand again, but she evaded him. He'd promised to marry her sister and, even though Linota didn't know it, Katherine had still betrayed her by her own actions this evening. Katherine hated herself at this moment. But she would make it all right when she got Linota back. Her sister would marry one of the most powerful men in the country and would have an army of servants to take care of her every need. Linota would want for nothing; it was the best Katherine could do for her.

Jarin dropped his hand and Katherine's heart hurt. If Linota was in here—and Katherine really hoped she was—Katherine could never touch him again. A little part of her died at the thought even though she knew she should never have touched him in the first place.

He made his way over to a small wooden door and banged it, the pounding sounding loud in the cold night air.

There was no answer.

He began to look around his feet.

'What are you doing?'

'Looking for a rock of a suitable size to smash the lock,' came his clipped response.

He picked something up from the door and began to hit the hinge with considerable force. Katherine flinched at the sound of snapping wood. The door gave way with a bang. Jarin didn't wait for her to follow as he bounded inside and ran up the flight of stairs in front of them.

Katherine followed and tripped over her dress at the first step. She landed on her hands and knees, the wood biting into her palms. By the time she'd pulled herself upright Jarin had disappeared.

She heard a woman's startled scream and she began to run.

The top of the stairs opened up into a single room; candles flickered casting ominous shadows around the space. Jarin was in front of her, fists clenched and jaw rigid. Another man she didn't recognise was facing him, his stance defensive, but Katherine only had eyes for Linota.

Her sister was huddled in the arms of a middle-aged woman, her eyes wide and her skin pale.

'Linota,' Katherine breathed.

Her sister looked up. 'Katherine!' she cried. She

pulled herself upright and the woman holding her dropped her arms.

Linota leapt to her feet and rushed over to Katherine's side, flinging her arms around her and nearly knocking her off her feet. 'There you are. I've been so worried about you.'

Katherine frowned. Surely that was for her to say. Linota was the one who was missing, not Katherine.

Linota held Katherine out at arm's length. 'Erik told me you'd been hurt. Are you all right?'

'Erik?' said Katherine numbly. Why was her sister on first-name terms with that scoundrel?

'Yes, Erik, he's been looking after me since those horrid men grabbed me. He said we couldn't trust anyone apart from Emma and her husband. Oh, I've been so worried about you.'

Katherine stared at her sister wordlessly. It should be a relief. Her sister hadn't been hurt and she hadn't been frightened and it was a comfort to know that, but… Now Katherine was facing a different problem. She was going to have to tell Linota that she'd been captured and that these people, who she clearly regarded as protectors and friends, had betrayed her. She was going to break it to Linota that her reputation had been compromised by the very man she'd thought was her saviour. She was going to have to break her sister's innocence.

Nobody else in the room had moved and the atmosphere crackled with tension. It finally seemed to seep through to Linota that something was wrong.

'What's going on?' asked Linota, turning back to face the room.

Nobody answered.

'Emma?' said Linota, her voice trembling as she addressed the woman whose arms she'd been in only moments ago.

'I'm sorry, pet,' said the woman, her gaze dropping to the floor, away from Linota's questioning eyes.

'Sorry...? Katherine, what's happening here?'

Katherine rubbed her eyes. Now that Linota had been found safe and well, exhaustion hit her, weakening her knees and making her eyes heavy.

'Katherine,' said Jarin, his voice laced with steel. 'Take your sister to the bottom of the stairs. I'll join you both shortly.'

'What's he going to do?' asked Linota as Katherine gently tried to tug her sister from the room. 'He's not going to hurt them, is he? They've been so kind to me over the last two days. Don't let him hurt them, Katherine.'

'Nobody's going to get hurt,' said Katherine, as she began to tug Linota harder. 'The Earl just wants to talk to them.'

Jarin grunted and Linota twisted in her arms.

'I'll explain outside,' said Katherine gently. 'Please, trust me.'

Linota's lips twisted, but she allowed herself to be guided out of the room and down the narrow steps to the front door.

No sounds came from the room above them as Katherine led Linota out on to the deserted street. Katherine didn't know if this was a good or bad thing.

'Are you truly all right?' she asked Linota as she looked over her sister's skin. In the darkness it was difficult to tell whether she'd suffered any physical damage from her ordeal, but maybe there were bruises underneath the unfamiliar clothes she wore.

'I'm fine, but I've been so worried about you. Erik said you fell off your horse while riding and that you were knocked unconscious.'

'That is true,' said Katherine, touching the bump on her head, which she'd almost forgotten about. 'It was only a small accident. What I don't understand is how you came to be in a room above a baker's shop. You were carried off by a group of men, Linota. I was so scared!'

'I wasn't with those men long enough to be very frightened. By the time I started to panic Erik had caught up with us and he dealt with the men.'

Even in the darkness Katherine didn't miss the light in Linota's eyes that shone when she mentioned Erik's name. Her hands curled into fists. How dare Erik take advantage of her sister like this? He had betrayed her trust and used her innocence against her. By treating her kindly he'd made her a docile captive.

'Erik Ward has betrayed you,' Katherine said flatly. 'He is ransoming you in order to get money out of Jarin.'

Linota inhaled sharply. 'No, he wouldn't do that. He cares—'

'He would and he has,' said Katherine bluntly.

Katherine could sense that Linota was going to protest again, so she simply laid out the events of the last few days, taking care to keep her emotion out of the retelling. Katherine sensed that if she railed against Erik she would lose Linota's sympathy and the knowledge made bile rise in her throat. The man had won her sister's confidence, but how had he done it? If Erik had seduced Linota, then Katherine would tear him apart with her own hands.

By the time she had finished her tale Linota was very still, her hands clasped tightly in front of her and her head bowed.

'I'm sorry, Linota,' said Katherine when it became apparent her sister wasn't going to say anything. 'I…' But she didn't finish.

At that moment Jarin appeared, pushing the other two occupants of the house into the road. The man's hands were tied behind his back and he stumbled on the uneven surface of the road.

'I'm sorry, my lady,' whispered the woman to Linota.

Katherine heard Linota let out a soft cry and her heart broke. Her sister had never had friends before and the one woman she'd met and whom she had trusted had turned out to be her jailer.

Jarin set the pace for their return to the fortress, his long legs striding powerfully through the dark streets of Borwyn town. As he walked he pushed the bound man along in front of him. The woman, who seemed concerned for the man's comfort, scurried along beside him. Katherine and Linota trailed behind.

Katherine tried to engage Linota in conversation, but after several failed attempts she gave up. Her sister was obviously shocked by the turn of events and would probably feel better for a long soak in some warm water and a good night's sleep.

Katherine was pleased not to be heading back along the beach. She didn't think she could cope with another scramble through the cave's narrow tunnel, especially now that she would be unable to hold Jarin's hand.

The entrance to the Borwyn fortress loomed forebodingly in the darkness and Katherine shivered as they approached.

'What will happen to them?' whispered Linota as they reached the gate.

'I don't know,' said Katherine honestly.

Jarin hadn't spoken to her since they'd been alone on the street. His shoulders were rigid as he marched along. She wanted to reach out and soothe the tension she sensed raging beneath the surface of his skin, but she knew she couldn't. That had never been her role and it never would be.

As they approached the menacing entrance, Jarin finally turned and spoke to her. 'When we arrive, I want you to take your sister straight to your room. I will instruct Mistress Sutton to bring up some warm water so that she can have a bath along with some clean clothes for her to change into. I will send for you both as soon as I have news.'

Jarin didn't wait to hear Katherine's response and she was hit with an overwhelming feeling of loss as he turned his back on her. Over the last few days, when they had been in each other's confidence, he had become her dearest friend, but that appeared to be already in the past. She would have to get used to being nothing to him now—nothing more than a sister-in-law he rarely saw. Within a day or two they would carry on their journey to Castle Swein and she would stay there after Linota married. She would barely see him again. She muffled a sob as she towed Linota in her wake. Linota must never know how Katherine felt for the man who would become her husband.

Jarin ensured they had an escort back to their room, but he didn't spare them another glance. The last Katherine saw of him, he was in deep discussion with the marshal of the guards as they both surveyed their prisoners.

Back in her room, Katherine helped Linota undress and climb into the bath. Katherine kept up a steady stream of chatter, but Linota remained as silent as stone.

Katherine's hands trembled as she dried Linota. She had found her sister physically unharmed, but it felt as if she'd lost her anyway. Now she truly was alone.

Chapter Seventeen

Linota was sleeping deeply. She still hadn't spoken to Katherine other than to thank her for her help in getting her ready for bed. Her expression had been strangely blank. Katherine had explained that Jarin had offered to marry her. Linota had nodded as if they had been discussing the weather. There was nothing of the happy, young girl Katherine was used to and it made her stomach churn.

She'd thought she'd known what anger was like, but nothing she'd ever experienced was comparable with how she felt about Erik. If she was left alone with him, she knew she'd be able to tear him apart with her bare hands.

Then there was Jarin.

Jarin, who had promised to marry Linota to save her from ruin, had made Katherine shiver with desire, but now she felt nothing but bone-deep shame. Linota had witnessed enough betrayal in her short life. She didn't need her traitorous sister to add to it. It was the right thing for Linota to marry Jarin. It was the best match

Linota could hope to achieve and the privileges that marriage would bring would make up for all that Linota had missed out on while growing up.

Yes, Katherine and Jarin had shared some passionate kisses, but he had never discussed feelings with her. Instead, he had given her something infinitely more precious. He had given her belief in herself. She would no longer accept the description of 'the *plain* Leofric sister'.

The fact that, in the process of giving her this new self-belief, she had fallen for Jarin would have to remain a secret she kept buried deep inside.

Katherine had known life wasn't fair ever since she'd witnessed her father's execution, but never before had she truly appreciated how cruel it could be. She had betrayed the one person she had loved her whole life. She would bury those feeling deep inside and not let anyone know that she was as guilty of treachery as her father.

She curled up on the cushions and stared out into the darkness of the night; sleep seemed an impossibility.

There was a soft knock on her chamber door. She lifted her head and stared at it. Surely this couldn't be Jarin?

The knock came again.

On trembling legs she made her way to the door.

She pulled it open gently. Her heart sank to see Mistress Sutton and then she reprimanded herself. She should not want or crave Jarin's company.

'The Earl wishes to see you in the Great Hall,' Mistress Sutton said primly.

Katherine glanced back to the bed.

'If your sister is sleeping, his lordship said not to wake her. I will wait with her.'

She nodded at Mistress Sutton. 'I'll come now.'

She slowly closed the door on the woman and crept over to the bed. Linota appeared to be in a deep sleep. Katherine leant over and brushed a kiss against her sister's forehead. Linota didn't stir.

She collected her cloak and threw it around her shoulders. Away from the fires in the room the air was frigid. She cast one last look at her sister and then stepped out into the corridor. It was time to find out what Jarin wanted.

Her heart pounded as she made her way to the solar. Events must be moving quickly otherwise she was sure Jarin would have left her alone until morning.

She'd known men and women slept in the Great Hall, but it was strange to see them settling down for the night in the very place they mingled during the day. She'd never witnessed it before and part of her wanted to stay behind and observe it, though she knew it was rude to stare.

Jarin was up on the dais, talking intently. Her heart stopped when she realised his companion was Erik.

She knew she wouldn't be able to dissemble. Erik was guilty of a great crime against her family and she would not forgive him for it or be able to pretend that she knew nothing.

'Good evening, my lady Katherine,' said Jarin, standing at her approach.

She dropped him a quick curtsy, glad when her hair fell on to her face and hid her expression from Erik. He wouldn't be able to see the contempt that she was sure was shining in her eyes.

'Shall we retire to my private rooms?' Jarin asked. 'I think we would be more comfortable if we spoke there rather than in front of an audience.'

Katherine hid her hands into the folds of her cloak to hide the fact they were shaking and followed the two men down a short corridor into a much smaller, cosier room.

Jarin's private room was as comfortable as the rest of the fortress. A thick rug stretched across most of the floor and a fire burned brightly in the hearth. Around the room, candles burned, making the room lighter than she was used to seeing at night.

The door closed behind Erik and then the three of them were alone.

Jarin rubbed his forehead. When he'd sent for Katherine he'd not been thinking straight. He'd wanted to see her again this evening. He wanted to know if Katherine was resolute in her determination to see him wedded to Linota, which shouldn't have been his prime concern, but seemed to be the question he wanted an answer to most desperately.

Although Erik had betrayed him by taking Linota, he and Katherine had managed to return her to the castle without no one being any the wiser, especially not her ferocious brother who would certainly demand retribution. No one need know that Linota had spent time alone with a group of men and then just with Erik. Her status as a pure maiden would not be called into question. If Jarin was free from his commitment to marry

Linota, then that would mean he could marry whom he pleased. His chest tightened; he would be free to marry Katherine.

At some point over the last three difficult days he had discovered the woman he was meant to be with. It was no longer just about desire. The feelings he had for her were far stronger than that.

Of course, she might not have him. He'd told her things about himself that no one else knew. Everyone else saw the image he wanted to portray, but she knew the real man behind the mask. Perhaps now that she did she would find him wanting.

Her kisses suggested that she found him attractive, but was that enough on which to base a marriage? Knowing her and her complete lack of belief in her own beauty, he wondered if she would think any offer from him would be for Ogmore's dowry.

Now he was regretting not waiting until tomorrow to see her. She wanted to be there when he confronted Erik, but that didn't mean she should be. It was not going to end well and he didn't want her getting upset in the process.

He ran his fingers through his hair; there was no going back now. Erik would find out they had rescued Linota soon enough and he might run before Jarin got the answers he needed.

He turned to his former friend. 'We found Linota.'

Erik's eyes widened and Jarin watched as realisation dawned on his face.

He waited a beat. 'Why did you do it, Erik? I don't understand.'

Erik glanced at the door.

Jarin moved to block it. 'I need to know, Erik. I thought we were friends.'

Erik snorted and looked back at him. Jarin took a step back as the anger in Erik's eyes seared through him. Until now he'd hoped, against all the evidence, that Erik was innocent, but the depth of his steward's hatred was plain to see. Erik loathed him.

'You don't know anything. We're not friends,' Erik spat out. 'We're brothers.'

Everything inside Jarin stilled. 'Brothers?' he said dully.

'Brothers,' Erik repeated. 'Only you're too wrapped up in yourself to realise it.'

The world tilted and Jarin reached out to grab the back of the nearest chair. Erik was his brother. His flesh and blood and he'd not even noticed. How was that even possible? Did everyone know but him? He really was as self-absorbed as Erik believed.

'How long have you known?' Jarin asked, his mind reeling.

'That I'm Borwyn's bastard?' Erik snarled. 'All my miserable life.'

Jarin took a step away from the man he'd always considered his closest companion.

'Why have you never said anything?'

Erik's lips twisted. 'Our ever-loving father threatened me with dire consequences if I breathed a word to anyone. Don't think you were the only one subjected to his violent mood swings and bruising punches. I wasn't good enough to acknowledge as one of his real sons.'

Jarin swallowed. He had spent most of his childhood hiding from his father, afraid of the fists that would inevitably fall, that was true. But how had he not noticed Erik was suffering alongside him?

'I would have helped you if you'd told me,' said Jarin honestly.

He might have had his own problems growing up, but he knew he would have helped the boy he'd always regarded as his brother anyway. Finding out they were related should have been a joyous moment, not one filled with anger and hatred.

Erik's hands curled into fists. 'I didn't want or need your help.'

'Why did you take Linota?' asked Katherine.

Erik jumped. He'd obviously forgotten her presence.

Jarin instinctively moved in front of her. He didn't trust the man. This person was a stranger.

Erik's lips curled. 'Does it matter why I've done it?' He paused and looked at Jarin for a long moment. Jarin wished he could read his friend's mind but it seemed Erik was lost to him. 'I did it for the money,' Erik said at last.

'You've done this for money? That doesn't seem like you,' said Jarin, shaking his head.

'You don't know me,' snapped Erik, colour sweeping across his face.

Jarin couldn't let that statement go. 'Yes, I do. You're the boy who stole bread from the kitchen so that I could eat after our father had locked me in my room. You're the person who carried me when I couldn't walk because he'd beaten me so badly. I've seen you nurse hedgehogs back from the brink of death because you care about people and animals that can't take care of themselves. I know you.'

Erik shrugged. 'People change.'

'But why? Please help me to understand this Erik.'

'Now you want to know about me? You've had years, Jarin. Years in which you could have asked me if I needed you. It's too late now...'

Jarin nodded,. 'Did our father turn you against me.'

'No!' said Erik, anger filling his eyes once more. 'I'm my own man. I make my own decisions.'

Jarin shook his head. 'Our father hated me. He couldn't bear it that I was the son who was going to inherit the earldom so he took the only thing that really meant something to me—your friendship—and he destroyed it. He manipulated you like he manipulated everyone.'

Erik snorted. 'Once again you think you have it all worked out. Believe what you want. I'm leaving.'

He advanced on Jarin, who stood firmly. Jarin would not let Erik go without answers. 'Let me past,' growled Erik.

'I don't want—'

But Erik didn't wait for him to finish. He tried to push past Jarin but he wasn't about to let Erik go. He needed answers. He reached out and grabbed hold of Erik's shoulder. Erik snarled and tried to twist out of Jarin's firm grip. Jarin held on tighter and Erik's fist plowed into his stomach.

Jarin grunted, but remained upright.

'Let me go,' roared Erik.

Jarin only tightened his grip. 'Calm down.'

His words had the opposite effect and Erik raised his fist again. Time seemed to slow down. Erik's fist was moving towards Jarin's head when Jarin heard a feminine 'No!' A small hand tried to push Jarin aside. He barely moved, but it was enough. Erik's punch landed on the side of Katherine's head rather than his own.

Her whole body snapped sideways and crumbled to the floor.

Time stood suspended as the two men looked down at her.

Erik broke the silence. 'I'm so sorry. I didn't mean…'

But seeing Katherine, so tiny and defeated, had unlocked something in Jarin. He wasn't going to fight his brother for himself, but for the woman he loved…

Before he had time to think he'd spun and punched Erik so hard that his brother stumbled backwards, his eyes wide with shock. Erik didn't even raise his hands to defend himself as Jarin punched him once more. This time it was Erik who fell to the floor unconscious. The result didn't bring him any satisfaction. Instead, the sight of his former friend, his half-brother, lying there, beaten, brought Jarin back to his senses.

'Katherine!'

He raced to her side. She was breathing steadily, but she didn't wake as he knelt beside her.

'Katherine, Kate, my love. Please wake up.'

He shook her arm gently. 'Kate, please.'

But her eyelids didn't flicker and a cold knot of fear settled in Jarin's stomach. He couldn't lose her, not now when he'd finally realised what she meant to him.

'Guards!' Jarin yelled.

Two men burst through the door. 'Fetch a physician and Mistress Sutton, she's in the guest chamber,' he barked out.

One man ran back out, the other stayed.

‘What do you want me to do about…?’ The remaining guard nodded towards Erik’s crumbled from.

Jarin hesitated. It would be safer to lock Erik in the dungeon, but Jarin couldn’t bring himself to send his brother to that stinking pit. He would deal with Erik later. All that mattered now was Katherine.

‘Take him to his chamber. Lock him in and make sure he’s guarded. I’ll send the physician to him after he’s seen Katherine. Don’t trust anything Erik tells you; he is not to leave his room under any circumstances and, if I find my orders have been disobeyed, there will be dire consequences.’

He didn’t turn as the guard heaved Erik out of the room.

Jarin gently strokemusd Katherine’s hair away from her delicate face. She muttered something and turned towards his touch.

‘I’m so sorry, my love. You keep on getting hurt, but I promise this is the last time. I will make sure you are safe from now on.’

Somewhere in the last few days he’d fallen in love with Katherine. It wasn’t the raging, superficial infatuation he’d felt for his first wife. Yes, the overwhelming desire was still there, but a new, deeper and stronger feeling was sweeping through him. He knew that he would lay down his life to keep her happy. This was what his mother had been trying to tell him all along. She’d wanted him to marry someone he loved, not just with his body, but with his heart and soul. Now that he’d found her he couldn’t lose her.

Mistress Sutton was the first to arrive. She didn’t comment on the fact that he was kneeling on the floor stroking Katherine's face and he was grateful. Nothing could have dragged him from her side at this moment.

'She'll be fine,' pronounced Mistress Sutton after a brief examination. 'She only needs bed rest.'

The physician confirmed the same and then left to see to Erik.

'I'll call a guard to have the girl returned to her room,' said Mistress Sutton.

Jarin's fingers curled possessively around Katherine's arm. 'I don't want to disturb her sister. Linota needs her sleep. Katherine can have my bed.'

'I don't think that's appropriate, my lord.' Mistress Sutton sniffed.

Jarin smiled despite himself. Mistress Sutton had virtually raised him and, although she never failed to follow correct etiquette when addressing him, he knew she wouldn't stand any nonsense from him.

'I will sleep in the solar,' he said. 'You can keep watch over her.'

Mistress Sutton nodded, her lips thin.

'There's no need to summon a guard. I will carry her.'

Before Mistress Sutton could argue with him any more he lifted Katherine into his arms. She was so light, there was hardly anything of her.

Mistress Sutton was hard on his heels. It was rather dispiriting that she thought he would try to seduce an unconscious woman. Did nobody have a good opinion of him?

Mistress Sutton pulled back his bed clothes and Jarin placed Katherine carefully down on the mattress. He tucked the covers around her and stood back.

'You can leave now. I will stay with her,' said Mistress Sutton.

'But...'

'My lord, you cannot stay in here,' said Mistress Sutton sternly.

Jarin nodded. He allowed Mistress Sutton to propel him from his own room with only a blanket to keep him warm.

He stood in the passageway outside his chamber and took a deep breath. It hurt him to think that Katherine would wake and he wouldn't be there to comfort her. He hoped the fact that he had placed her in his own room would tell her how much he cared for her.

It had felt so right to see her in his bed, as he'd known it would. It was easy to imagine her there for the rest of their lives.

He rubbed his chest. What if she didn't feel the same way about him? He didn't have the best record in reading the truth in those closest to him. He shook his head. He'd have to ask her. She wouldn't lie to him. If she didn't return his feelings, he would find out soon enough.

Chapter Eighteen

Katherine's head throbbed. She rolled on to her side and breathed deeply. Jarin's scent was everywhere. How was that possible?

Her eyes flickered open and she frowned. This wasn't the bed she had been expecting to wake up in. She tried to push herself upright, but the room swam and she groaned.

'Ah, so you're finally awake.'

She turned her head to see Mistress Sutton peering down at her.

'Wha…?' she croaked.

'Try not to exert yourself,' the older woman said kindly. 'You've had a nasty bump to the head.'

It all came flooding back. Erik had been about to hit Jarin again. He'd already hit him once and she'd found she couldn't breathe as Jarin had bent double in pain. She'd known that he was too honourable to hit Erik back and she couldn't let him get hurt again. She'd tried to push Jarin out of the way of Erik's flailing fists and then the world had turned black. Had Erik hit her instead? It would explain the pain searing through her skull.

'I will inform his lordship that you are awake. He has been most anxious,' said Mistress Sutton.

Jarin couldn't have been far away because he was by her side very quickly.

'How are you feeling?' he asked, gently touching her forehead.

'My head hurts.'

'I'm sure it does. What on earth were you thinking?' His eyes were kind despite his words.

'You weren't defending yourself. He would have hurt you.'

Jarin smiled. 'I think he was trying to escape rather than wound me but still, I would rather he punched me for all eternity than see you hurt.'

Katherine's heart fluttered. 'That's just silly.'

Jarin smiled down at her and she looked away. She couldn't bear for him to look at her like that. He would never be hers and yet her heart wasn't listening. When he looked at her in that way, her heart kept trying to persuade her that he cared for her in the same way she did for him and that was a dangerous line of thought because if it was true then they were *both* guilty of betrayal.

'Does Linota know what happened?' she asked.

'No. I thought you would want to be the one who told her. She is resting at the moment. Mistress Sutton has been to check on her and reports that she is well, if a little quiet.'

Katherine closed her eyes. She had to hope that Linota would return to her normal self when she got over the shock of her ordeal. Knowing that she was going to make a good marriage would help her mend quickly.

'What of Erik?' asked Katherine.

'He's locked in his room. I have several guards standing watch, but so far he has made no move to escape or to wreak any further damage. I spoke to him briefly this morning. He's being very closed-lipped about the whole ordeal. He was shocked that your saddle had been deliberately damaged. I genuinely believe he had no intention of physically hurting you or your sister.'

'Did he try and fight you again?' she asked, her heart hammering wildly at the thought.

'No. After you crumpled to the ground...' Jarin closed his eyes tightly and then opened them again, fixing her with mesmerising stare. He cleared his throat. 'After he hit you, his aggression disappeared. He was strangely wooden this morning. I asked him what he'd hoped to achieve with his actions and he merely shrugged.'

'Do you think it really was about the money?'

'No. I don't know but I think it all comes back to our father. The man wanted me to be alone and the only way he could achieve that was by turning Erik against me. I am sad that he managed to achieve it, but I won't let the bastard win. I won't give up on Erik. I will keep trying to get him to speak to me. I hope we can rebuild our friendship in time, but I want to leave it for a while so we both calm down.'

'You seemed pretty calm yesterday,' said Katherine, picking at a loose thread.

Jarin frowned. 'That was before he punched you to the ground. I will not forgive that in a hurry. I lost my temper quite spectacularly after that. In a way I'm glad you were unconscious for that bit.'

Katherine's heart stilled. She was amazed that seeing her hurt could turn the calm Earl frantic.

'Will you forgive him for everything else?' she asked.

Jarin sighed and lowered himself on to the edge of the bed. 'My father was a horrible, manipulative man. I'm glad you never met him. He would have delighted in turning Erik and me against each other, especially as he knew that, at the time, Erik was the only person I cared about. It would have given our father a sick pleasure to know that Erik would work against me even after his death.'

'What will you do with him?'

'I can't bring myself to punish him for what he's done. That's what my father would have wanted, but that's not the man I am. I want to bring peace to my lands and I can hardly start that by banishing or executing my half-brother.' Jarin sighed. 'I hope to talk to him and make him see reason. I want to try and rebuild our relationship, although my trust in him has gone. If he refuses to meet me halfway, then I will have to banish him from Borwyn. But I will not have him executed.'

Jarin's eyes were sad. Katherine wanted to pull him to her side and hold him, but she kept her hands to herself.

'Katherine…' Jarin paused and rubbed the back of his neck. 'Katherine,' he repeated. This close, Katherine could see his pulse beating in his throat. He licked his lips and she realised he was nervous. She pressed herself back into the mattress, bracing herself for what was to come.

'I was thinking,' Jarin continued slowly, 'now Linota's been found…now that she's safe and well, perhaps there is no need for me to marry her after all.'

The air rushed out of Katherine's lungs. Linota had only been found yesterday evening and already he was trying to distance himself from her family. She had expected better from him. She had believed he was honourable and that he would not break his promise to her. Had everything he told her been a lie?

'But you promised,' she croaked.

He nodded slowly. 'I did. But…things have changed, haven't they?'

Their eyes met and her gaze snagged on the intense blueness of his.

'Nothing's changed,' she managed to say.

He couldn't promise Linota a golden future and then take it away from her. Linota had been damaged by her experience, but becoming one of the greatest ladies in the land would help her recover. She would want for nothing if she was Jarin's bride. Yes, his finances were strained at the moment, but Ogmore's dowry would help and now that he had discovered the source of his problems he would only go from strength to strength. The marriage was the best thing for Linota's future.

'Are you sure?' said Jarin quietly.

'Quite sure,' said Katherine firmly.

'Then I will go and speak to her now,' said Jarin, pushing himself to his feet.

Katherine wanted to cry out to him. To tell him to wait. He didn't need to ask Linota so soon. But she knew that was ridiculous. The sooner he and Linota were formally betrothed, the sooner Linota's future would be secured. And that was what she wanted above all things, even if her own heart broke in the process.

Chapter Nineteen

Jarin ran a hand through his hair and turned to speak to Erik before he realised he was alone. He couldn't get used to his friend's absence. Erik would have a joke for him, something to take his mind off his current situation.

Jarin folded his arms and leaned back against the wall. Erik wasn't here beside him, but that wasn't what was giving him the feeling of a noose slowly tightening itself around his neck.

He was waiting for an audience with Katherine's brother. The man should have seen him straight away to accord him the respect his status deserved as one of the most important earls in the country, but the knight was obviously trying to make him sweat—a clever tactic, but annoying because it was working. The longer he waited the tighter the noose felt.

A tall, thin man appeared. 'Sir Braedan will see you now.'

Jarin rolled his eyes. Why make such a drama out of this? By now Braedan would know Jarin intended to offer for Linota. Jarin was sure Katherine would have told her brother as soon as she arrived, since she was so keen on the match. Jarin rubbed his hand across his face; he'd thought that while he'd been falling for Katherine she'd been doing the same with him. He'd obviously been wrong. The look of horror on her face when he'd suggested not marrying Linota convinced him of that.

He'd rather die than see Katherine married to someone else, which told him all he needed to know about his feelings for her.

He followed the tall, thin man through several corridors and into the Great Hall. Jarin's irritation increased another notch. Why hadn't he been told to head to the Hall? Its location wasn't a secret and now he was being led like a sheep to pay homage to the lord and master of the castle. It was as if Braedan Leofric was deliberately trying to humiliate him, which Jarin supposed he was.

'Borwyn,' said the man himself, stepping down from the raised dais to meet him.

'Leofric,' said Jarin.

Sir Braedan was obviously used to using his height and bulk to intimidate people and he fixed Jarin with a silent glare. Jarin was the knight's equal in stature and stood his ground, waiting for him to speak again. Jarin would not be the one to break the silence.

'I've spoken to my sisters,' Braedan said. 'They have given me the strangest account of their last few days. Do you wish to expand on that?'

'Linota spoke to you?' Jarin asked, surprised.

During the two-day journey from his castle to here, Katherine had fussed around Linota like a mother hen.

Linota hadn't said a word and Katherine had become tenser and tenser as the scenery had rolled past. He'd longed to take Katherine in his arms and comfort her, but she had made it very clear she wouldn't want that. She didn't want him at all.

'No, Linota hasn't spoken, a fact that concerns me greatly,' said Leofric, a frown on his craggy features. 'She was taken from you in broad daylight. How did you let that happen?'

Jarin opened his mouth to respond and then closed it again. He was on the back foot here and wasn't about to get defensive over something that had been out of his control. He'd resolved the situation and both Leofric sisters were now safely home. He had nothing to apologise for.

'I am sure that the lady Katherine explained everything to you satisfactorily,' he said instead.

Sir Leofric raised an eyebrow. 'Don't you want to add anything?'

'I do not.'

Leofric regarded him for a long moment. Jarin held his eye, refusing to back down an inch.

'I trust the man who took her is being suitably punished,' said Leofric eventually.

Jarin swallowed. 'He is locked up and unable to escape,' he said.

He didn't add that he had no idea what to do with his half-brother. Ever since Erik had accidentally hit Katherine, the fight had appeared to go out of him. Jarin didn't want to punish Erik even though he deserved it. His half-brother had suffered enough being the bastard son of a cruel father and a uninterested mother. Jarin didn't want to see his former friend suffer any more. He hoped that, in time, they might be able to salvage something of their friendship, but they wouldn't be able to do that if Jarin came down hard on him.

'Katherine tells me that you plan to marry my sister, Linota,' said Leofric.

Jarin forced himself to nod. 'I do.'

'We shall need to make sure it is done quickly before any hint of what happened comes to light. My family and I are wary of malicious gossip, as I'm sure you understand.'

Jarin nodded again, focusing on a point above Braedan's right shoulder. His soul screamed out to him that marrying Linota was wrong. He would never be able to treat her as anything other than a younger sister. To lie with her would be abhorrent. Not because she wasn't beautiful—objectively he knew she was very comely. But she wasn't Katherine, with her ever-changing expressions, her tiny curves and her passionate longing to know the outside world. To get Linota with child would be nothing more than a duty. She would have everything that she desired, but she would never have his heart. That, for better or worse, belonged to Katherine.

'Good, I'm glad you are agreed. The wedding will take place in three days. Ogmore has sent me a letter in which he outlines the dowry he is settling on both of my sisters. It's a very generous offer. I will, of course, add something, but it will not be on the same scale.'

Jarin forced himself to nod once more. He was in danger of looking like a puppet. He'd expected a weight to be lifted from his shoulders once the deal was done, but now a stone had settled itself in his chest and he could barely breathe.

'We should toast this union, don't you think?' said Leofric. 'Now that we are going to be brothers.'

Jarin wanted to plant his fist in his future brother-in-law's face. He knew this offer of a toast was not the friendly gesture it first appeared. Leofric wanted to question him and probably hoped that a strong drink would help loosen his tongue.

It was true, though, that they were going to be brothers and so he nodded his acceptance. Leofric gestured to the thin man that drinks were needed and Jarin resigned himself to spending more time than he wanted with Katherine's brother.

The only good thing his experiences with his father had taught him was how to hide how he truly felt about anything and everything. It didn't matter how much Jarin imbibed, he wouldn't tell Leofric that he was marrying the wrong sister.

Chapter Twenty

'I thought you might like to eat dinner with just the two of us this evening,' said Katherine, carrying a trencher laden with Linota's favourite meats. 'I hope I've selected a little of something that you'd like.'

'Thank you,' said Linota quietly.

Katherine put the food down at the end of the bed. 'Did you see that our new sister has finished your dress? She is a far better seamstress than I am. You are going to look very fine tomorrow; of course, you always do, but nobody will be able to take their eyes off you on your wedding day.'

Katherine prattled on, filling the silence with aimless talk. She moved around the room, straightening things on the dressing table. Neither of the girls made any attempt to eat the food that Katherine had brought to their room.

Katherine's heart hurt with every beat.

'Katherine.' Linota's voice cut through her idle talk.

Katherine's heart leapt. For the first time in days Linota's voice sounded normal.

'Yes.'

'I'm not going to marry the Earl of Borwyn tomorrow.'

Katherine stilled, her hand resting on the handle of a hairbrush.

'Did you hear me, Katherine?' asked Linota.

'Yes, I heard you. Why not? Is it happening too quickly for you? I'm sure Jarin won't mind if you want to put it back a day or two.'

'I'm not going to marry Borwyn at all,' said Linota calmly.

'But...'

'I should never have agreed to it in the first place. I was in shock and not thinking properly.'

'But he is such a good match for you.'

'No. He's not. I don't want to marry him. I'm not going to.'

Katherine made her way to the bed and sat next to her sister, taking her hands in hers. Her heart was pounding in her chest.

'Is this your nerves talking? I believe it is quite natural to have doubts the night before a wedding.'

Linota stood, pulling her hands out of Katherine's. 'I know you have had this match in your mind for some time; even before we met him you were extolling his virtues. Prior to leaving Ogmore's castle, I would have been satisfied to marry such a man. I'm sure he will make someone a perfectly pleasant husband, but not me. So much has happened in such a short period of time and I am not the same woman I was only a week ago. One day, when I am feeling stronger, I will tell you all about it, but not now. Just know that when I agreed to marry Borwyn I was not myself. I thought it was a solution to a problem that doesn't really exist.' Linota turned to Katherine, her eyes shining. 'We are free now, Katherine. We don't have to marry to escape our mother. I cannot and will not marry the Earl of Borwyn.'

'But...'

It was Linota who now took Katherine's hands in hers. 'I'm sorry. I know you have put a lot of effort into making this match happen and I know I sound ungrateful, but I would not be a good wife for Borwyn and I would not make him happy. I would make him miserable. I can see that he's a good man with a kind heart and he deserves better.'

Katherine's heart pounded painfully. 'I don't understand why you don't want to marry him. He is the best of men.'

Linota touched Katherine's cheek. 'Why don't you tell him you think that?' she said softly, her eyes filled with an emotion Katherine couldn't read. For the first time in their relationship it was as if Linota was the older sibling. The experience of being abducted and betrayed had aged her beyond her years and Katherine wasn't sure if she should be worried or glad.

'I...'

'You and he have become close, I believe. Will you tell him of my decision? I will let our brother know. I'm sure he will rant and rave at me, but he won't force me to marry someone I don't want. He is also a good man, despite his rather fearsome countenance.'

Linota stood and, before Katherine could stop her, she left the chamber.

Katherine stood abruptly and then sat back down

again. How would she tell Jarin? He'd experienced so much rejection in his life and it wasn't fair that he would have to face it again. Even worse, he was going to lose Ogmore's promised dowry. He needed that to help restore his estate's finances. This mess was all because of her. She sunk her head into her hands and let out a moan. She didn't know how she would even look him in the face, let alone break the news to him.

She stood again, slowly this time as if her movements were under water. She had to go to him right now. It was only fair and waiting wouldn't make it any easier for either of them.

She moved through the castle unthinkingly. The evening meal was still ongoing in the Great Hall. Their brother was absent from the table, as was Jarin.

Her heart was in her throat as she made her way over to her sister-in-law. Had Jarin already been made aware of Linota's decision? What did his and her brother's absence mean?

'Where is the Earl of Borwyn?' Katherine asked Ellena, her brother's new wife.

'He hasn't come down for his meal yet,' said Ellena. 'Is everything all right? Linota has taken Braedan off for a private chat. I was relieved to see her more animated, but from the look on your face it is perhaps not as good news as I hoped.'

It wasn't Katherine's place to tell Ellena of Linota's decision. 'Everything is fine,' she said vaguely. 'I will talk to them all later. I'm sorry for disturbing your meal.'

Ellena frowned, but Katherine didn't wait around

to be questioned more. She turned and headed away from the hall.

It would be wrong to head to Jarin's chamber. It was his private space and she didn't think her brother would like it if she went to the room without a guard for her protection. But he couldn't be left in ignorance about Linota's decision and it wasn't fair to tell him in front of anyone else. Not telling him was worse than protecting herself.

Yet she found herself outside his chamber door and knocked. Half of her was hoping he wouldn't answer. Maybe he was visiting Eira or talking with a member of his retinue.

She waited.

In the quietness of the corridor she fancied she could hear her own heart pounding.

The door creaked open and Jarin's broad body filled the doorway.

'Katherine Leofric,' he said, crossing his arms over his chest. 'Of course you are here and without an escort. I'm not even surprised any more.'

She frowned. Why did he always focus on her safety? It wasn't as if she was wandering outside right now. She was safe in her brother's castle. 'I need to talk to you.'

'What is it that's so important it couldn't wait until I see you during the evening meal?'

'It's...look, can I come in?'

Jarin's eyes widened. 'Are you insane? No, forget that, I know you don't like it. We settled on foolish, didn't we? You can't just barge into a man's chamber. He might expect things from you that you aren't willing to give.'

Katherine folded her arms. 'You are insufferable.'

'Ah, that's a new one. I thought I was an obnoxious boor.'

'You're that, too.'

A crooked smile crossed his lips. 'Your good opinion of me never wavers, does it? I suppose if you're intent on coming in you might as well. But, I beg you, don't make a habit of this.'

He stood aside and she swept past him into the room.

Her annoyance at him held until she was standing in the middle of his chamber. His dress robes were arranged on his bed and the enormity of what she was about to do hit her.

'Katherine, what's wrong?' he said, stepping towards her.

He stopped when he was a few paces away.

'It's...' Words failed her.

She didn't think for one minute that Jarin was in love with Linota. They hadn't spent long enough together to form an attachment and she knew enough about him to know that he wouldn't keep kissing *her* if his heart was truly engaged. The loss of the union would affect him financially and she knew that this would be the bigger blow to him.

'Kate...' He paused and her heart stumbled. No one had ever called her Kate. It was what a dear friend would do and now she was going to destroy that friendship forever.

'Whatever the problem is, please tell me. You must know that I would do anything to help you.'

She saw the truth of it shining in his eyes and her

toes curled. She was about to let him down in such a terrible way.

'There's nothing wrong with me,' she said, her voice coming out as barely a whisper. 'It's Linota.'

'What's wrong with her?' he asked gently.

Katherine took a deep breath. 'She has said she won't marry you. I'm sorry.'

'I see.' Jarin blinked slowly. 'Did she say why?'

Katherine looked down at the floor. 'No. Only that she would not be a good wife for you. I'm so sorry, Jarin. I know it wasn't a love match, but I also know how much you need Ogmore's settlement.'

She looked back up at him; the expression on his face was impossible to read.

Jarin nodded slowly. 'Ogmore's dowry would have been…helpful, but it is no longer essential. Erik admitted to me he was aware of someone deliberately inciting trouble at my borders and did nothing to stop it. Now that I know the person responsible I will put a stop to it. I am sure my coffers will recover quite quickly. Borwyn is a vast, asset-rich estate, after all, and I'm determined to work hard.'

'Right,' said Katherine, blinking back inexplicable tears. It was a good thing that Jarin wasn't experiencing any heartache or difficulties because of this, but for some reason Katherine's throat ached with the effort not to cry. 'Good.'

'I'm sure no one will expect me to stay now that the wedding is off,' said Jarin briskly. 'I shall inform my men that we will leave at first light.'

'Yes,' she said, unable to look at him.

There was a lengthy silence. There was so much she

wanted to say, but her throat was locked in misery. A small part of her, the part that was so tiny she hadn't even wanted to admit its existence even to herself, urged her to yell, *But what about me? Did those kisses mean nothing?* It was the part of her that had hoped, without expectation, that he might offer her marriage now that his engagement to Linota was over. Not because he loved her, but because he needed Ogmore's dowry. It seemed not even that incentive was enough to induce him to marry her.

'This is a parting of ways then,' said Jarin. 'Unless...'

Katherine nodded woodenly. 'Yes, a parting of ways,' she repeated numbly.

Before she knew what was happening he'd pulled her into a tight embrace, his mouth taking hers in a bruising kiss. He released her just as quickly and turned away.

'Goodbye, Katherine,' he said, his back to her.

She turned and fled.

Chapter Twenty-One

Jarin strode along the battlements, checking that everything was in order. This daily check, always at different times, was one of the many changes he'd made in the last three months. He stopped briefly to talk to his new marshal of the guards. The man was eminently capable and Jarin appreciated his calm, measured reports at the end of each day. Reports he now insisted on as part of his routine. Gone was Jarin's relaxed approach to leadership. He no longer craved being liked as long as he was respected. Although, he had found that respect seemed to lead to liking. He was certainly getting a warmer reception from his people now that he was firmer in his dealings with them.

He strode on, nodding briefly to the guards he passed. A lot of them were new faces. He'd sent many old retainers, who had been loyal to his father, to posts on his borders, splitting up factions and ensuring he had a tight ring of trusted men around him. He no longer relied on one person to give him information. He had to work even harder than before, but it was worth it. His wealth was showing signs of recovery; he was still some considerable way off from returning it to what it had been at the height of Borwyn prosperity in the past, but he had no doubt that he would reach and surpass that in the coming years.

He reached a point on the wall and, despite himself, slowed down and stopped. A soft sea breeze ruffled his hair and he reached out and touched the stone wall. He tried not to think about Katherine during the day. She visited too often in the night, her soft body promising him things that vanished in the cold light of day. But this spot was where they'd talked, where she had made him proud of the man he had become—the real him, not the one he showed to the world. The man he'd shown only to her. He closed his eyes as more memories assaulted him, hammering him as hard as a physical blow to his chest.

He hoped that whatever she was doing right now she was happy, even as another part of him knew that he would never be truly happy without her. He hoped someone was finally taking care of her in the way she deserved.

He took a deep breath, then turned away from the place and re-entered the fortress. He slowly descended the spiral staircase. He was about to do something that was either spectacularly stupid or divinely inspired. Only time would tell which.

He paused for a moment outside Erik's chamber. It had been nearly two months since he'd stopped locking his half-brother in and over a month since he'd stopped having the man watched. It hadn't seemed to make much difference. Erik barely left his room and when he did he was a pale imitation of his former self, weight had fallen off him and his eyes were full of a deep sadness.

Jarin took a deep breath and then pushed open the door.

Erik was slumped in a chair, gazing listlessly at the fire.

'Busy as usual, I see,' said Jarin, striding over to the window and pushing the shutter open. A waft of spring air rushed into the room, partly dispelling the stale stench, but not quite.

'What would you have me do?' Erik asked as he scrunched his eyes against the light.

'Wash, for a start,' said Jarin. 'And when you've done that I've got a job for you.'

Erik sat upright in his chair. 'A job for me? Are you insane?'

Possibly, thought Jarin, looking down at his brother. But then, if he was going to be the sort of man Katherine Leofric knew he could be, he needed to help Erik, no matter what he'd done. It was neither of their faults their father had been the way he was. It didn't mean they had to suffer going forward.

'I need someone to escort some goods to Ogmore,' said Jarin briskly. 'You know the way and you're hardly busy right now. You seem like the ideal choice. You can leave tomorrow morning—after that wash you so badly need.'

Jarin turned to leave. This was a big gamble and he hoped his trust was not misplaced. If he was wrong, Jarin was at a loss as to how to proceed.

'I let you down,' said Erik.

Jarin turned back to look at Erik. He'd moved and was now sitting more upright, watching him intently.

'I think you let yourself down more.'

Erik nodded slowly. 'I swear I will never let you down from now until I the day I die.'

'I know.'

Sensing Erik had more to say, Jarin took a few steps back into the room and pulled up a chair. For a long moment neither of them spoke and then Erik began, the words tumbling and spilling out of him. Erik told Jarin things about his childhood, secrets that Jarin hadn't even guessed at and a web of lies and betrayal that had Jarin sick to his stomach. It was a story that had Jarin wanting to dig up their father's body only so he could kill him all over again. He wanted to rail against the man, but he held his tongue and waited for Erik to finish his story.

When he had, Jarin knew he had been right not to punish his half-brother for his betrayal. They were both victims of a viciously cruel father, Erik possibly more so. Now was the time to move forward and help his brother to heal. He said as much to Erik, who closed his eyes and rested his head against the back of his chair.

'I should have told you the truth from the beginning. I don't deserve you as a brother or a friend,' said Erik quietly.

Jarin laughed, 'I'm not sure about that.' He made to stand. 'Given the circumstances I think I would have acted in the same way.'

'Is there any news on…the Leofric sisters?' asked Erik, his eyes still closed, but every line in his body taut.

The answer obviously mattered a great deal to Erik.

Jarin was unsure as to whether it was because Erik had developed real feelings for Linota during the ordeal or because he wanted the women to have suffered no lasting damage from his actions. Perhaps it was both.

Jarin cleared his throat. 'I have not heard from them directly, but I believe both of them have received marriage offers recently. Sir Braedan is considering them.'

Whenever Jarin thought about Katherine marrying some faceless man he wanted to punch something, hard. For a man dedicated to peace he had been experiencing a lot of violent thoughts recently and nearly all of them were tied up with Katherine.

Erik nodded, glanced at the fire, then back at his half-brother. 'I had it wrong from the start, didn't I? Linota Leofric didn't interest you at all. It was always Katherine.'

A flicker of fear raced up Jarin's spine and he forced himself to remain calm. He had decided to trust his half-brother again; he had to believe that Erik wouldn't harm Katherine. Besides, she was a good two days' ride away from Borwyn. She was safe and that was the important thing.

'I'm sorry I ruined that relationship for you. She seems like a good woman,' said Erik softly.

'You didn't ruin anything,' said Jarin. 'There was nothing for you to ruin. Katherine wanted a good marriage for her sister and when that didn't work out she had no further use for me.'

Erik snorted. 'You don't seriously believe that.'

Jarin shrugged. There were times when leaving Katherine seemed like the most foolish mistake he'd ever made in a life littered with them. In those instances he believed he should never have left Katherine's side without telling her he loved her. She might not have felt the same way, but at least she would have known. If nothing else, it would have given her some of the confidence she so badly lacked.

Other times, he convinced himself he'd done exactly the right thing. If he'd told her he loved her at their last meeting she wouldn't have believed it. She would have thought he was only after Ogmore's dowry and that would have destroyed him.

'You do think she had no interest in you!' said Erik when Jarin didn't respond. Erik shook his head disbelievingly. 'The lady Katherine looked at you as if you were the sun, the stars, the everything. She allowed herself to be punched to the floor because she didn't want you to get hit. You're seriously losing your touch if you think she wasn't interested.'

Jarin really didn't want to discuss Katherine with anyone, but he found himself grinding out, 'She gave me no encouragement.'

Erik waved his hand to one side. 'You mean she wasn't like Viola, leading you a merry dance. She is a young, innocent woman, Jarin. Of course she didn't try and tempt you to her bed. She wouldn't know how to! You need to go to her before her brother accepts another offer.'

Jarin stood. 'I'll think about. In the meantime, you get that bath we talked about.' He strode from the room before Erik could say anything else.

Without stopping, Jarin marched to the Great Hall. He had disputes to settle. It would take many hours and then there was the evening meal. These days, he always attended, even if all he wanted to do was rest for a short while. He had realised how important it was for him to be seen by his people and to be seen as a lord who was in charge and in control.

Right now he had to concentrate.

He took his place on his chair at the centre of the dais. Two men stepped forward and began an extensive argument over a boundary.

Jarin didn't hear a word. Katherine had looked at him as if he were the sun?

Had he made a terrible mistake? He could set off for Castle Swein tomorrow. But what if he was too late? The offer of marriage had to have come some time ago for rumours of it to have reached him here at Borwyn. She might have already accepted it; she might already be married to the faceless bastard.

He clenched his fists and stared at the two men as they wittered on about stretches of land.

Jarin tugged at his neckline. If Leofric had accepted the proposal on Katherine's behalf, but the marriage hadn't taken place then he still had time.

'Gentlemen,' he said, standing and cutting short the endless debate. 'You seem like sensible people. Sort this mess out between you. If you don't, you'll both receive a fine. Now, if you'll excuse me.'

The Great Hall was packed with people wanting his time and attention, but he was about to exercise his right as lord and master of the fortress and ignore them all. Their quarrels would still be here when he got back.

As he strode from the hall a young page called to him, 'My lord…'

'Not now,' said Jarin as he continued to head to his

private apartments. He needed to get underway. If he travelled light he could be halfway to Swein by tonight.

'You said to notify you straight away if word came from Castle Swein,' said the young lad, hurrying to catch him up. 'You've had a letter, my lord.'

Jarin froze.

A letter.

From Castle Swein.

With shaking fingers he took the proffered paper from the young lad's hand.

What on earth could this missive contain? Please God, do not let it be an invitation to Katherine Leofric's wedding. He didn't think his heart could stand it.

Chapter Twenty-Two

Katherine twisted on her feet, watching the way her shadow moved across the sand. She'd filled out in the months since arriving at her brother's home. Now it looked as if she finally had curves. Small ones, but they were definitely there.

Images of Jarin's firm hands moving over them flickered across her mind. She pushed them ruthlessly to one side. She'd hoped after three months her mind would have stopped doing this to her, that it would have stopped presenting her with images that could never be. But if anything the images were getting stronger and were coming more often.

She took the path up from the beach and on to the mainland, the guard assigned to keep her safe following at a discreet distance. She waved to a group of fishermen who were already back from their morning haul. They waved back. Occasionally she would stop and talk to them—their stories were endlessly fascinating—but not today.

She made her way back to the castle. It was much

smaller than the vast fortresses of Ogmore and Borwyn, but it was such a friendly, prosperous place and the people within had taken her and her sister to their hearts.

She stopped at the stables on the way to the keep. Her new horse, Haf, whickered in pleasure at her approach. She found a carrot in a bucket of vegtables left by the door and presented it to her horse. She stroked Haf's nose as the horse munched happily on her snack.

'I'm sorry I won't be riding you this morning,' she said to the mare. 'I've promised Ellena I'll help her with some sewing, although goodness knows why she wants my help because my skills have not improved no matter how many lessons she's patiently given me.'

Haf snorted and Katherine took that as agreement.

She waved to the stable master as she left. He was a gruff old man, but he treated Katherine with considerable kindness and had been teaching her to ride. She was slowly getting the hang of it and had even galloped across the beach with her brother the day before. The feeling of the wind whipping through her hair had been exhilarating.

She let herself into the keep and made her way to Ellena's private rooms.

Ellena and Linota were already there. They were sewing an intricate pattern at the centre of a piece of cloth. Katherine had been relegated to the edges, but that was fine with her. It was more about the three of them getting together to chat than for practical purposes.

'Have you given any more thought to Lord North's proposal, Katherine?' asked Ellena.

Katherine stabbed the cloth with her needle and

promptly pricked her own skin. She sucked her finger as she thought about her response. Lord North's proposal was a good one. He was of a similar age to her with a comfortable position and rumour had it that he wasn't a bad man. He would make a good match for her. Braedan had told her that she could make up her own mind; he wouldn't force her either way.

Katherine and Linota had been shocked to discover that Ogmore still intended to provide them with a sizeable dowry each and Braedan had also said he would add to it. Linota had already turned down one proposal of marriage. Katherine had yet to make up her mind about Lord North.

She knew she should at least arrange to meet the man. Despite her dowry, she might not get another offer and she didn't want to be a burden on her brother's estate for her whole life. Something—or, more accurately, some*one*—was holding her back from making a decision.

Even now, months later, she was cursing herself for not telling Jarin she loved him the last time she'd seen him. When it had become common knowledge that Ogmore's dowry was still intact, she'd cherished a hope that Jarin would return, but they'd heard nothing from him at all.

'Braedan and I have been planning a celebration at Easter,' Ellena continued when Katherine didn't answer. 'My father and mother will attend. We could invite Lord North so that you could get to know him.'

Katherine nodded when she really wanted to shake her head vehemently, which she supposed gave her the answer she needed. She was not going to marry Lord

North. It wouldn't be fair when she was still in love with Jarin.

'And we are planning on inviting the Earl of Borwyn,' said Ellena. 'It would be good to extend the hand of friendship to him, don't you think?'

Katherine's heart leapt and fell painfully.

'I don't think he will come,' she said, when it became obvious a response was expected from her.

'I think he will,' said Linota quickly.

Katherine didn't miss the look that passed between Linota and Ellena.

'What makes you think so?' she asked. Her heartbeat sped up. Did they know something about him that she didn't? Had he already married and nobody had told her? It was too soon for her to see him again if he had a bride on his arm. She would have to fake an illness so she could hide in her chamber. It would hurt too much.

'Oh, Katherine,' said Linota, laying down her embroidery. 'I don't understand why he left in the first place. What did you say to him that last evening? Did you tell him you thought he was the best of men like I told you to? Because I don't think you can have done. The attraction between you was so intense it was like standing next to a fire whenever you were together. I felt as though I would burn from it sometimes.'

Ellena nodded. 'I noticed it on my wedding day. Neither of you were able to take your eyes off each other, even then.'

Katherine felt the blood drain from her face. The one thing that had got her through the endless days without Jarin was the knowledge that nobody knew how she felt about him. Now she didn't even have that.

She mumbled something unintelligible and began sewing with an intensity she'd never mastered before.

Ellena took the hint and began to chat about inconsequential things with Linota.

The rest of the morning passed slowly and Katherine was glad when Ellena suggested they take a break. The straight line she was meant to be attempting looked decidedly uneven.

'I think I will take a walk,' she announced and then stood up before either woman could talk her out of it.

She loved being outside. Now the spring was getting into its stride the woodland was changing every day. She'd spied a small group of fox cubs the other day and she'd enjoyed watching them play together, the youngsters making her laugh with their antics.

Katherine made her way through the forest and settled herself in her favourite spot: a secluded den amongst the trees, which provided her with a natural seat. She lay back and rested her head against the moss. Through the tangle of branches above her, she could make out the bright blue of the sky. She closed her eyes; the colour reminded her of Jarin's irises. One day, she hoped, not everything would remind her of the man she loved, but couldn't have.

The snap of a twig had her sitting bolt upright, her heart thundering wildly.

She looked around and then rubbed her eyes. As if she'd summoned him by thought alone, Jarin was standing in front of her, a faint smile across his firm lips.

For a long moment they looked at each other, his gaze as piercing as ever.

Then, without thinking, she jumped up and ran towards him.

He opened his arms and she flew into them, burying her face in his solid chest. His arms tightened around her and she slid hers around his back, running her hands over the muscles that bunched under her fingers.

His long, firm fingers tilted her head to face his. His eyes searched her face and he opened his mouth as if to talk. She didn't want him to; she didn't want to know what brought him to her side because then she would know when he was going to leave. She stood on tiptoes and kissed him.

He gave a small grunt of surprise, but responded quickly, moving his lips firmly over hers, opening her mouth and stroking her tongue with his. Heat rushed through her and the world fell away. All she was aware of was Jarin, his lips, his tongue and his glorious body. For the first time in months her heart sang with pure joy.

Her hands stole into his hair and she ran her fingers through the thick locks, rejoicing in his groan of pleasure. The skin on the back of his neck was soft. Her fingers slid through the neckline of his outfit. His body was warm to the touch. She skimmed her fingertips along the ridge of his shoulders, mapping the shape of him.

She found herself airborne as he carried her the few steps back to her woodland seat. He lowered her gently to the ground and she held on to him tightly, unwilling to let him break away from the kiss even for a moment.

She didn't know how long this unexpected gift would last and she wanted to take her fill of him, to know him in every way.

They were both breathing heavily as his lips trailed the length of her jaw and she gasped in delight as his stubble grazed against the sensitive skin of her neck.

She tugged at the fastenings on his tunic and he reached up a hand to help her. Together they pulled it off and Jarin threw it to one side. She slipped her hands beneath his shirt and revelled in his sharp inhalation as her fingers traced the firm contours of his stomach.

She barely registered his hands undoing the ties to her own outer garment, but she noticed the cool air rushing over her, quickly replaced by his body heat as he lowered himself on to her once more. His mouth returned to hers and their movements became jerky and frantic as their hands grasped and explored each other.

She could feel his arousal against her leg and she instinctively moved against him. He growled and gripped her ankle. For a moment she thought he was holding her in place and her heart skipped a beat. But then his hand began to move up the curve of her calf and over her knee, his fingers burning a trail against her sensitive skin. He reached her hips and her dress bunched at her waist. He seemed to hesitate for a moment and so she grabbed his arm and moved it so that it continued on its journey.

He lifted his head briefly to pull her dress over her head, throwing it in the same direction as her tunic. His eyes, when he met her gaze, were glazed and nearly completely black.

He propped himself up on his forearm and looked down the length of her body. She fought the urge to cover herself up. There was nothing she could do to improve her figure. She could not suddenly grow curves, but his ravenous gaze suggested he liked what he saw.

The wind brushed over her tiny breasts, causing them to pucker. She heard Jarin's intake of breath and then it was her turn to cry out as Jarin gently traced their outline with his forefinger. Slowly, he lowered his head and took the other nipple in his mouth. The sensation caused her to buck from the ground and she felt his smile against her skin.

While his mouth teased her breasts, his hand brushed over the skin of her stomach, his fingers sliding into the soft curls at the top of her thighs.

'Oh,' she whispered as his fingers stroked her sensitive flesh.

She'd never known, never realised, it was possible to feel this way.

His mouth returned to hers and he began to kiss her again. She arched against him as his tongue began to mirror the strokes of his fingers between her thighs, softly at first, but with increasing pressure as she began to writhe beneath him.

She began to fumble with his remaining clothes. She wanted his skin against hers. For him to experience the same sensations she was.

'Are you sure?' he whispered against her mouth.

'Yes,' she whispered back. 'Quite sure.'

She wanted this. She wanted to know him in every way possible before he went from her life again. So what if this was wrong? Nothing had ever felt so right to her before.

He tugged the remainder of his garments off and she took a moment to breathe in the sight before her.

The skin of his muscular chest was pale. She reached up and ran her fingers through the light smattering of blond hair until she reached his nipple. She circled it with her fingertip as he had done to her. He inhaled sharply and she smiled, pleased to have elicited such a response from him.

He settled between her thighs, his hardness pressing on her soft skin.

She moved restlessly beneath him and he smiled, pressing a gentle kiss against her mouth as he slowly began to edge into her.

She gasped as his length began to fill her and then she cried out as a sharp pain whipped across her belly.

'I'm sorry, my love,' he murmured into her hair. 'The pain…it will fade, I promise.'

For several heartbeats they lay together, unmoving apart from the soft kisses he ran along the length of her jaw and on to the soft, sensitive skin under her ear. The sharp sting slowly subsided and she drew her fingers over his broad shoulders. The strange, restless feeling began to build in her again and she wriggled beneath him.

He groaned and claimed her mouth anew, moving inside her now, slowly at first and then faster as she began to claw at his back.

Pressure was building. Her body was racing towards a point. There was nothing apart from his body moving above hers. A new, powerful sensation was building and she was racing towards it, then it burst through her, starting at her core and unfurling through her body, sending wave upon wave of pleasure flooding through her. She cried out and clung to him.

He called her name as he rocked into her, seemingly as lost in the moment as she was. He collapsed on to her, his solid weight pressing her into the moss, his mouth once more claiming her in a searing kiss.

The new, beautiful shudders slowly faded away from her body, leaving her with a bone-deep contentment.

Jarin propped himself up on his forearms and gazed down into her eyes. Her heart soared. The look in his eyes made her feel truly beautiful for the first time.

He rolled on to his back, pulling her with him so that she nestled against his shoulder. He gently pressed his lips to her forehead. She never wanted this moment to end.

From her vantage point she could see down the length of his body and for the first time she wished she could draw. How she wanted to capture the image of him so that she could study it whenever she chose.

His long fingers stroked her back and she slipped one leg over his so they were entwined. Neither of them said a word.

She knew reality would have to intervene sooner or later, but for now she was content to stay in this little bubble of complete happiness.

She couldn't say how long they lay there under the canopy of the trees, but slowly the fingers that stroked her became more demanding, sliding down her back and over the bare skin of her buttocks, pressing her closer to his body.

Her hand moved down his chest and over his stomach, exploring the muscles that bunched under her fingers. She continued over his hips and dipped close to his erection, which strained towards her once more.

She traced its length with the tips of her fingers, marvelling at how soft the skin was beneath her hand when it had felt so hard inside her.

She took her time exploring it, learning the places that made him moan with pleasure as her fingers glided over him. She glanced at his face; his eyelids were half-closed, his lips parted. A strange sort of power stole over her as she realised she had made him look like this, as if he was almost insensible with desire.

She placed a light, teasing kiss against the corner of his mouth. He grabbed her before she could move away and kissed her deeply, his tongue firm and demanding.

He began to move in the hand that held him, his hips thrusting as they had when he'd been inside her, his groans pulled at something deep inside her.

He broke off the kiss. 'I want you again,' he growled.

She nodded and made to roll on to her back but he stopped her.

'No, this way.'

He pulled her up so she was straddling him and then he sank into her, groaning as he filled her to the hilt.

This time there was no pain, only pleasure.

His hands were in her hair, pulling the braids free until it hung free around her face, falling on to him and brushing his chest.

'I've pictured you like this a thousand times,' he said, slowly thrusting into her.

She couldn't believe it, yet the look on his face told her it was true.

His hands slid over her breasts, cupping and squeezing them both. She gasped and began to move over him.

This time their movements were less hurried and

frantic. She took the time to trace her fingers over every inch of his skin. She wanted to remember everything about his body for when he was gone.

The wave of pleasure when it came was a slow build, unfurling and crashing through her steadily, though no less intensely than the first time.

She watched as he broke and came apart inside her, his big hands holding on to her hips.

She slowly sank back down on to him, resting her head on his chest; he kissed her forehead, her eyelids and then her lips.

This time she stayed lying on him, her head resting over his steady heartbeat.

Beneath her, his breathing slowed before dropping into the lazy rhythm of sleep. Although drowsiness tugged on her, she kept her eyes open. She didn't want to miss a single moment of their time together.

She could tell when he woke as his body stirred beneath her. She tightened her grip on his shoulders and then she slid from him, coming to rest in the crook of his arm.

She never wanted to move. His body was her home, her refuge, but she knew it was time for their interlude to come to an end.

Her stomach rumbled, reminding her that she hadn't eaten that day. Hunger seemed so mundane after what they'd experienced.

Jarin covered her belly with his large hand. 'I should have brought some food with me,' he murmured into her hair. 'I hadn't intended on staying out so long.'

'Where are you travelling to?' asked Katherine, pulling herself upwards slightly so she could look down at his face.

She didn't really want to know the answer, but perhaps it would be less painful to imagine him going about his business if she knew where he was headed. She could picture him doing whatever he did all day as she went about her life without him.

He gave her a strange smile. 'I'm not travelling anywhere.'

'Then what are you doing here?' she asked, gesturing to the surrounding wood.

He glanced down at his naked body and then looked back at her, raising one eyebrow.

Heat rushed over her face. 'You can't tell me you came out to the woods expressly with the intention of… of doing this.'

'No,' he said. 'That is true. It didn't cross my mind for one minute that I would spend the afternoon making love to you in the forest, although I must say that I'm very glad it did happen. I did come out to the woods to look for you, however.'

'How did you know where I would be?' she asked, startled.

Jarin rolled his eyes. 'Your brother told me where to find you.'

Her hand flew to her chest. 'Braedan knows you're here. But how does he…?'

Jarin grinned, the expression more boyish than anything she'd seen on him before. 'I must say, when he isn't glaring at me, Braedan can be all right. We might, in time, become friends. I believe his words were, "She is happier when she thinks she is not being looked after so the guards keep a discreet distance".'

Katherine gasped and grabbed at her dress.

Jarin laughed. 'Don't worry, I sent them away when I arrived. I thought we should talk in private. Although we haven't done much talking yet,' he added ruefully.

'Perhaps you are right. A guard should follow me all the time,' she said pertly. 'Look what happens when they don't.'

Jarin laughed out loud.

She tried to pull the dress back over her head but Jarin drew her towards him and stopped her with a kiss. 'Don't be angry with me, Kate, my love.'

She held herself rigid against his body for a long moment, but he knew what he was doing with his mouth and very shortly she was pliant in his arms once more.

He raised his head. 'If I'd known all it took was a kiss to stop you from arguing with me, I would have done that on day one.'

'You didn't want to do that in the beginning, remember.'

He tilted her chin up so that she was looking directly into his eyes. 'I wanted to kiss you from the first moment I saw you in the Great Hall at your brother's wedding. You looked so furious, you kept muttering to yourself and then you turned to your sister and smiled. It took my breath away.'

Katherine's heart stopped. She didn't believe it and yet…and yet the truth of it was shining out of his eyes.

Jarin threaded his fingers through her hair and brought her mouth back to his. The world fell away again for a long moment until he pulled away.

'What was it you were so angry about during the wedding? Was it what I said about your family?'

Katherine nodded slowly. 'I was furious with you.' It was almost difficult to remember the rage that had pulsed through her during the ceremony. It was so different to how she felt right now.

His eyes clouded. 'I deserved it for what I said.'

She shrugged. 'It doesn't matter.'

'It matters that I hurt you. I promise to try never to do it again, although I can't always promise I will get it right.'

Katherine smiled and reached up to his beloved face. She couldn't tell him that it would hurt beyond agony when he went away again. There was nothing he could do about that; it was her misery to bear alone.

'What did you come to see Braedan about?' she asked.

She wondered how long it would be before he had to return home. Could they steal another morning together out in the woods before he did?

'I came to see him about you,' Jarin said slowly but firmly.

'Me?' She pointed to herself as if to clarify.

Jarin smiled. 'You.'

Slowly, realisation dawned on Katherine. Jarin still needed Ogmore's money and Linota wouldn't have him. Her heart beat quickly. Would marriage to Jarin without love be better than living without him? He obviously desired her. Was that enough? *Yes*, cried her whole body. *It would be enough.* To be able to spend the rest of her life with him even if he didn't love her the way she loved him would be a paradise she had never believed possible.

'What is going on in that complicated mind of yours?' asked Jarin, gently brushing her forehead with his fingertips.

She had to know the truth from him. She knew he would always be honest with her and, even though it would hurt, she knew life would be worse if he pretended to love her. 'Is this about Ogmore's dowry?'

He shook his head and smiled at her, pressing a kiss against her mouth. 'No, it's not about that. I thought that's what you would think. It's one of the reasons I have stayed away from you for so long. That and...' He shrugged. 'No, I had to make sure I could offer for you on my own terms. I have spent the last few months securing my finances. Borwyn is not the great earldom it was in the past, but I am positive it will be again in the future. I do not need Ogmore's dowry to make that happen.'

Misery clawed at Katherine's heart. Once again, Ogmore's dowry was not enough to tempt him to marry her; that wasn't why he was here. She pulled herself out of his arms and sat upright. She should get dressed. They would need to return to the castle before anyone realised they'd been gone for so long.

'Do you want to know the other reason I stayed away?' Jarin asked softly.

Katherine swallowed. She couldn't answer him.

Jarin gently pulled her back into his arms. 'I didn't believe you cared for me the way I care for you. When I suggested to you that I didn't need to marry your sister, the look of horror you gave me convinced me that you didn't. I think, perhaps, I should have started that conversation by telling you how I felt about you, but I was too afraid. I have been rejected by people who should have cared for me all my life and I didn't believe you would feel as strongly for me as I do for you.' He turned her so that she was facing him. The look on his face set her heart pounding. 'Your sister's letter changed that.'

Katherine tried to pull herself upright once more, but his arms were like bands of steel. 'My sister wrote to you! What did she say?'

Jarin reached over and patted his clothes as if searching for the letter.

'There is no need to show it to me. I still can't read. It turns out I don't have the patience to learn. What does it say?'

Jarin's eyes crinkled at the corners. 'It was very brief. She said only that you were miserable and that she thought that was due to my absence.'

Katherine's heart stopped. 'I thought I had hidden it well. I have been busy, I have learned to ride, I have explored, and I have laughed and talked during all our meals together. How did she know I was sad?'

Jarin smiled and gently ran his fingers down her neck. 'She doesn't say, but I'm glad she knew and I will be grateful for ever that she wrote to tell me. It gave me hope. I was going to come to see you anyway. I had decided you needed to know how I felt about you even if you didn't feel the same way.

'And even though Linota's letter wasn't an absolute guarantee that you would be pleased to see me, it was enough for me to hope that you would. Katherine, look at me, please.' She raised her gaze until she met his.

His eyes burned and the expression she saw in their depths took her breath away. 'I have no need for Ogmore's money, but I do have a need for you. I love you, Katherine Leofric. These last few months without you have been the worst of my life. Please tell me you will do me the honour of becoming my wife.'

Katherine blinked. Surely he couldn't have said all that? Somehow she found her voice. 'You love me? You want me to become your wife?'

Jarin laughed. 'Yes, I love you. If you will have me, then I will spend the rest of my life making sure you know how much. Hopefully then you will fall as deeply in love with me as I am with you.'

Katherine's mind whirled. This couldn't be possible. 'But look at you…you are so beautiful and I am…'

Jarin brushed her hair away from her face. 'No, don't do this, Kate. Don't put yourself down again. I wish you could see yourself the way I do. You are so beautiful: your golden hair, your caramel eyes, which turn a different colour depending on the light…your petite waist. I could spend the rest of my days watching you and I would die a happy man.'

'Oh.' Katherine didn't know how this could be possible, but the truth of it shone from his eyes.

'And even if you weren't beautiful,' Jarin continued, 'I would still love you because of the way you are, your generous heart and your courage. So please, don't ever put yourself down again.'

Katherine reached up and touched his lips with her fingertips, hardly daring to believe what she'd just heard.

Jarin cleared his throat. 'What is your answer, my love?'

For a moment Katherine could only stare at him. Her sole coherent thought was that he loved her and he thought she was beautiful.

'Answer?' she repeated.

'Will you marry me?'

'Oh, that...' Her heart skipped. From the look on his face it seemed as though he doubted the outcome. How could he, even for a moment, doubt that she returned his feelings?

'Yes, that.'

It amazed her that his voice shook as he spoke; he was nervous. He really didn't think she could care for him the way he felt about her. It was incredible, but it was true.

'Of course I will marry you. I love you.'

The smile Jarin gave her made her heart hurt. He pulled her towards him and held her tightly against his chest.

A soft breeze picked up and brushed against her back. She shivered.

'Shall we return to the castle and tell everyone our news?' he suggested.

'There's no rush,' she said and pulled his head down to meet hers once more.

Epilogue

'Faster, Papa, faster. We are nearly there.'

Jarin's arms moved quickly as his oars cut through the water. His oldest daughter bounced in delight.

'Just a few more pulls, Papa.'

The boat grounded on soft sand, signalling that they had arrived. Jarin jumped out and dragged the boat up the beach until it was no longer in the water and helped Ann and his younger daughter, Helen, out of the boat. They ran screeching across the sand, delighted to have arrived even though it was only a small journey from the mainland.

Jarin reached down to and pulled Katherine to her feet. Even after all this time his warm hands still caused a tingle to race through her body.

'Thank you, my lord,' she murmured as he helped her over the edge of the boat.

He grinned at her and pulled her into his arms for a swift kiss before they set off after their daughters.

This small island, not far from the coast where their fortress stood imposingly on the cliff's edge, wasn't

France or a faraway country she'd always dreamed of, but it was her family's sanctuary. It was where they came when they needed a break from the demands of castle life. All the people that depended on them for their livelihood knew not to disturb the Borwyns when they were here.

Katherine's feet sunk into the soft sand, her breathing coming in hurried pants. It was hard to move across the beach at the best of times, but today it was especially difficult.

'Mama, come on. You're so slow,' called Helen.

'It's because she's so fat.'

Beside her, Jarin laughed softly although he was quick to turn his laughter to a frown when Katherine glanced at him. 'You mustn't call your mother fat, Ann,' he said solemnly, although Katherine could hear the laughter in his voice.

Ann looked up at her parents. 'But you told me I must always tell the truth.'

Katherine stopped walking to rub the base of her spine.

'You must be truthful *and* kind,' explained Jarin.

Ann blinked up at him once, her blue eyes so like her father's. Truthful and kind appeared to be a concept too complicated for their seven-year-old. She ran off to join their younger daughter, who had given up waiting for her mother and was busy chasing oyster catchers, which ran away from her tiny, grasping fingers.

Katherine ran her hand over her rounded stomach. 'Do you think it will be a boy this time?' she asked wistfully.

'I hope it's another girl,' said Jarin. 'The men in my family don't tend to turn out well.'

'That's not true. I mean, Erik's turned out to be a wonderful brother-in-law.'

Jarin laughed. 'I should have learned not to fish for compliments from you by now.'

Katherine laughed, too. 'You don't need flattery. You know what I think about you already. I couldn't hope for a better husband and father to our children.' She sobered. 'I would love a little boy for you. Just think of all the things you can teach him. He will always know how much he is loved by you and by me and he will grow to be a fine man like his father. But another girl would also be perfect. I do adore those two, even if they are turning into harridans. I don't think I've ever been called fat before.'

Jarin laughed and slipped his arm around her. 'You're still tiny despite the fact that your figure resembles an apple.'

'I'm as round as I am tall,' she said cheerfully. It had been months since she'd seen her feet and there was still another month to go until this one was ready to come out, but she didn't mind. Each pregnancy was a joy to her, a miracle she'd never dreamed possible until Jarin had come into her life and made her his wife.

'You are beautiful.'

Even after eight years, Katherine never tired of hearing Jarin tell her so. Every day he made her feel it too. 'You're biased, but I'll take the compliment.'

She turned so that she was facing him and tried to wrap her arms around him, but her stomach got in the way.

Jarin laughed at her efforts and turned her sideways so that he could slip his arms around her shoulders.

'You, Katherine Borwyn, are the most beautiful Countess in the country.' He pressed a kiss behind her ear.

'I'm one of the only Countesses in the country,' she parried.

'Are you arguing with me?' Jarin raised an eyebrow.

Katherine laughed up at her husband. 'Yes.'

'Good,' he said, 'because you know how I like to win...'

And he pressed his mouth to hers. Beyond them their daughters' laughter floated dreamily through the air.

* * * * *

If you enjoyed this book, why not check out
Ella Matthews' stunning debut

The Warrior Knight and the Widow